Dornford Yates
GALE WARNING

J. M. Dent & Sons Ltd
London Melbourne

First published in Great Britain by Ward Lock & Co. Ltd 1939
This paperback edition first published by J. M. Dent & Sons Ltd 1985

This book is set in 10/11½ Linotron Plantin by
Inforum Ltd, Portsmouth
Printed in Great Britain by
Richard Clay (The Chaucer Press) Ltd, Bungay, for
J. M. Dent & Sons Ltd
Aldine House, 33 Welbeck Street, London W1M 8LX

British Library Cataloguing in Publication Data

Yates, Dornford
Gale warning.—(Classic thrillers)
Rn: Cecil William Mercer I. Title II. Series
823'.912[F] PR6025.E56

ISBN 0-460-02268-7

Gale Warning

'Sometimes, at great garden parties, literary luncheons, or in the quiet of an exclusive gunroom, a laugh rings out. The sad, formal faces for a moment relax and a smaller group is formed within the larger. They are admirers of Dornford Yates who have found out each other. We are badly organized, we know little about ourselves and next to nothing about our hero, but we appreciate fine writing when we come across it, and a wit that is ageless united to a courtesy that is extinct.'

Cyril Connolly

DORNFORD YATES is the pen-name of Cecil William Mercer, the son of a solicitor, who was born in Walmer, Kent, in 1885. He was educated at Harrow and Oxford, where he became President of the Oxford University Dramatic Society. He then qualified as a barrister, working for a time on the trial of the notorious 'Dr' Crippen. But his legal practice left him plenty of time for writing, and with half an eye on his cousin 'Saki' (Hector Hugh Munro), who was by that time a famous writer, Mercer began to publish stories in the *Windsor Magazine*. At the outbreak of World War I he joined the County of London Yeomanry and served in Egypt and Salonika. After the war he resumed his writing and was soon launched on a new and immensely successful career. He wrote over thirty books – light-hearted farces like *Berry and Co* as well as adventure stories such as *Blind Corner* and *She Fell Among Thieves*. Although he created 'clubland heroes' of great charm and sociability, he was himself an unclubable man. He married twice, and lived in France for many years. Forced to leave France when World War II broke out, he moved to Rhodesia, where he died in 1960. His ashes are immured in the north porch of St John's Church at Umtali.

CONTENTS

1	Without the Law	1
2	Tulip Lane	16
3	I Wait for the Stroke	30
4	On Parade	43
5	Close Quarters	55
6	The Kingdom of Heaven	71
7	The Toll of the Road	88
8	The Stolen March	101
9	Audrey's Way	115
10	The Château of Midian	126
11	My Lady's Chamber	139
12	Cold Blood	152
13	Barabbas Receives	167
14	Mansel Mops Up	183
15	Aftermath	193

To Jill
to whom I owe so much

CHAPTER 1

Without the Law

I think I might have made a good land-agent, but I know of no other calling which I should have failed to disgrace. In a sense this was not my fault, for my father was a land-agent, as had been his father before him, and I was brought up in the tradition almost from the day of my birth. Then, when I was twenty-two, my father and his master were killed by a falling tree, and the proud estate—my world—was sold to a man of affairs and was turned into building-plots.

It was nearly two years later, when I was on my beam-ends, that George St Omer of Peerless, stifled a yawn.

'I'm going to bed,' he said; and got to his feet. With a hand on the door, he turned. 'By the way, I'm parting with Collis. I've told him to leave next June. And I want you to take his place—at six hundred a year.'

Before I could find my tongue, he was out of the room.

Now Collis was land-agent of Peerless, which had been the seat of the Earls of St Omer for more than three centuries.

* * *

George lived by himself at Peerless, in great simplicity. Where his father had kept forty servants, he kept a man and his wife, and he lived in the servants' quarters of his ancestral home. But death duties have to be paid, and the money he saved indoors was spent upon the acres without. He grudged the estate nothing—he once sold his favourite hunter to buy a barn a new roof: but love is not expert knowledge, and so he employed a land-agent—not to spare himself, but for Peerless' sake.

I had stayed with him several times since his father's death, and when he made the announcement which I have reported above, I was spending a week at Peerless and hunting three days out of six.

When I tried to thank him next morning, he closed one eye.

'Mathematics, my boy,' he said. 'I'm a business man. You'll be very much better than Collis—and cheaper, too. I pay him eight hundred a year, and he's worth about four. So you stand by for

June. We'll meet in Town in the spring and fix things up.'

(He never told me the truth—that he had caught Collis clean out. The fellow had been robbing St Omer right and left. But George would not prosecute or even discharge the man, because his sudden dismissal would have prejudiced what future he had.)

All I had in the world at that time was a capital sum of four hundred and fifty pounds, but I was determined to pull my weight at Peerless and, in view of the well-paid post so soon to be mine, I arranged to take a course of instruction which should, so to speak, put an edge to my ability. The fees were high, and I had to live in a style which I could not afford; but I made out that I could just do it—and have some twenty pounds over, when June came in.

No man ever worked harder than I did that winter and spring: I applied myself unto wisdom with all my might. And then, one April morning, my summons from George arrived in the form of a telegram.

Let's dine at Scotts tomorrow is that all right

I replied by wire that it was—and travelled to Town the next day with a leaping heart, eager to make George free of the dreams I had woven for Peerless out of the stuff I had learned.

I reached the restaurant early, to find, as I had expected, that George had reserved an alcove, where we could talk undisturbed: so I sent for an evening paper and took my seat—with my face to the busy staircase down which St Omer must come.

Then a boy came down with the paper . . .

It was the latest edition—the 'late night extra,' I think—the first to publish the news of St Omer's death.

His car had overturned that same afternoon . . . not very far from Bedford . . . whilst he was driving to London . . . to meet me at Scott's. George was lying dead at a wayside inn. And here was I at his table . . . waiting to talk of Peerless and see the smile in his eyes and show him that I was the man for the post I should never fill.

* * *

How long I sat staring at the paper, I do not know, for I was, so to speak, knocked out. I had lost my familiar friend, the only friend I had had—not that I needed others: one friend like George St Omer was as much as a man can ask. I had lost my admirable Crichton—the man who did all things well, all of whose ways were so handsome, to whom I had always looked up. I had lost my *deus ex machina*—the man who had come to my help, who was to have made my fortune. . . . 'Was to have.' My prospects had died with George. The time and the money which I had spent on my course had been thrown away. And now I was 'up against it' as never before. And so, as I say, I sat staring, oblivious of time and place, when the casual words of a stranger cleared my brain.

'I wish you'd got an alcove,' he said.

As the head-waiter began to express his regret—

'This one's free,' said I, and got to my feet.

The head-waiter opened his eyes.

'Isn't his lordship——'

'His lordship's dead,' I said.

'Dead, sir?'

I picked up the paper and put it into his hand. Then I took my coat and hat and made my way up the staircase down which George would never come.

It was a rough, wet night and I hung on my heel for a moment, to put on my coat before I took to the streets. As I did so, a hand on my shoulder made me look round.

By my side was standing the stranger to whom, a moment before, I had given the alcove up.

'I think you're John Bagot,' he said.

'Yes,' said I, staring. 'I am.'

'Well, my name's Mansel,' he said. 'And I was a friend of St Omer's—I knew him extremely well. He was speaking of you last week. Please come back and dine with me. His death has shaken me up, and as you knew him so well—well, I think perhaps it'd be a relief to us both.'

'You're very good,' said I, 'to try and temper the wind. But——'

'Please come—for my sake,' said Mansel. And then, 'I mean what I say.'

'But you're not alone,' said I.

'No, a man called Chandos is coming. But that won't matter at all. He knew George better than I.'

I confess that I felt something dazed, and a hand went up to my head.

Then—

'All right,' I said, and turned. 'Did you know he was dining here?'

'Yes,' said Mansel, 'I did. And I knew you were dining with him. After you'd dined together, he was to have brought you along to meet Chandos and me.'

Then he slid an arm under mine and led me back down the staircase which George would never descend. And soon after that I was drinking a champagne cocktail in the alcove which George had reserved.

* * *

Dinner was a thing of the past, and Mansel, Chandos and I were sitting in Mansel's flat in Cleveland Row.

Mansel was addressing me quietly.

'I said I had something to tell you, and here it is. George met his death today, but not by an accident. That is the verdict which the coroner's jury will return. But Chandos and I know better. *St Omer has been bumped off.*'

I heard myself say, 'Who by?' and I found myself up on my feet.

Mansel wrinkled his brow.

'Well, I don't know who did the job, but I know who gave the order for the job to be done. He's a rather—inaccessible wallah. For convenience, we call him Barabbas: we don't know his proper name. We trod on his corns last week—St Omer, Chandos and I. And this is his riposte.'

I sat down, trembling a little.

'Are you going after him?' I said.

'Until we get him,' said Mansel, 'or he gets us.'

'Well, count me in,' said I. 'I'm broke to the world and I don't know where to begin: but if you'll let me help, I'll do the work of two men for the run of my teeth.'

'No need for that,' said Mansel. 'A week ago today, we witnessed St Omer's Will. He wrote it out himself and he told us what he had done. He's left you twelve thousand pounds—unless there's another "John Bagot, of 33 Shepherd's Market when he's in Town." '

I dared not trust my voice: and after a little silence Mansel went on.

'But before you come in on this deal, you must know where you stand. I mean, in a sense, George bought it. Barabbas is not a nice man, but he hadn't done George any harm. Yet George went out of his way to tread on his corns. Tread? Stamp. The swine'll go lame for years.'

'I'm glad of that,' I said thickly. 'And I don't care a damn where I stand: I want to know what to do.'

'I wish I could tell you,' said Mansel, and got to his feet. 'But as I can't, I'll put the cards on the table for you to see what they're like. I need hardly say that they're—rather private cards. I mean, if their existence were dreamed of, the game would be up.'

'I can hold my tongue,' said I.

Mansel smiled.

'So George maintained,' he said. 'And he was a pretty good judge. Although you didn't know it, you've been, so to speak, spare man for the last six months.'

'Spare man?' said I.

'Spare man,' said Mansel. 'You see, for some time now, St Omer, Chandos and I have occasionally done some poaching—on the preserves of the police. In other words, we have more than once combated crime which the police were unable to combat because, like everyone else, the police are bound by the law. They weren't in days gone by. The Bow Street Runners, for instance, employed every trick of the trade. But that's all over now, and the police have to fight in gloves. And that is where we have come in—for we fight without gloves. We take the criminal on at his very own game.

'Now let me say this. We have no standing at all. I know them at Scotland Yard, and they know me. And if I can give them a tip, they'll take it without any question because they know that they can count upon me. But we cannot call upon them or even tell them what we are doing, because, if we did, they would have to tell us to stop. And so I repeat—we have no standing at all. If I was arrested tomorrow, they'd have to let me go down.'

'Yes, I see that,' said I, and put a hand to my head. 'I'd no idea, of course. George never breathed a word . . . and I thought I knew him so well.'

'So you did,' said Mansel. 'You were his closest friend. But, you see, this wasn't his secret. . . . And now, if you'll listen to me, you shall hear some facts that you won't hear anywhere else.'

With that, he set his back to the chimney and told his tale, speaking without emotion and keeping his strong hands folded, after the way of a child.

So far as I can, I will set down his very words.

'You may or may not remember that, six nights ago tonight, burglary was attempted at Blanche Mains, a Dorsetshire manor, owned by the Earl of Larch. The Press made much of the affair, for a house-party was in progress and a Royal Duke and Duchess made two of the guests. As is so often the case, the attempt was made while dinner was being served, but the burglars were disturbed by a servant and, leaving the job undone, made good their escape. The papers went on to describe the jewels which, there can be no doubt, the burglars had hoped to secure. Those which the Duchess had with her were irreplaceable.

'So much for one item of news.

'Some papers reported another—of less account. This was that upon the same night, not very far from Blanche Mains, a big, closed car left the road at a very high speed. It overturned and caught fire, and the three men sitting within it were burned to death. Who they were, nobody knows—and nobody very much cared, because "The Blanche Mains Outrage" overshadowed their shocking fate. One unkind fact stood out—they could not have been the burglars, because they were driving *towards* the scene of the crime.

'So much for the second news item—and now I'll tell you the truth.

'No burglary was ever attempted. It was a case of robbery under arms. The Larches and their guests were at dinner at a quarter past nine. The room was dim, for, as lots of people do, they were dining by candle-light. And so they never noticed that the places of the servants had been taken by four armed men. And then the lights went up, and the Duke was sitting still—with the mouth of an automatic against each ear.

' "I shouldn't move," said someone. "Much less make a noise."

'The injunction was supererogatory. The Duke was up against it, and everyone else was almost afraid to breathe. In a deathly silence the women were stripped of their jewels and the candles put out. Then the lights went out, and the thieves were gone. The whole thing took less than two minutes—a perfect show. It really was damned well done. The telephone line had been cut, and when the lights went out, they went out for good.

'Outside, two cars were waiting—the first with a man at the wheel. And now mark this. The engine of the first car was running, but that of the second was not. It should have been running, too: but the petrol had been turned off, and so it had stopped. The consequence was that the second car was left standing, while the first, with the jewels inside, went off a blue streak. So the gang was split up—I should have told you before, that, if you include the chauffeur, there were eight men on the job.

'Now all of the eight were masked. It follows that the three who entered the leading car did not perceive that a man who was not their chauffeur had taken their chauffeur's place. In a word, they had no idea that they were being driven by a well-known peer of the realm.

'They should have been driven to Blandford. A car was waiting there, to carry them on. But St Omer drove them elsewhere—into the net, in fact, which Chandos and I had spread. We and our servants were waiting in a convenient lane. Once the car had entered, it couldn't get out, and the thieves would be at our mercy and would have to disgorge their spoil.

'Well, in fact, it worked out very well. St Omer drove like hell clean into the net and had stopped and was out of the car before the three knew where they were or what was what. I need hardly say that we were prepared for a scrap: but, before we could interfere, something we hadn't bargained for took matters out of our hands. . . .

'Thieves are suspicious people, and when their nerves are frayed they are apt to jump to conclusions which are not true. And that's what the leader did. Alarmed and disconcerted, he jumped to the conclusion that the others were letting him down, and there and then he shot the two of them dead. Well, when a man's done two murders, he's ripe for three: I, therefore, took the precaution of doing the hangman's job. Then we put them back in their car, and George and Chandos, between them, attended to their cremation without any fuss. This took place at Red Hanger, where their remains were discovered the following day. The jewels I took straight to the Chief Constable, whom I happen to know. In fact, I reached him before the news of the crime. And since all had ended well, he instantly saw the wisdom of keeping the whole thing quiet.

'Well, the honours must go to St Omer—no shadow of doubt about that. Everything hung on him. And he balanced his life on one finger when he got into that car. But Chandos, here, was too broad, and I was too high. . . . So when they bumped him off, in fact they got the right man.

'The trouble was he'd been spotted. He told me he thought he had been the day before. You see, he was in touch with the chauffeur—a devilish delicate job. He'd met the fellow in Town, to hear what he knew; and someone who knew the chauffeur had noticed St Omer's face. And when the game had been spoiled and the chauffeur had disappeared, they put two and two together and thought about George.

'Well, now let's come to Barabbas. It's not too much to say that none of these things would have happened, but for that master mind. He is a "fence" or receiver of stolen goods. As you probably know, no robberies would be committed, but for the "fence": and, though you may not know it, in all important robberies the goods have been appraised by the "fence" before ever the crime takes place. The thief, so to speak, "sells forward." . . . But Barabbas goes very much further than any ordinary "fence". He does not wait for the robber to come to him: instead, he goes to the robber and indicates what he wants. And he tells him how to steal it and offers him rather more than the ordinary "fence" would give. Indeed, it amounts to this—that today Barabbas controls quite a number of thieves. Though they would hotly deny it, they are, in fact, his agents, working for him and faithfully paid by results. And since he can pick and choose, it follows that all his agents are devilish good at their job.

'Well, he sent his best men to Blanche Mains: if the chauffeur may be believed, he'd set his heart on receiving the Duchess' jewels. He meant to have them—this time. . . . Not only did he not get them, but he lost three valuable agents—all thanks to George. So now you see why he was cross. Still, to do George in was foolish: he might have known that we shouldn't stand for that.

'We've met once or twice before, though not, of course, in the flesh. We've had one or two encounters: his brain against ours. But now the game has become a personal matter. Had George been killed that night, it would have been the luck of the game: but George was deliberately murdered, and that is—beyond a joke.

'Of course I'm not complaining. I have no cause for complaint. We three were without the law, and it is without the law that people get hurt. Then, again, without the law you have no right to question what others do. But you have a right to resent it and, if you can, to get back.'

There was a little silence.

Then—

'How did George meet it?' I said.

'I've no idea,' said Mansel. 'At seven o'clock this evening I got this note.'

He took an envelope from his pocket, drew out a sheet of paper and put it into my hand.

There were no words—only figures: but these were eloquent.

3 - 1 = 2

Mansel continued quietly.

'That told me that George was gone, for Chandos was here with me. And ten minutes later my man came in with the paper in which you read the news.'

In silence I gave back the note and tried to marshal my thoughts.

I had been badly shaken by George's death, and Mansel's revelations had dazzled my jolted wits. I had been ushered abruptly into another world, where shadow proved to be substance, and fiction, fact: I had been shown the region which George had ranged: I had, so to speak, been conducted without the law. But all this, as in a dream—until I had seen that note. The thing might have been a wand. As I read those sinister figures, the mist of uncertainty cleared and I realized with a shock that I was sitting with men who moved in a work-a-day world with their lives in their hands. Mansel had said that George had been recognized: but he had not troubled to say that he and Chandos were known—that what had happened to George might happen *at any moment* to either of them.

And at that moment the bell of the flat was rung.

* * *

I think that I must have started, for Mansel smiled.

'Takes getting hold of,' he said. 'But once you've flirted with danger, you've got to go on. Without it, life seems too humdrum. You go on all right for a while and you're glad of a rest, but after a bit . . .'

'It's rather like drink,' said Chandos, and knocked out his pipe. 'After a bout you swear off it and go upon your lawful occasions like any respectable man: but when the time comes round for another bout, all your good resolutions go down the drain, and ——'

Here the door was opened and a man-servant entered the room.

'Yes, Carson?' said Mansel.

'It's Lady Audrey, sir.'

Mansel's eyebrows went up, and Chandos got to his feet.

'I'll do what I can,' said Mansel, 'but she's certain to want to see you.' He turned to me. 'You must excuse me, Bagot. I don't suppose you knew it, but Audrey Nuneham was engaged to be married to George. She is—no ordinary girl: she was aware of our activities and would, if we had allowed her, have played her part. I've been trying to find her since seven—I thought she was out of Town.'

'I'll have to be going,' I said.

'No, no. Not yet—unless you want to be gone.'

'Oh, no: but——'

'Then don't go yet. We've quite a lot to discuss.'

A moment later Chandos and I were alone.

Chandos was younger than Mansel and gave the impression of being immensely strong. (He later told me that Mansel was stronger than he: but that I beg leave to doubt, though Mansel's powers of endurance were most exceptional.) He was tall and broad and deep-chested, his fair hair was gray at the temples, and his eyes were set very wide: his face, though not handsome, was goodly, by which I mean that to look on him did you good, so pleasant was his expression and so honest and fearless his gaze.

'Audrey,' he said quietly, 'is a very great-hearted girl. She'll mourn, but she'll mourn in secret—no one will ever know. She won't go sick—she'll see red. And I think she'll want to rush in. But we can't do that here. We don't know which way to go.' He sighed. 'Never mind. I expect you've read "Forestry Practice." What did you think of that work?'

For the next twenty minutes or so, we strolled upon ground that I knew, comparing notes and discussing woods and pastures and flocks and herds: and I very soon found that Chandos knew his subject and was a better farmer than many a man so called.

At length he came to the point—for now that I know him better, I have no doubt at all that he had but been leading me up to the water he wished me to drink.

'I'll tell you what,' he said slowly, 'I wish you'd come down and have a look at my farm. I don't have a bailiff: I do what I can myself. But you, of course, are an expert . . . I mean, unless I'm mistaken, we've time to burn, and a week or two in Wiltshire would do us good.'

'You're very kind,' I began . . .

'I propose to use you,' smiled Chandos. 'And so will Jenny, my wife. She belongs to Nature. She can do what she likes with any beast of the field. But seeing's believing, so come. D'you think you could manage Monday? I'll drive you down if you can.'

And there the door was opened, and a girl with a scornful look came into the room.

I cannot believe that any man, high or low, that ever met Audrey Nuneham, will ever forget the first time she crossed his path. For myself, my whole being thrilled, just as a bowl will quiver to some particular chord—not because she was so good-looking or because her air was so proud, but because her charm was compelling and had ridden over my spirit before I knew where I was.

Though her manner was careless, vitality burned in her eyes, and I never saw on a woman a keener, more resolute face. Her head was well set on, and her features were fine and clean-cut: she was tall and slim and well-made; and had she married poor George, they would have made a wonderful pair; but as I looked at her with that in my mind, I knew that I, as his friend, should have fallen far short of the standard set by his wife.

Chandos was by her side before Mansel had followed her in. For a moment he faced her squarely. Then he bowed his head and lifted her hand to his lips.

'Thank you, Richard,' said she. 'I'll take it as said.'

Mansel spoke over her shoulder.

'This is John Bagot, Audrey. He knows who you are.'

I bowed, and she nodded her head.

'George mentioned your name,' she said shortly—and left it there. She moved to a chair and sat down. 'D'you think he's in England, Richard?'

'That's my belief,' said Chandos. 'I can't back it up.'

'You think he came over for Blanche Mains, and, when he went down over that, he stayed on to get George?'

'I don't think he came over for Blanche Mains: but when we crabbed that show, I think he came over hot foot to—answer us back. I think he stage-managed what happened this afternoon:

and, if I'm right—well, he couldn't have done it from France.'

'Will he stay to get you or Jonah?'

Chandos raised his eyebrows.

'I shouldn't, if I were he.'

'Why not?' said Lady Audrey.

'Because murder for murder's sake is a dangerous thing to do in this particular land. That being so, I shouldn't do it twice running. If it comes to that, I don't think his men would march. Then, again, I think it likely that he hopes to have frightened us off. If I'm right, he'll wait and see. But I don't think he'll wait in England—I don't quite see why he should.'

'If you were he, when would you leave?'

'Tomorrow morning,' said Chandos. 'I shouldn't wait on this weather, if I lived in the South of France.'

The girl leaned forward.

'The *South* of France?' she said sharply. 'What do you know?'

'Nothing at all,' said Chandos. 'But, surely, only a fool would live in the North.'

'Paris?'

'I don't think so. Barabbas is without the law: and when an outlaw's *chez lui*, he likes to be able to see who's approaching his house: and if he lived in Paris, he couldn't do that. But all this is pure speculation. All that we know for certain is that he lives in France.'

'And you're going to let him go back?'

Chandos looked at Mansel, who put in his oar.

'We can't very well stop him, Audrey. We don't know what he looks like: we don't know what name he goes by, or where he is.'

'What about Sermon Square?'

'Sermon Square,' said Mansel, 'is the only link we have. If that link is broken, we're done. And if he dreamed that we had it, Barabbas would snap it at once. So we've got to conceal our possession, until it has served our turn. In other words, it's a highly delicate link, and the strain which we put upon it must be correspondingly slight.

'At 22 Sermon Square, there are five business firms. With one of those business firms our man is in touch. That's all we know—for the moment. Well, the first thing to do, of course, is to find out which of the firms is the one we want. That shouldn't be hard—inquiries should tell us that. But when we have found that out, we shall have a bad time, for Sermon Square is a very hard place to watch—without being seen. That's probably why it was chosen. It isn't a square at all: it's a short, well-lighted, blind alley, some thirty feet wide: and from any one of the windows of 22, a man can command the alley from bottom to top.'

'Nothing "to let"?' said the girl.

'Nothing at all,' said Mansel. 'What observation is kept will have to be kept from the street.' He put his hands to his temples and pushed back his hair. 'Audrey, you must be patient: this isn't a fence we can rush.'

Audrey Nuneham frowned.

'I don't want to rush any fences. But once the man's out of England——'

'He'll be very much more easy to deal with. Be sure of that.'

'Perhaps. But we'll have to find him. And even the South of France is a pretty big place to comb.'

'I shouldn't think of trying,' said Mansel. 'I propose to be led to his aerie—from Sermon Square. But Sermon Square is in balk. The problem we've got to resolve is how to start from a place *to which you must not resort.*

'It's the long way round, of course. But what other way can we take? Do please remember this—that William and I are marked men. We are, therefore, weighted out of any spectacular race. The moment we leave the background, whatever we're doing is doomed. Sermon Square is a bridge, but if he or I try to use it, the bridge will cease to exist.'

There was a little silence.

Then——

'Are you going to the inquest?' said the girl.

'No,' said Mansel, 'I'm not—for that would be waste of time.'

'On the principle of "Let the dead bury their dead." I see. Are you going to the police?'

'Certainly not,' said Mansel. 'It's no good my going, unless I tell them the truth. And if I tell them the truth the inquest will be adjourned—and all concerned in the murder will instantly fade away. Our man included, of course. Secure or no, no man takes any risks when the murder he's done is out.'

'In fact, you mean to sit still?'

'Extremely still,' said Mansel. 'Because, if we put a foot wrong, it may cost us the game. I'm awfully sorry, Audrey. I know a bit how you feel. But you simply cannot short-circuit a show like this.'

Lady Audrey raised her eyebrows.

'By what you say, there's not going to be any show. The melodrama is over. The curtain came down at Bedford this afternoon.'

'Melodramas,' said Mansel, quietly, 'don't end like that.'

Lady Audrey looked at Chandos.

'Can I have a cigarette?'

The box was by me: so I opened and offered it her.

She looked me up and down before taking a cigarette.

'Ah,' she said. 'The remount. And how do you feel about things? Are you going to watch and pray—for a magic carpet and two invisible cloaks?'

As I lighted her cigarette—

'Remounts are green,' I said. 'They have to be schooled. And if they won't be schooled, then they have to be cast.'

'I'll school you,' said Lady Audrey.

'So you shall,' said I. 'But not in the field.'

'No one would know who you were if you went to Sermon Square.'

'I quite agree,' said I. 'But after I'd spent a few hours there, they'd have a damned good idea.'

'Not if you were a waiting chauffeur. I'll lend you my car.'

'That sounds all right,' said I. 'But it wants working out.'

'Does it, indeed?' said the girl. 'And how many months would it take you—to work the conception out?'

'Audrey,' said Chandos quickly, 'he's perfectly right. The blue suit and peaked cap are nothing. He would have to *be* a chauffeur—the chauffeur belonging to someone with business in Sermon Square. I mean, he couldn't drive up with an empty car. Then, again, there will be other chauffeurs of other cars. They'll talk to him, while they're waiting, and he must be able to keep his end up with them. Finally, what's he to watch for? "A reed shaken with the wind?" '

'He'd be wasting his time if he did. I can show him a couple in Cleveland Row.'

'Be fair,' said Mansel, gently. 'Making bricks without straw is not a spectacular job. What is more'—he glanced at his watch—'it is not a job which people can do when they're tired. If they try, they lose their labour. I've done it—that's how I know.'

'I'm not tired,' said Lady Audrey.

'I know; but we are,' said Mansel. 'Bagot was up at four and William at five, and, though I rose at eight, I didn't get to bed until three. So, you see, we're not at our best. Let William take you back now—to Cavendish Square. If you'll stay in bed till midday, I promise I'll come and see you at half past one.'

'I'm much obliged,' said the girl and got to her feet. She looked me up and down. 'You'd better come too, I should think: and sing me to sleep.' She moved to the door and swung round. 'In fact, I can spare you—all three. I know how to take a taxi and how to turn out the light. As for staying in bed till midday . . .'

'Go on,' said Mansel, quietly, with his eyes on her face.

For a little she faced him squarely. Then she looked down and away.

'What if I won't—confine myself to the house?'

'I shan't come and see you,' said Mansel, 'at half past one.'

'In other words . . .'

'We shall keep our own counsel, Audrey, from this time on.'

She stood very still for a moment, her underlip caught in her teeth. Then she turned her face to the wall and burst into tears.

Before I had time to think, Chándos had picked her up and had carried her out of the room.

* * *

Near half an hour went by before Mansel returned.

'She's all right now,' he said. "And Chandos is taking her home. I'm awfully sorry for you, but please be sorry for me. To put it across her like that, tonight of all nights . . . But something had to be done. If she'd gone, as I knew she was going, to Sermon Square—well, that would have finished that clue, and as sure as I'm speaking English, it's all we've got. It's pitiably slender, of course: but it does give us something to go on, something on which we can focus what wits we have.

'George St Omer got it—out of the chauffeur he squeezed. Twice that fellow set down at 22 Sermon Square. The same man each time—one Rudy: that was the wallah I shot. Once they got caught in the traffic, and Rudy was worried stiff for fear he was going to be late. Mark that, if you please—a public enemy worried, in case he was five minutes late. There's only one explanation of such a contradiction in terms. *Rudy had an appointment with somebody greater than he.*

'And now you should go to bed. I expect you'd rather go home: but, if you don't fancy the walk, I'll put you up here.'

I said I would rather go home and arranged to 'report for duty' in two days' time.

Then he saw me out of the flat, and I stumbled to Shepherd's Market after the way of a reveller whose wine has gone to his legs.

I think I may be forgiven. I had worked from four that morning till four that afternoon: that evening my world had crashed: and another world had risen out of the ruins, before I had picked myself up.

CHAPTER 2

Tulip Lane

The next day I returned to Sussex, to pack what stuff I had there and take my leave of the men who had taught me so well.

The Secretary, whom I saw first, was kind enough to deplore my decision to cut short my course: but I told him that the post which I had hoped to secure had been suddenly filled, and that, as such posts were today extremely rare, I must not pursue a shadow, but seek what substance I could in some other walk of life.

'I see your point,' he said. 'But it's wicked waste. And I can't see you as a bank-clerk.'

'Neither can I,' said I. 'A porter at Covent Garden is more in my line. When d'you think the Director can see me? I'd like to catch the four o'clock train.'

The Secretary looked at me thoughtfully, stroking his chin.

'He's busy just now,' he said slowly. 'Say half-past two.'

I thanked him and went off to pack—and to bid farewell to the many friends I had made, both of men and beasts.

At half past two I entered the Director's room.

'Ah, Bagot,' says he, 'sit down. I've only five minutes to spare, so we've got to be quick.' I did as he said, and he threw himself back in his chair. 'Cairns tells me you feel you should go, and, in view of what has happened, I think you're right. Well, I'm very sorry to lose you, and if I'd a place to spare, I'd ask you to join the staff. But, though I can't do that, I do not agree with you that "a porter at Covent Garden is in your line." A talent must sometimes be buried; but it must not be defaced. So I've written a letter here for you to present yourself to some people I know.' I made to interrupt, but he put up a hand. 'I happen to know they're short of a man like you. They're an old-fashioned firm of surveyors, and most of their work has to do with the countryside. Reports and valuations of farms and estates. That means you'd be out and about two-thirds of your time. Two days a week in the office—not more than that. What the screw will be, I don't know: but, unless they're already suited, I think they'll jump at you when they read what I've said.'

Rebuff such kindness, I could not. How many eminent men would have done so much for a beggar they scarcely knew? Besides, I could hardly explain that I was without the law.

I stammered my thanks somehow, received the letter he gave me, shook his generous hand and bowed myself out.

As I made my way to my quarters, I reflected that Mansel would help me to hand such benevolence back.

I think I slept in the train, for I do not remember the journey and I know I was still very tired. And Shepherd's Market seemed dreary, after the give and take of the genial Common Room. As much as anything else, this sent me early to bed, and I should have been asleep by a quarter to ten, if something had not happened to blow my dullness to bits.

As most people do, I suppose, I always empty my pockets before I undress, and among the things I took out was the letter the Director had given me, to show to the firm he knew.

As I laid it down on my table, I thought, had things been different, how grateful I should have been for the chance it gave: but now I should never present it, because I had already accepted a post of another kind.

Then I saw the superscription—and I think that my heart stood still.

C. V. Lacey Esq.
Howson and Dewlap,
Surveyors,
22 Sermon Square,
London, E.C.

Not 7, or 12, or 20—*but 22.*

* * *

My first idea was to go straight to Jonathan Mansel at Cleveland Row. Then I saw that I must not do this, because, if his flat was watched, I might be recognized later in Sermon Square. So I wrote him a careful letter and took it myself to the post.

I told him what had happened and what I proposed to do, and I begged for an early answer, because I wished to do nothing until I had his consent.

When I came back from the post, I did not retire, but paced my room for ages, revolving this prank of Fortune's and all it might mean to our cause.

To put it no higher than this—if Sermon Square was a link between Barabbas and us, it was now no longer a link which we need be afraid to touch. As Howson and Dewlap's clerk, I should be free of the precincts the enemy used. More. My credentials were flawless: no one in Sussex had known that I was St Omer's friend. In a word, our first problem was solved, for now we could safely approach the only place in the world from which we could start.

Of course I went further than that. But the foolish hopes which I dandled were very soon overtaken by much more practical fears. With a shock, I perceived that the post upon which I was counting might well be already filled . . . that Mansel might be out of Town, when my letter arrived . . . and, what was a thousand times worse, that I might have been seen with Mansel and Chandos at Scott's. This last reflection brought the sweat on to my face, for, if I had been so seen, my appearance at Sermon Square would snap that link out of hand. And then we should be done . . .

When I had worn myself out in this fruitless way, at last I saw the wisdom of going to bed, and this made me wild with myself for wasting two hours of slumber, with such a morrow in view. But, despite the state I was in, I slept very well, and a letter from Mansel arrived before I was dressed.

That fact will show perhaps better than anything I can set down how highly efficient Jonathan Mansel was. He had had my letter at eight, and exactly half an hour later my orders were at my door—careful, considered orders, as I shall show. Most men think, and then act: but he could act whilst he was thinking and could begin to put into practice a plan he had not yet made.

Who it was that bore the letter, I never knew—except that it was not Carson or anyone else connected with Cleveland Row.

With one shoe on and one off, I read the following words.

My dear Bagot,

It's perfectly clear that you're going to pull your weight.

Present your letter this morning, as soon as you can. If the post is already filled, say you'll work for a month for nothing, if only they'll take you on. Swear they'll never regret it. Beg and pray. You have simply got to get in.

Once you are taken on, forget that you ever met me. Put your back into your job, and think about nothing else. Welcome the days when your work keeps you out of Town. You've got to be down in the saddle, before you play any tricks.

By four this afternoon you will be a member of the City Conservative Club, Mark Lane. (This is five minutes' walk from Sermon Square.) From there you can always telephone to Minerva 4343. Ring up that number this evening, to say how you have got on. And always acknowledge my letters to that address.

Read through this letter again, and then burn it up.

Yours ever,

Jonathan Mansel.

I read the letter through twice, thrust it into my pocket and put on my second shoe. Then I rang twice—for breakfast, finished dressing and went off to buy my paper at a neighbouring shop—a thing I always did before breakfast, when I was sleeping in Town. By the time I was back in my rooms, my breakfast was served, but, before I sat down, I read Mansel's letter again and then put it into the fire. I ate and drank and I fancy I read the news. Then I put on my hat and went out and called the first taxi I saw, to take me to Sermon Square.

But all these things I did subconsciously. One sentence of Mansel's letter obsessed my mind. 'You have simply got to get in.'

* * *

I cannot better Mansel's description of Sermon Square—'a short, well-lighted, blind alley, some thirty feet wide.' It ran up from Pigeon Street to an old churchyard, where grass and leaning tombstones were pointing an artless fable which no one had time to read. Here a four-foot passage led down a flight of steps and presently past a tavern, into Mark Lane. The square itself was quiet, though all about it, of course, the roar of the City's traffic made itself heard. At the churchyard end of the square there was just enough room for a car, which was not too long, to be turned about; provided this space was kept clear, there was room for four cars to be berthed along one side of the square: but once those berths were taken, chauffeurs could come and go, but they could not wait.

22 Sermon Square was the very last house—that is to say, it abutted upon the churchyard, and its doorway faced the passage of which I have spoken above. Its number was misleading, for there were but ten houses in all; but since they were none of them ancient, the numbers, no doubt, had survived the much smaller dwellings which they had displaced. Each house had a common staircase which served four floors, and a row of plates on the jamb of the open doorway declared the names of the firms to be found within.

Howson and Dewlap's office was on the ground floor.

I must confess that when first I saw the name, I wished that my drive to the City had taken as long again. On the way I had tried to prepare the case I might have to present, but I am no advocate and I could think of no way of gilding the downright suggestion which Mansel had told me to make. Of course, if the post was still vacant, my letter of recommendation should carry me in: but I had a definite feeling that I should have no such luck, but should have to fight for a concession which a business man and a stranger would see no reason to give. But I knew that, now I was there, to wait, so to speak, on the brink would only make matters worse, so I settled my tie and my hat and then walked into a room at the foot of the stairs.

A clerk of about twenty-five looked up from behind a counter as I came in: then he returned to his business of filling a fountain-pen. I watched him patiently. But when, the pen being ready, he drew a newspaper towards him and began to fill in his answers to some competition there set, I saw that he found my politeness stuff for contempt.

'Attend to me, please,' I said sharply. 'Is Mr Lacey in?'

The clerk looked up.

'Have you got an appointment?' he said.

'No, I haven't. I've got a letter.' I laid this down on the counter. 'I wish him to have it at once.'

The clerk rose and came to the bar. Taking the letter up, he turned it about. Finding the envelope open, he drew out the sheet and read it—a thing that I had not done. And then he looked up, to meet the look in my eye . . . I like to think that that shook him, for he hastily stuffed the sheet back and made his way round the counter and up to some private door. He knocked and was told to come in, and when he reappeared, he asked me to take a seat. But, so far as he was concerned, the damage was done. If the post I desired had been filled, I meant to take his.

And so I did.

Charles Vincent Lacey was a quiet, keen-eyed man, some sixty years old: but if his hair was gray, his manner was young, and he had that easy dignity which no one can ever acquire.

'Mr Bagot,' he said, 'I'm sorry. You're just too late. The post was filled yesterday morning, and that's the truth. I'm really very sorry. From what Colonel Ascot says, you'd have suited us very well.'

'I think I might have,' said I. 'I'm not afraid of work and I want to get on. And here I could have done that. I should have been learning daily . . . I've another job in view, but that'll mean standing still—or, what is worse, sliding back. Still, it's thirty shillings a week, and I've got to live.'

'Thirty shillings a week?' said Lacey. 'What job is that?'

'Office-boy,' said I, 'to a stock-broking firm. I don't mind the work a bit, and I'll lay that I do it better than some I've seen. But I wish it was in other surroundings.' I pointed to a book on a shelf. 'They don't read *Thacker on Drainage* in Mincing Lane.'

'But this is all wrong,' cried Lacey. 'Why, I pay that waster outside three pounds a week.'

'All's fair in war,' said I. 'He isn't worth that.'

Lacey stared upon me, finger to lip.

'Am I to understand that you want his job?'

‘With all my heart,’ said I. ‘I don’t mind wiping his eye and I shouldn’t be wasted here.’

‘I’d see to that,’ said Lacey. ‘Are you sure you mean what you say? An office-boy’s pretty small fry. He has to say “Sir,” and he doesn’t sit down in my room.’

‘I’ll do my duty,’ I said, ‘wherever I am. But I’d much sooner do it here than in Mincing Lane.’

‘Hours nine to six,’ said Lacey, ‘and Saturdays nine to one.’

I smiled.

‘I’m used to a day’, said I, ‘that begins at five.’

Lacey gave a short laugh.

‘The thing’s unheard of,’ said he, ‘but when can you come?’

I got to my feet.

‘That rests with you, sir,’ said I. ‘Today, tomorrow, Monday—whenever you please.’

‘Let’s make it Monday,’ he said. ‘Report to Mr Bonner that morning at nine o’clock.’

‘Very good, sir. I’m very grateful.’

‘Don’t be a fool,’ said Lacey. ‘The boot’s on the other leg.’

‘Good day, sir,’ said I, smiling.

‘Good day, Bagot. I don’t think you’ll stand it long, but that’s your lookout.’

I bowed myself out.

As I came abreast of the counter—

‘Get the job?’ said the clerk.

‘No,’ said I. ‘It’s gone.’

‘Yes, I knew it had,’ he sneered, ‘when I showed you in. But I thought you might as well buy it. Perhaps that’ll teach you to order people about.’

‘I’m much obliged,’ said I—and spoke no more than the truth.

The remnants of my compunction had been destroyed.

* * *

Now, much as I longed to do so, unless I disobeyed Mansel, I could not report my good news till the end of the day, and since it was only just ten and I had nothing to do, I decided to study my surroundings and make myself at home with a district which till now I had never seen. I, therefore, purchased a map and spent the whole of the day exploring the busy environs of Sermon Square. Since I did not go far afield, by half past five that evening I knew the neighbourhood well and could leave or approach my office by five or six different ways. For a furlong from Sermon Square, I knew every court and alley and how they ran, and I remember thinking that I was probably doing as pickpockets used to do, so that if they were chased by some victim, they would stand a much better chance of making good their escape.

And then, at a quarter to six, I something nervously entered the City Conservative Club.

I need have had no concern.

When I gave the porter my name, he smiled and thanked me and gave me a note and a letter addressed to me. Then he asked if I would not like to see over the house, and when I said 'Yes,' he instantly summoned a page and told him to take me round.

The inspection did not take long, for the rooms were few, but the atmosphere was delightful after the strife without. Comfort and peace prevailed wherever I went, and the house itself was unbelievably fine. Its panelling, staircase and ceilings were precious things, and I afterwards learned that it had been the city mansion of some great lord.

As I had expected, the note was from the Secretary, informing me of my election and stating the fees which were due. The letter was from Mansel and covered a banker's draft for five hundred pounds.

> I don't know how you're placed, so I send you this. You shall pay me back when you get your twelve thousand pounds. Sorry to be so abrupt, but we must not take any risks and I like to think you'd do the same by me.
>
> J.M.

Some clock was striking six when I entered a telephone box which was cunningly set in a closet under the glorious stair.

'Minerva 4343.'

After a moment I heard a voice that I knew.

'Who is that speaking?' it said.

'This is John Bagot,' said I.

'At last,' said Lady Audrey. 'What have you done?'

'All's well,' said I.

'Thank God for that. I had a dreadful feeling the job would be gone.'

'It was,' said I, 'but—they gave me another instead.'

'Good for the remount,' said she. 'What is it and when d'you start?'

'Office-boy,' said I. 'And on Monday next.'

'Dear God,' says she. 'Was that the best you could do?'

As soon as I could speak—

'I'm sorry,' said I, 'but they hadn't a partnership free.'

'It can't be helped. Did you get a letter tonight?'

'I did,' said I.

'All right. Now listen to this. You can always get me here between half past six and eight. And that is when I shall ring up, if I want to get you.'

'I'll always be here,' said I.

I heard her sigh.

'This waiting business,' she said. 'How long will it be?'

She spoke as though thinking aloud, and such was her tone it must have touched anyone's heart. Indeed, in that moment I knew that I would ten times rather she took me unfairly to task than let me be a witness of her distress.

'Not very long,' said I. 'And I haven't wasted today. I know this country backwards for quarter of a mile.'

'Good man,' said she—and made me feel suddenly rich. 'I'd give five years of my life to have your job.'

'I know,' said I, 'but somebody's got to do yours.'

'I haven't a job. I'm only a dictaphone.'

'But not for long,' said I.

'That's up to you. Goodbye.'

Before I could say 'Goodbye,' she had hung her receiver up.

* * *

The next day, in my zeal, I did a ridiculous thing.

I thought it would be imprudent to haunt for two days running the purlieus of Sermon Square; so I took a binocular with me and climbed the winding stair to the top of the Monument. I had hoped from this high place to be able to gain some knowledge which, lest I attracted attention, I dared not seek from below: in other words, I had hoped to survey at leisure some one of the outside walls of 22 Sermon Square. (These walls were three, because, as I have shown, the house was the last of its row: one was facing the square, one the church and its yard, and one a seven-foot passage, called Tulip Lane.) Only a fool would have harboured a hope so vain: but I was more used to the country than to the puzzles which bricks and mortar can set.

Had it not been for the church, I should never have even located the square I sought, for I saw next to nothing but roofs and I could not even follow the lines of the streets I knew. The church, as luck would have it, I saw very well, because from where I stood I was looking up Sermon Square: and for that same reason, of course, the walls which I wished to survey were wholly obscured from my view. In a word, I stood west of the house: and the west was the only quarter from which it could never be seen.

I could see no other eminence, likely to serve my turn—except, of course, my landmark, the church of St Ives. This, I knew, must command the whole of one of the walls—and must itself be commanded by every single window that faced that way. But for this fatal defect, it would have done wonderfully well, and if visitors were not permitted to prove the leads, four great down-pipes, like ladders, were waiting there to be climbed.

With a sigh, I put up my glasses and thrust temptation away . . .

At five o'clock that evening I went to the club, to find a letter from Mansel which did me good.

> We had champagne last night, on purpose to drink your health. From every point of view, the job you have managed to get is better than any other that I can spell.
>
> I'm going to give you one week in which to form your habits and settle down. Please use it faithfully—and think of nothing at all but the work you are paid to do. And then we'll get down to things.

That day the inquest on George St Omer was held. No one had seen the smash: and, in view of the evidence given, no one could blame the jury for bringing in the verdict they did. 'Accidental Death.' Indeed, so far as I know, nobody ever remarked that his injuries might have been caused by a violent assault. There was no reason why they should. The job had been very well done.

The evening papers, of course, reported the proceedings in full, and, as much because of their headlines as anything else, I was very reluctant to ring Lady Audrey up. But I had to acknowledge the letter which I had received, so at seven o'clock I went to the telephone.

As before, she answered herself.
'Is that John Bagot?'
'To let you know,' said I, 'that he got a letter tonight.'
'I see. What's the City like?'
'Quiet,' said I. 'It's Saturday afternoon.'
'It will be still quieter tomorrow.'
'No doubt about that.'
'Then take a day off,' says she. 'I mean what I say.'
'I understand. Till Monday.'
'What did you do today?'
'I wasted my time,' said I.
'That's my prerogative.'
'I don't agree,' said I.
'Of course you don't. "What's Hecuba to him?" '
' "Or he to Hecuba?" '
I heard her draw in her breath.
Then—
'Have you ever watched a fool untying a knot?'
'Not for long,' said I.
'Exactly,' says she. 'Well, that's what I'm doing now.'
'I take it,' said I, 'I'm the fool.'
'It's not your fault, John Bagot; but what do you know? How can an unskilled man do a skilled man's job?'
'I'm sorry,' I said. 'It's terribly trying for you. But I'm going to get there somehow.'
Lady Audrey sighed.
'Oh, dear, you do mean so well. Never mind. Till Monday, then.'
'Till Monday,' said I. 'If anything happens——'
'Nothing will happen,' said she. 'Be sure of that. Nothing will ever happen. There's no reason why it should.'
Before I could make any answer, she had cut off.
I returned to the smoking-room, smarting from the cuts she had dealt me, yet glad in a way to have been her whipping-boy. After all, it hadn't harmed me: and if it had done her good . . .
Mansel, of course, was right to forbid me to come to the City the following day. It would have made me conspicuous. As like as not, on Sundays no members entered the City Conservative Club. Not more than half a dozen were in it now.
It was now a quarter past seven, and since I was there, I decided

to dine in the club. So I sent for a glass of sherry and lighted a cigarette and then read once again the dialogue of the play which had been presented near Bedford that afternoon.

How many people, I wondered, knew that it was a drama which had been produced? A dozen, perhaps, in the world. The players themselves had no idea they were acting—gravely speaking the lines which had been put into their mouths. Inspector, surgeon and earnest constable: St Omer's cousin and heir: the pompous coroner 'and his disciples twelve'—all of them saying their pieces, according to plan. And the whole of the British public shaking its head and lapping the nonsense up. . . .

Little wonder that, facing these facts, Lady Audrey Nuneham was not at her best.

* * *

After an excellent dinner, I left the club about ten, proposing to walk for a while and then pick up a cab.

The streets were so empty and quiet that it would have been asking for trouble to go through Sermon Square; but there seemed to be nothing against my walking down Tulip Lane, for though, in fact, it was slightly out of my way, no one I met would know that and, as a convenient short cut, it was very much used.

Now, as I have shown already, 22 Sermon Square backed on to Tulip Lane, which means that the lane ran parallel with the square. But whereas the square was cut short by St Ives' churchyard, the latter, so to speak, gave way to the lane, which ran on past its railings and past the door of the church.

Turning into Tulip Lane, I lifted my head.

One glance was more than enough.

Every window on either side was dark and most were fitted with reflectors, which, though no doubt they lighted the rooms they served, effectually screened those chambers from curious eyes.

I walked on down the lane, proposing to stop and look round when I came to the door of the church, for from there I knew I could see the whole of the flank of 22 Sermon Square. But I never got so far, for before I had reached the railings which fenced the churchyard, I saw to my surprise a light in the church.

I slackened my pace, staring.

And then I saw my mistake.

It was not a light in the church. *One of the stained-glass panes was reflecting the light from a window of 22 Sermon Square.*

I think it was then that I saw that what is dangerous by day may be safe by night and that, now that darkness was come, no one could see a man on the leads of the church. And a man on the leads of the church could command the room that was lighted in 22 Sermon Square.

As I came to the churchyard railings, I glanced behind. So far as I could see, I had the lane to myself.

The railings were high enough, but I covered two spikes with my hat and clambered over this not very promising stile. Stooping low, I moved between tombstones and over, I fear, a good many unmarked graves, but I hoped that the dead would forgive me because, after all, I was seeking to serve one of them. And then at last I came to the wall of the church—and an elegant flying-buttress to hide me from Tulip Lane.

I set my back to the wall and took my first look at the window from which the light came.

To my delight, I could see clean into the room, but since this was two floors up and not twenty paces away, I could only see the ceiling from where I stood. But the window was not so high up as the leads of the church, so that if I could only climb up there before the light was put out, I ought to be able to see all there was to be seen.

With that, I turned to the down-pipe I knew was at hand, thanking my stars that I had surveyed by daylight the way which I meant to go.

Looking back, I remember that I was possessed with a fear that the light in the room would go out before I could reach the leads. What I thought I was going to see, I have no idea. I do not believe that I ever got so far. And that, no doubt, was as well, for if I had questioned the instinct which ordered me up to the leads, I think that I must have seen how childish the enterprise was. Though I saw five men in the room, I should have gained nothing at all, *because I had nothing to tell me if they were the men I sought.* But, as I say, I never thought of these things. My one idea was to see right into that room.

The down-pipe was square-shaped and massive and was stoutly tied to the wall every five or six feet, and since it was flanked by windows the stone frames of which were carved, to climb it was just as easy as I had supposed: indeed I deserve little credit for anything done that night, and I even remember cursing because I had not thought to take my binocular off—the soldier cursing because he has remembered his sword.

Be that as it may, I managed to gain the leads, and there sitting down behind the open-work screen, which served for a parapet, I could see straight into the room, which belonged to the second floor of 22 Sermon Square.

A man was sitting at a table, under a powerful light. I could not see what he was doing, except that he seemed to be sitting back in his chair: but I saw that his hair was white, or else very gray.

All at once I thought of the glasses—which, had I not been so hasty, I should have left behind.

These were very powerful; and after a little adjustment, they brought the man so close I could see the ring on the hand with which he was stroking his chin.

I never saw him full face, for to me he was sitting sideways and he never looked round: but the view which I had of his profile left nothing to be desired.

It was the kindly face of a man of some sixty summers in excellent health. He was clean-shaven; his thick hair was nearly white, and his colour was fresh: his features were rough, but strong: and he made me think of an old-fashioned, country parson of whom his parish is not only fond, but proud. That he had a sense of humour was perfectly clear, for he was reading some paper and smiling at what he read. Indeed, once or twice he literally shook with mirth, and I found myself laughing with him, so honest and unaffected was his merriment.

Then he turned over a page, and I saw that the paper before him was *The Evening News*.

Now, as I have shown, I had had the best of reasons to study the papers that night, and I was ready to swear that there was no humorous matter upon the front page of the paper which I have named. Two columns had been devoted to the inquest upon poor George, and the coroner's vivid account of what he presumed had occurred had been taken out of its place and printed in heavy type. . . .

I have no excuse to offer. I never saw—even then. But when, some two minutes later, my genial friend returned to the paper's front page and, taking a pair of scissors, *cut out the two columns and the head-line which stretched across the whole of the sheet*, then the scales fell from my eyes and I knew that he was the man, to find and to spy upon whom was all the object I had in coming to Sermon Square.

CHAPTER 3

I Wait for the Stroke

The discovery shook me so much that I began to tremble from head to foot and I could not hold steady the glasses to which I owed all that I knew: but I watched him cut out the rest of the full report, fold the two cuttings together and then slide them into a buff-coloured envelope. Then he picked up a pen and addressed it and sealed it up, and I think there can be no doubt that that night it went to Barabbas, wherever he was.

Now, if I had had any sense, I should have left the leads without any delay, for now I had only to watch the door of the house and, if I could do so safely, to follow him when he came out: but although he left his table, I sat there watching until the light was put out, and then, of course, I knew that my chance was gone and that I must stay where I was, for the down-pipe was not a staircase and he would be out of the house before I was down from the leads.

A street lamp was lighting the doorway of 22 Sermon Square, and I saw him come out and look round and then walk across to the passage which led to Mark Lane.

I will not dwell on the feelings with which I watched the monster pass out of my sight, whilst I sat on the other side of the gulf I had fixed between us in my stupidity. But at least this blunder showed me how much I had yet to learn and that I should be worse than useless, unless I was ever ready to take up the running when Fortune had done her share.

I had won something, of course, but, had I but used my wits, I might have won so much more that I could take no pleasure in what I had done: and when, descending my down-pipe, I thought of the disappointment which Mansel and Chandos would hide, I could have done myself violence for what I had failed to do. Then I thought of Lady Audrey—and nearly fell down the twelve feet between me and the turf.

She would show me no mercy. She had chastised me with whips: but now she would chastise me with scorpions. 'A fool untying a knot'—and before the night was out I had proved the truth of her words. I could bear the scorpions as I had borne the whips; but I did not want her to beat me; I wanted myself to force the scorn from her face and set in its stead a look of gratitude. In my heart I valued her censure more highly than Mansel's praise; but I wanted her just admiration—because I admired her so much.

I looked no further than that. For one thing, she was in mourning for one of the finest fellows I ever knew, and though she might put off her sackcloth after a while—well, when a girl has worn emeralds, she takes little interest in jade. Then, again, I had no money, except my twelve thousand pounds; and she was bred to grace Peerless and not some land-agent's lodge. And so I was not such a fool as to harbour the faintest hope. But Fate had kicked me upstairs and fairly thrust me into my lady's chamber, and, since I was there, I wanted to win her smile. If I liked to adore her, that was my private affair. But I did not wish her simply to suffer my presence because I had been introduced by somebody greater than she.

The prey of these selfish emotions, I stumbled through the churchyard and back into Tulip Lane, for though I was tempted to climb into Sermon Square and take, for what it was worth, the way which my man had taken eight minutes before, I had seen three policemen go by whilst I was up on the leads, and as my end of Sermon Square was very much better lighted than Tulip Lane, it would have been asking for trouble to go that way.

Once in the lane, I hastened round the block into Sermon Square, but of course the passage was empty and, though I walked down Mark Lane and then, turning west, all the way to Ludgate Hill, the man I wanted to see was not to be seen.

The incident being over, I knew that I must report it as soon as I could. When all was said and done, I had some valuable news: to suppress it for forty-eight hours would be the act of a fool and, what was still more to the point, my tale was not one I could tell on the telephone.

After a lot of thinking, I rang up Lady Audrey from Charing

Cross, and fifty minutes later, in obedience to her instructions, I took a train from Paddington, travelling west.

When the train was well under way, I left my seat and walked down the corridor. Mansel's servant, Carson, was standing outside a compartment the blinds of which were drawn down, and as soon as he saw me approaching, he opened the door.

Without a word, I went in, and there were Mansel and Chandos and Lady Audrey herself.

* * *

'I'm sorry,' said Mansel, 'to be so hard of access, but Carson says I'm being watched, and he's usually right. Well, that doesn't matter to me, but it matters to us. And that's where a train comes in. If you've got a ticket waiting and you run it sufficiently fine, you can always steal a march by taking a train. And now we should love to hear what it is you know.'

I told what there was to tell, while the train slid out of the suburbs and into the countryside and the three sat still as death, with their eyes on my face.

When I came to the end—

'I'm most awfully sorry,' I said. 'I see the mistake I made and I've no excuse. If I'd had the sense of a louse——'

'What would you have done?' said Mansel.

'Left the leads,' said I, 'the moment I realized that he was our man: lain in the grass by the railings, until he came out of the house: watched which way he went: and then whipped over the railings and followed behind.'

'I see,' said Mansel. 'And now I'm not going to spare you—I'm going to put it across you once for all. You have done magnificently: but when you talk like that, you not only talk as a fool, but you scare me stiff. If you had gone after that wallah, you would have torn everything up. I'll tell you why. Because men like that are accustomed to being followed, but you are not accustomed to following men like that.'

That was as much as he said, but his tone was very sharp and the blood came into my face: and there followed an awkward silence, which I did not know how to break.

Then a hand came to rest on my arm.

'What a shame,' said Lady Audrey. 'He's done so terribly well.'

'More,' said Mansel, smiling. 'He never answered me back.'

'Neither did I,' said Chandos, 'when you told me off in a meadow some years ago.'

'In a word,' said Lady Audrey, 'my record is safe.'

Then all three spoke very warmly of what I had done. But I had had my reward. My task-mistress had actually taken my part.

'And now,' said Mansel, 'to business.

'Thanks entirely to Bagot, we're over the first big fence: it doesn't look so bad now, but it was a hell of a leap. Bagot has gained in one night what might very well have taken us months to obtain.

'You see, all I knew was this—that of the five firms in that house, only two were firms which we could count out. One was Howson and Dewlap, and the other was a firm of solicitors on the first floor. To one of the others, then, I knew that our man belonged. But think of the task that presented. . . . And think of the time we'd have wasted—on two firms out of the three . . .

'Well, we have been spared that nightmare. Bagot now knows by sight Barabbas' *chargé d'affaires,* and I can give you the name of the firm to which he belongs. Benning and Sheba, General Agents, London and Valparaiso. That, of course, is a blind, though they certainly have an office in Valparaiso: and if you went to them and asked them to ship a car, they'd probably do it all right—through somebody else. Very well. He is Benning and Sheba, of 22 Sermon Square.

'Now, what do we want from him? We want Barabbas' address.

'Well, it won't be in his office—I think you may lay to that. And I think it more than likely that when he addressed those cuttings, he didn't address them direct: he probably sent them to Paris, from where they will be sent on. And whenever Barabbas writes, he probably does the same. I mean, I know I should. Postmarks aren't always blurred.

'That means we can wash out the post—we shall get nothing there. And men like Barabbas don't talk on the telephone. But, happily for us, we are dealing with business men: and big business cannot be written—it simply *has* to be talked. You can correspond all right for weeks at a time, but sooner or later you've simply got to meet, if business is to be done.

'Now it is my firm belief that Barabbas comes to England as seldom as ever he can. Movement attracts attention: and once a fence has attracted attention to himself, he may as well shut up shop. So I think that, like all good fences, Barabbas sits still. I think he came to England after the Blanche Mains show. But that would have stung a limpet into a dance. As a general rule, I believe Barabbas stays put. Very well. If Barabbas stays put in France, how does he manage to talk to his *chargé d'affaires*? The answer, of course, is obvious. His *chargé d'affaires* goes to see him, now and again.

'Soon or later, then, the man Bagot saw tonight will leave England for France—to have a talk with Barabbas, wherever he happens to be. And that will be our chance. I've no idea when he will go or what route he will take. But, when he goes, we must go with him, for he will lead us up to the fountain-head.

'Now, when people are going on a journey, they usually start from their homes: or, to put it no higher than this, it is at their homes, and not at their offices, that their visible preparations for a journey are usually made. The first thing, therefore, to do, is to find out where Bagot's man lives.'

He paused there, and Lady Audrey opened her mouth.

'An office-boy,' she said, 'can talk to a caretaker. It's a hundred to one the caretakers live in the basement of 22 Sermon Square. They have the keys of the rooms and they keep them clean. And they know quite a lot of their patrons—a good deal more, perhaps, than their patrons think.'

'That's perfectly true,' said Chandos. 'But if you know that, Audrey, why, so does the fellow that Bagot was watching tonight. And it's Sermon Square to a soak-pit that he has got those caretakers where they belong. All done by kindness, of course. Toys for the children at Christmas, and that sort of thing. And if Bagot approaches them, before we know where we are the fat'll be burnt.'

'William's right,' said Mansel. 'I'm sorry, Audrey: but we've got to go round the long way.'

'By which you mean . . . ?'

'That Bagot must point out this fellow to somebody else—someone who knows how to follow a highly suspicious man. Neither William nor I can do that, because we are known: neither Carson nor Bell can do that, because, as our servants, they have been seen with us: but, as luck will have it, I've got someone just as good. He is to be Bagot's servant, if Bagot will take him on. But that's for later, of course: he mustn't be seen with him yet. His name is Rowley, and he used to be in the service of a very great friend of us both.

'All City men, even office-boys, go out to lunch: and Bagot, of course, will conform to that excellent rule. So, it is to be hoped, will Bagot's man. Either going or coming, therefore, the two are certain to meet before very long. And when they do, Bagot will put his right hand—not into his trouser-pocket, but into the pocket of his jacket, as if he were feeling for something which he had lost. Rowley will see the gesture, and Rowley will do the rest.'

'How will Rowley know me?' said I.

'He knows you already,' said Mansel. 'He was on the platform tonight. But I don't want you to know him, till we're over this fence. Oh, and by the way, I shouldn't lunch at the club. After six it doesn't matter so much, for people begin to clear out about half past five. But when I arranged your election, I did not count on your being an office-boy.'

'Inconsistency rampant,' said Chandos. 'D'you think it's safe for him to be seen going in?'

'For the moment, yes,' said Mansel. 'He looks like a member, and not like an office-boy: and few, outside Howson and Dewlap's, will know he's an office-boy. There *is* a very slight risk: but I think we've got to take it, because, as a line of communication, the club is ideal.'

Lady Audrey lifted her voice.

'Suppose all goes as we hope. Mr Bagot shows him to Rowley, and Rowley follows him home—and Rowley then finds out that the fellow is leaving for France on the following day.'

'We must leave that night,' said Mansel, 'and pick him up on arrival—"somewhere in France." I promise you, Audrey, so far as mere man can do it, we shall leave nothing to chance. Bell will cross the Channel on Monday, to fix up some sort of base on the other side. He gets on well with the French and he's very, very good at that sort of thing. He ought to have everything ready in six days' time: and then he'll sit down and wait: he's not coming back. So that, though we may have to leave at a moment's notice, at least we can always be sure of a flying start.'

Lady Audrey regarded him straitly.

'I believe you have reason to think that when Mr Bagot's man goes, he will go by road.'

'I have this reason to think so—that that is what I should do. You see, from his point of view, it is absolutely vital that he should not do that very thing which we hope so much that he will—lead some unauthorized person up to his master's lair. Not that he loves Barabbas: but if Barabbas goes down, his occupation is gone.

'Now, if a man travels by train, or even by air, he cannot choose his company, and however much he mistrusts it, once he is moving, he's got to stay where he is. But what is very much worse, from a criminal's point of view, he has to use stations or ports, as the case may be: and, quite apart from the fact that stations and ports are beloved by plain-clothes men, the movement in those places is such that, however skilful he is, he can never be sure that he isn't being watched by somebody there. But if a man goes by road in his private car, he *can* make sure that he isn't being followed or watched. I mean, I think that's clear. Half a dozen times in the day, he can, if he pleases, confirm that desirable fact. And if he's not sure, he can stop or turn or go back. Better still, he can lie up by day and travel by night, when the lights of a following car would instantly give it away.'

Lady Audrey drew in her breath.

'If you're right, and he goes by road and travels by night . . .'

'Quite so,' said Mansel. 'It's going to be very hard. But remember we're four to one, and that's going to be a great help.'

I saw the stars leap into my lady's eyes.

'My God, d'you mean that, Jonah? You'll really let me come in?'

Mansel smiled.

'Up to the neck, my dear—if you'll swear to do as I say. I'm bound to warn you, you may have a pretty rough time. I don't say you will, but you may. No bath and no bed for two days, or possibly three. It all depends on where Barabbas hangs out. And if you fall by the way, we must let you lie.'

'Don't worry,' said Lady Audrey. 'I shan't do that. And what do I care if it's rough? I'd sleep in my clothes for a month, if that would help us to get that butcher down.'

'We know you would,' said Mansel, 'and that's why we want you in. For your sake only, I'd rather that you were a man.' He turned to me. 'Audrey,' he said, 'is one of those very few women who have a way with a car. I can almost believe that she could drive in her sleep. And her sense of direction is the finest I ever saw.'

'And as those two gifts,' said Chandos, 'are precisely what is required—I'm assuming, of course, that our man will travel by road—not to use them would be suicidal: you can't get away from that.'

My lady inclined her head.

'Thank you both,' she said gravely. 'I promise I won't let you down.' She turned to me. 'You mustn't believe all you hear. On my day out I'm not too bad on the road, but Richard is better than I am, and Jonah can drive a car backwards smoother and faster than most men can drive one in first.'

'Which is absurd,' said Mansel. 'And now I'm going to be brutal, pull the rip-cord and bring our balloon down to earth. "I'm assuming," said William just now. So are we all: and it's done us a power of good. Agreeable speculation is just like a Turkish bath. But now we must take our cold plunge—and go back to Sermon Square.

'I hope that before very long the scene will shift, and, as I told you just now, I shall do my best to ensure that, when it does, we can walk straight on in the next. But it may not shift for some time. Bagot may come and go, yet not set eyes on his man; and though there's always the church, Benning and Sheba's late sittings are probably very rare. It's no good not facing these things . . .

'Bagot will start work on Monday—and concentrate all he knows upon keeping his job. He will also avoid Tulip Lane and the leads of the church of St Ives. Once is enough, when enough's been as good as a feast. At lunch-time he'll keep his eyes open—no more than that. Be ready, of course: but on no account look for your man. And don't try and pick out Rowley: his eye's not dim.'

He stopped, to glance at his watch.

'Time to burn,' he said. 'But Audrey gets out at Swindon and Bagot at Stroud. Most inconvenient, of course: but that is the worst of being without the law. And no one need be afraid of going to sleep. Carson is on duty as call-boy, and he won't fail.'

With that, he closed his eyes, and after a little Chandos began to doze. But I was too much excited to take any rest, so I sat back and waited till Lady Audrey should speak.

For a while she stared out of the window on to the flying country she could not see. Then with a sigh she looked round, to glance at Mansel and Chandos and then at me.

'You must be tired,' she said.

I shook my head.

'I haven't done much today.'

'I don't agree,' she said shortly. She settled herself in her corner and put up her elegant feet. 'And I shouldn't have called you a remount. I might have known that George wouldn't make a mistake.'

'It was true enough,' said I.

'Well, it isn't now. You've—"passed out." In future I'll call you "John." And if you can manage "Audrey"—well, that's my name.'

'If you please,' said I, and felt more than pleased myself.

'Tell me honestly—how do you feel about things? Shall we ever discover Barabbas?' Before I could answer, she lifted a little hand. 'Don't say "Of course we shall," for we're past that stage. Pretend you're a looker-on, and then say what you think.'

'I think,' said I, 'it's only a question of time.'

'We're red-hot now because we're straight from the fire. But after a while, you know, an iron grows cold.'

'This one won't,' said I, and meant what I said. 'Barabbas will go to Hell—no doubt about that. But I want to take his ticket and see him off. George was damned good to me.'

To that she made no reply, and when I looked up, she was staring out of the window, with one of her hands to her mouth.

'I'm sorry,' I said. 'I'm afraid I speak as I feel.'

Her head was round in a flash.

'Try not to be a damned fool.'

I swallowed.

'To tell you the truth,' I said, 'I'm not very good at women.'

'Dear God,' says she, 'and when did you find that out?'

'Two nights ago,' said I, 'when I spoke on the telephone.'

There was a little silence.

Then—

'You say,' she said, 'that you think it's a question of time. But in your heart you know it's a question of luck.'

'Not altogether,' said I. 'Let me put it like this. We are going to go all lengths to get what we want: we are going to spare no labour and no expense: we are going to take every precaution that man can take. Well, people who do these things are very well placed for dealing with what is called luck. If it's good, they can pounce upon it and suck it dry: if it's bad, they can cope with it better than people less well prepared.'

'Very specious, John; but, supposing we get so far, we shall need the devil's own luck to keep in touch with your gentleman's car in France.'

'I don't know the country,' said I. 'But I've always understood that it's much more open than England.'

'It is,' said Audrey. 'And the traffic is very slight. But if there's plenty of room, there are plenty of roads, and if I didn't want to be followed, I guess that I'd have my way.'

'I can't argue with you about that. But human nature should help.'

'What d'you mean by that?' said Audrey.

'He'll put us through it to start with—no doubt about that. Twist and turn and double, *in case* he is being trailed. And then, being human, he'll make up his mind that he's safe and stick to the path. Precautions pall very fast, when, for all you know, they may be a waste of time.'

'You're begging the question,' said Audrey. 'If ever a man of that type makes up his mind that he's safe, you may bet he *is* safe. Never mind. Are you as good at French as you are at women?'

'Just about,' said I. 'I can't speak a blasted word.'

'Dear God,' says she, 'that's a help.'

'I depend upon you,' said I, 'to talk and to drive.'

She stared upon me open-mouthed.

'Thanks very much,' said she. 'And what will you do?'

'I shall keep you straight,' said I. 'If I can do that, I believe we ought to get home.'

Audrey glanced round the carriage, as though for support. But Chandos' lips were pursed and Mansel was smiling—apparently in his sleep. With a sudden movement, she pushed back her thick dark hair.

'All square,' she said. 'And I thought I was good at men.'

'I should think you are,' said I. 'Very good indeed.'

She shook her head.

'You've shown me, John, that I have a lot to learn. And now I'm going to do what I can to doze. And you'd better do the same. You've earned a better night than you're going to get.'

With that, before I could answer, she shut her eyes—which was as good as saying that our conversation was closed. For this I was sorry—if for no other reason because I had not yet ventured to accept her invitation to use her Christian name. Still, I comforted myself with the thought that, when she got out at Swindon, to mumble 'Good night, Audrey,' ought to be easy enough, and settling myself in my corner, began to review the events of the last few hours.

But Nature loses no chances. . . .

In point of fact, I suppose I was very tired. Be that as it may, the next thing that I remember was Carson's voice in my ear, announcing that in five minutes' time we should run into Stroud. And there was Mansel smiling and Chandos cleaning a pipe, while Audrey's corner was empty, as though she had never been there.

* * *

I shall always remember gratefully my time with Howson and Dewlap, short though it was. Everyone in that office was kindness itself. The work, of course, was nothing; it was the post. I made such a glorious cock-shy . . . yet nobody threw any sticks. The grave-faced Mr Bonner, the junior clerks, the busy typists, the cheerful switchboard girl—one and all were as sympathetic as people could be. Mr Bonner gave me papers 'which he thought I might like to read': the clerks told me where to lunch and related the manners and customs which Howson and Dewlap kept; the typists brought me tea; and Miss Taylor, the switchboard girl, who did my duty when I went out to lunch, watched over me like the angel I think she was. With the partners, of course, I had little or nothing to do: and for this I was truly thankful, for Lacey had shown me great kindness in taking me on, and since, when I left his service, I might have to do so without any notice at all, I had no wish to enter more deeply into his debt. If sometimes my hours seemed long, my duties were very light, and since to sit and do nothing was more than I could endure, I made one or two innovations, for which my successors have probably cursed my soul. They are not worth setting down, but Mr Bonner approved them with all his might, and to my confusion my wages were raised that week—a kindness which hit me harder than any rebuke could have done. I like to think that the measure I gave was good; but sailing under false colours is not the sort of progress that one can ever enjoy, and when your consorts go out of their way to be nice, the burden they lay upon you is heavy to bear. At night I slunk to the club, where the deference shown me by the servants made me feel ill at ease; and when I went back to my rooms, to find my things in order and comfort ready and waiting for my return, I felt ashamed of the rôle I was playing in Sermon Square. However, there was nothing to be done. Till Fate or Mansel released me, the game must go on. With twelve thousand pounds behind me, I must continue to pose as a 'down-and-out' and, as such, to accept a goodwill which many an honest beggar has never known.

Now I had fully expected that a very short time would elapse before I renewed my acquaintance with the man I had seen at his table that startling Saturday night: indeed, my only concern was lest the signal I gave should seem to Rowley to indicate somebody else; but this anxiety was wasted, for day after day went by, yet I never set eyes on my man.

Expectation gave way to hope, and hope to doubt. I lingered before shop-windows; I went for a stroll after lunch; I left my umbrella behind—and so had a good excuse for retracing my steps. But all these endeavours were vain, and though my hand was itching to give the sign, the sign was never given and Rowley had nothing to do but go empty away.

I never rang up Audrey, because I received no letters and I had no news to report; and she never rang me up, because, I suppose, she had no instructions to give. This suspension of our relation was something I had not foreseen, and I longed that something would happen, if only because in that case I should hear her most excellent voice. Indeed, as the days went by, I could hardly resist the temptation to ring her up, but I knew that if I did so without just cause, I should lose what credit I had with that very exacting girl. The loss would not be great, because, as a matter of fact, I had none to lose; but at least I had a clean sheet, and I did not want an entry upon the opposite side.

So sixteen days went by: and May came in in splendour, and the green of the churchyard trees was a sight for sore eyes.

It was on a Tuesday evening, the tenth of May, that I entered the club, as usual, at twenty-five minutes past six. As usual, I washed my hands and made my way to the elegant smoking-room: as usual, I ordered a drink and, as usual, I read the papers from end to end. But either because I was restless, or else because the papers had little to tell, I found myself at seven with nothing on earth to do. I had no letters to write—and if I had, I should not have cared to write them from that address. I had no book to read, for though there were some shelves in the morning-room, they were laden with dry-as-dust volumes whose names were enough to frighten a pedant away; but, since they were bound in calf, they made a brave show, and I fancy they had been purchased to serve as furniture.

For a while I struggled with a crossword—of course in vain: and then I remembered the volumes of *Punch* I had marked when the page who had shown me the house had led me into the silent billiard-room.

At once I knew I was saved—that night and for weeks to come, for there had been a set at Peerless and always, after hunting, it had been my great delight to stroll down its gallery of humour and study the spirit and manners of other days.

As thankful as any prisoner released from jail, I mounted the lovely staircase two steps at a time, to pause at the billiard-room door and honour the time-honoured order *Wait for the Stroke*. More as a matter of form than anything else, I peered through the little peep-hole which gave me a chance to obey, for I did not suppose that the table would be in use. But there I was wrong, for a game was indeed in progress and one of the players was, if I may borrow the phrase, addressing his ball.

I saw him well, for while the room was in shadow, his kindly face was flood-lit by the table's lamps: in fact I could see him much better than when I had seen him last.

So once more, though he never knew it, my eyes were fixed on Barabbas' *chargé d'affaires*.

The encounter was so unexpected that I stood for a moment or two as though turned into stone, but when I perceived how narrow had been my escape, my knees felt weak and the palms of my hands grew wet.

Had his opponent been playing and he standing back, I should have walked into the room when the stroke had been made. He would have looked round, of course, and our eyes would have met . . . and that, I believe, would have been the end of this tale, for the start which I must have given would have made a simpleton stare.

Though I had been spared this disaster, its bare contemplation embarrassed my shaken wits, and though I tried my best to think what to do, my brain could suggest no action, but only precipitate flight. And this I was sure was wrong. Though I could not see how to play it, I had been dealt by Fortune a valuable hand. Mansel or Chandos would have made a hatful of tricks. But I could think of nothing, but of throwing the cards away. And the game of billiards was very nearly over, for 'spot' was eighty-seven and 'plain' was ninety-two. . . .

Then a cough at my shoulder roused me, and there was a servant standing, with a tray in his hand.

'I'm sorry,' I said somehow, and stood away from the glass.

'It's quite all right, sir, thank you.'

He peered through the peep-hole himself, before going into the room.

It was his natural action that cleared my brain.

'What's the name of that member?' I said. 'The one with the thick, gray hair.'

The servant looked round.

'That's the Reverend Plato, sir.'

'No,' said I. 'The one in his shirt-sleeves, I mean.'

'That's right, sir. He is a reverend, though he doesn't wear clerical clothes. I don't think he practises. He's something in the City, I think. He lives at Virginia Water and comes up to Town most days.'

CHAPTER 4

On Parade

My instructions were clear.

> Give notice at once and leave on Saturday. Say that you cannot endure an office life.
>
> Continue to go to the club—from half past six each evening till seven o'clock. Go for the last time on Friday.
>
> Leave London for Paris on Tuesday and travel by train. (You must be prepared to stay abroad for some time.) Go to the—— Hotel and engage a small suite. Say that Madame will arrive the following day.
>
> Go to Le Bourget on Wednesday to meet the mid-day 'plane. Madame will come by that, and you are to greet her exactly as you would greet a girl-friend for whom you had taken the rooms. This is most important. If she can play up, so can you.
>
> From that time on you two will work together, and so her

orders are yours. But here is a special order for you alone. 'She is to talk and to drive, and you are to keep her straight.'

I will not set out my emotions, for they may be better imagined than written down: but I was so much excited that I could hardly think straight, and I had to take hold of myself lest my friends in Sermon Square should find my demeanour curious and wonder what was afoot. By strict application to business, I managed, I think, to conceal the elation I felt, but I must confess I was thankful when Saturday came, not only because I was stamping to get to France, but because I was sick and tired of deceiving those honest souls.

On Monday, as may be believed, I had a full day, for, although I had a passport, I had no more than ten hours in which to provide for an absence of several months: however, I did it somehow, and after packing till dawn, I caught the Golden Arrow and slept the most of the way.

I shall always remember that evening, for Paris was warmer than London and summer had really come in; and the world seemed big with promise, and business disguised as pleasure was in the air. The day which should have been ending seemed to have taken a second lease of life, and people appeared to be coming, instead of going away. The streets might have been a *foyer*—between two acts of some popular musical play, and in view of the part which I was about to enact, I do not think I could have demanded a more congenial setting for my entrance upon the stage.

The hotel was retired and private: its hall was empty and I could see no lounge: but the suites I was shown were attractive beyond belief, while the address of the staff, from the manager down to the pages, was irreproachable. No rake's progress was ever so dignified—a fact, I may say, which afforded me great relief, for though I was resolved to ignore it, I had in my heart been dreading the knowing complacence with which I was sure I should meet. In spite of the manners and customs prevailing today, I did not relish the notion of being credited with a conquest which in fact I had not made; still less did I like the idea of parading Audrey Nuneham as the victim of my desires: but the style of the place was so good and the deference shown to my orders was so correct that, so far as that house was concerned, I never deplored the impression which we were bound to convey.

That night I dined in my suite and, after strolling awhile, went early to bed. The next morning I walked about Paris until it was time for lunch: and after that I ordered a private car, which carried me out to Le Bourget by half past two.

As a special favour, for which I fought very hard, I was allowed on the apron on which passengers alight, and from there, at ten minutes to three, I saw the aeroplane land.

As her pilot taxied over, I began to regret my insistence on such a conspicuous place, for a number of less-favoured people were looking on and, as it were, making an audience, whilst I had the stage to myself. My nerves were only waiting for some such opening as this, and I can most truthfully say that now I know what it means to be attacked by stage-fright.

I certainly stood my ground, but that was because I felt unable to move: my mouth was dry as a bone, and I could remember nothing of what I had meant to say: and when, in a frenzy, I tried to recover myself, I think some devil must have possessed my mind, for I thought of Mr Bonner of Sermon Square and the trick he had of holding a pen in his mouth.

The machine must have come to rest and the little staircase been wheeled to its open door, but such was my state that I cannot swear to these things—in fact I remember nothing till Audrey Nuneham stepped out of the aeroplane.

As she did so, she lifted a hand—and my nerve came back.

Halfway to the staircase I met her, hat in hand.

'Audrey, my darling,' I cried: and, with that, I stooped to kiss her, and her arm went about my neck.

Then I drew her towards the building and said how splendid she looked and asked her about her flight; but she did better than that, for she locked her arm tight in mine and walked up and down on the apron, talking of all she had done and all we were going to do, till at last some official approached us and said that the Customs were waiting to clear what luggage she had.

As I opened her dressing-case for her—

'Have you got a car, my darling?'

'I have, my sweet.'

'Good boy. Do you like my dress?'

'I think it's perfect,' said I, and meant what I said.

Indeed, she looked a picture—in blue and white, with a fur slung over a shoulder and a diamond brooch in her hat. And though everybody was smiling, I know that I felt like a king, for a queen had handed me up to sit by her side.

And then we were in the car, and were whipping over the cobbles the way I had come.

Half an hour later, perhaps, we entered our suite.

* * *

Audrey stood looking round.

Then she pulled off her hat and pitched it on to a chair. And then she walked up to a mirror and looked at herself in its glass.

'Well, we're over that fence,' she said. 'But I wish you wouldn't give me these shocks. As the 'plane came up to the apron, I thought you were going to be sick.'

'Well, I damned near was,' said I. 'I wasn't made for these things.'

'Kissing strange women?' says she.

'Well, not in public,' said I. 'There must have been fifty people lapping it up.'

'What could have been better? One of those fifty people is now quite sure that, though I know Jonah and Richard, my visit to Paris has nothing to do with them. "Girls will be girls," they'll say—and write to our Mr Plato to say there's no cause for alarm. But I had to do all the work. You hardly opened your mouth.'

'That wasn't my fault,' said I. 'I couldn't get a word in.'

'You wicked liar,' said Audrey. 'You never tried.'

'Not at all,' said I. 'I thought it looked more natural to let you talk. If you'd dried up——'

There I met her eye in the glass, and the two of us laughed.

'Oh, John,' she said, 'you were sweet. The way you said "Audrey, my darling" . . . I nearly burst. But please do remember this—when a man's in love with a woman, he looks in her eyes.'

'I—I know,' I said feebly enough.

'Then for God's sake do it,' says she, 'the next time we're on parade. And now be a saint and order some China tea. I'm going to wash.'

The waiter had come and gone before I saw her again, and when I did, she was wearing a pair of dark glasses, such as are commonly worn against the glare of the sun.

'And why?' said I.

'Would you know me like this?'

'Anyone would,' said I. 'If you want to disguise yourself, you'll have to get a new face.'

This was true. Veil the great, brown eyes, and the temples came into their own, while the curve of her chin and the pride of her beautiful mouth looked almost more distinguished, because, I suppose, one rival had been suppressed.

She whipped the glasses off.

'They'll be better than nothing," she said. 'Such heaps of people wear them that I shall fall into a class.'

I shook my head.

'You'll never do that,' said I. 'And now may I know our instructions and where we stand?'

She took her seat at the table and poured out tea.

'We're to stay here two nights,' she said, 'and go out and about. Not to the bigger places: Montmartre is rather the portion of people like us. Then we shall leave for Amiens, and there we shall join up with Bell.'

'The base,' said I. 'We're not off?'

'Not yet, thank God—and I never thought I'd say that. But we must have a chance to get ready, if we are to follow Plato with any hope of success. Even I can see that . . . D'you remember our talk in the train?'

'Every word,' said I.

'Well, Jonah heard what you said, and he says you're right. If Plato goes by road, our worst time will be when he leaves the coast. For the first thirty miles, Jonah says, he'll lead us a hell of a dance; but if, at the end of that lap, we're still at his heels, he thinks he'll go tooling along and we ought to get home.

'Very well. The first thirty miles. You and I are in France to learn by heart the country for thirty miles round the ports. Dunkirk, Calais, Boulogne, Dieppe and Havre. We don't know which he'll go to, but, God be praised, they're not very apart; and Amiens makes a good centre from which to work. And Bell's got a car all ready, and I've got some glorious maps.'

'That's very clever,' said I. 'The odds were against us, of course; but this'll shorten our price.'

And that, I think, was true, for, though Plato turned and twisted, he would be turning and twisting in country he did not know; if he switched to the right or the left, he would know where he hoped to come to, but nothing more; but *we* should know where his road led to and, therefore, where he must go.

'Provided he goes by road.'

'Audrey,' said I, 'we must make up our minds that he will. If we are to bring this off, it's no good wondering whether our labour is going to be lost.'

She looked at me steadily, over the rim of her cup.

'The Gospel according to St John.'

'That's the worst of me,' I said. 'I "do mean so well." '

There was a little silence.

Then——

'Don't you like your tea?' said Audrey.

I sighed.

'I've drunk some filth in my time, but I can't drink this. Of course, I'm spoiled. Now the tea Miss Buchan made——'

'Who the devil's Miss Buchan?' said Audrey.

'Another girl-friend,' said I. Audrey choked. 'She's typing letters just now—at 22 Sermon Square. Now the tea she made——'

'D'you expect me to make your tea?'

'God forbid,' said I. 'But——'

'Tell me of Sermon Square, John. I used to think of you there, and you don't know how I wanted to ring you up.'

'My dear,' said I, 'I'll make you a present of this—I used to pray for a letter to be at the club.'

'Well, let's make up for lost time.' She flung me a charming smile. 'And you're right about this tea. Give me a cigarette to take the taste out of my mouth.'

Then she took her seat on a sofa, and put up her pretty feet, and I straddled a chair beside her and told her all I had done in the last three weeks.

It was a dull enough tale, but in the light of her interest it seemed to be a romance; no detail was too petty, and no description too full; she wanted to hear everything—and, because she wanted to hear it, everything seemed to acquire a new significance.

As at last I came to the end——

'And now do tell me,' said I. 'Was my information correct? Does he live at Virginia Water? And is he a clergyman?'

'Yes—to all three,' said Audrey. "According to Rowley, he has a delightful house—with an acre of woodland, which suits Rowley down to the ground. And he runs a boys' club, the darling, and plays a prominent part in local affairs. Full of good works, of course. Rowley also reports that his housekeeper's better-looking than housekeepers usually are, but the neighbours fully believe that she is his niece and that he is a man of God.'

'A car?' said I.

'*And* a chauffeur—a queer-looking card. But, again according to Rowley, he looks as though he could drive.'

'Oh, hell,' said I, without thinking.

'Now then, St John. . . .' She glanced at a tiny wristwatch and got to her feet. 'I'd like to go for a walk. Will you take your little friend out and show her the shops?'

With her consent, I ordered a car for the evening and told them to get two stalls for a musical show: and then we went out on foot, with her, of course, for guide, because she knew where to go.

I cannot believe that there was a shop in Paris which was worth looking into, of which she was unaware, but though such an exercise was not at all in my line, a hermit must have enjoyed it in Audrey's company. And I never would have believed that I could take any interest in women's wear, but when she grew excited about some silk or satin, spread out on a velvet board, I found myself infected and wondering how it would suit her and wishing I had the right to make it hers.

Of course we were 'on parade,' but nobody could have been sweeter or seemed more natural. She made it hard to remember that we were playing a game, taking my arm at the crossings and always sharing with me whatever she saw. And when I walked into a florist's and, finding that they could speak English, selected a basket of roses and gave her name and address, she caught my hand in hers and held it against her heart—the tenderest gesture, I think, that ever a woman made.

But one thing I never did. When I was calling her 'darling,' I never looked into her eyes. I never dared do that, because I could not answer for what she might see in mine.

When I fell in love with her, I cannot pretend to say—I think, perhaps, the first time I saw her, in Mansel's flat. But when that afternoon she stepped out of the aeroplane, then I knew I was mad about her, body and soul. In a way, this made it easy to play my part, for when I had kissed her lips, I was doing as I desired—though I felt rather badly about it, because I seemed in a way to be stealing a march. But what worried me ten times as much was the fear lest I should do something to make her suspect the truth, for that would be the end of a relation that meant the world to me, and though by *force majeure* we worked alone together for week after week, we should never again be easy with one another.

The position, of course, was absurd: I was free to make love to Audrey; but when I did so, I did so with my heart in my mouth.

* * *

By her desire, I did not put on dress-clothes, 'for I must do you credit,' she said, 'but I *will* wear a hat.' So I put on a dark-blue suit and hoped for the best. But when she appeared in the doorway in black and gold, then I knew that it did not matter how I was attired, for, once they had looked upon Audrey, no one would notice how anyone with her was clad.

I got to my feet and bowed.

'All right, St John?'

'Let me put it like this. I shall be the best-hated man in Paris, before the evening is out.'

Audrey smiled.

'You're quite good, when you try,' she said. She turned on her heel. 'And now come and do me up. That's the worst of this dress.'

I do not wish to labour the point, but I was not then accustomed to fastening women's clothes: yet twenty-seven 'bobbles' had to be wheedled through loops for the length of her spine. Since the loops were too small to admit them, the 'bobbles' would not go through, but when I pointed this out, my lady merely observed that that was as it should be, for then, once the 'bobbles' were in, they could not come out. Thus encouraged, I set to work, and after the first two or three, I got on very well, but our dinner arrived when six remained to be done, and we had to adjourn to her bedroom to finish them off.

Here I should say that, while there was only one bathroom, we each had a room to ourselves: mine, I suppose, was really a dressing-room, but at least it had a bed in it, and that was as much as I asked.

Whether anyone watched us that evening, I do not know, but, if they did, any doubts they had of Audrey's business in France must have been cast for ever out of their minds.

When the music-hall show was over, we drove to Montmartre, to eat an excellent supper and dance till two. I cannot answer for the company which we kept, but I can say with truth that none that I ever was in so well interpreted the spirit of revelry. The worship of Folly and Pleasure was unabashed; yet all were so gay and artless, so friendly and laughter-loving in all they did, that had some prelate arrived to rebuke their sins, I think he would have remained to share their *bonhomie*.

Audrey, of course, attracted much attention, and I do not think I should have been human if I had not been proud of the honour I seemed to have. She played up with a will, and I went the way of my heart—to give such a joint performance as I shall never forget. 'Present mirth hath present laughter.' And though I knew very well that the higher I soared the greater must be my fall, I fairly drained the cup which Fortune had put to my lips and let the frowning morrow take thought for itself.

Sure enough, I had my reward.

As we were dancing a valse——

'John, my dear,' breathed Audrey, 'I think we'll go after this.'

'Just as you please, my darling.'

I felt her lean back on my arm.

'Have you enjoyed tonight, John?'

My head came round to face hers, two inches away.

'My God, what d'you think?' said I—and looked into her eyes.

For a moment she met my gaze squarely. Then she looked down and away. The damage was done.

At once I strove to repair it.

'A few nights like this,' I murmured, 'and I should get very good.'

Audrey spoke over my shoulder.

'You're very good now,' she said.

With her words, the music slowed down and a moment later the dance was over and done.

'Thank you, *madame*.'

'And you, John dear.'

She slid an arm through mine, and I led her back to our table and called for the bill.

Three minutes later, perhaps, we were back in the car.

'Are you very tired?' said I.

'Not particularly. Why? D'you mean you don't want to go home?'

'I don't question my orders,' said I.

'I'll give you that,' said Audrey. 'You've—worked very hard tonight.'

I shrugged my shoulders.

'As long as you're satisfied.'

She made no answer to that, and we never spoke again until we were back in our suite.

Then she asked me to order some water, and when I had done so, she took her seat on her sofa and lighted a cigarette.

'All very well,' she said, 'but I want to get down to things.'

I nodded.

'Amiens on Friday,' said I. 'I think it would have been safe to go there tomorrow, instead.'

'So do I. But it can't be helped. When Jonah says what he wants, he means what he says. So tomorrow we'll go to Versailles—all the lovers do that.'

'I'm in your hands,' said I, and stifled a yawn.

Audrey opened her eyes.

'The quick-change artist,' said she. 'Don't wait up for me.'

'I'm waiting for the waiter,' said I.

'God give me strength,' said Audrey. 'And what's biting the evangelist now?'

'Sorry,' said I. 'It's reaction. I've had a difficult day.'

'Have you, indeed?' flashed Audrey. 'And what about me? Hugged and kissed by a man that I hardly know, and, instead of doing him violence, I have to fawn upon him and slobber back.'

Here a knock fell upon the door.

'Play up—sweetheart,' said I, and called 'Come in.'

The waiter came and went.

As the door closed behind him, I got to my feet.

Then I walked up to the sofa, and bent my head.

'Do me your violence,' I said.

My lady searched my eyes.

Then—

'Give me some water,' she said, 'and don't be a fool.'

'Or a cad. I'll do my best—but I haven't much hope.'

And, with that, I turned to the tray.

When I returned to her, I found she was up on her feet.

As she took the glass from my hand—

'I hate to ask you,' she said. 'But if I'm to sleep tonight, you'll have to undo this dress.'

I put my hands on her shoulders and turned her about.

'I'll undo what I've done,' said I. 'A symbolical act. How many fools would sell their souls for the chance?'

'Well, gently does it,' said Audrey. 'I can't help being a girl—and I value this frock.'

'God forgive you for that,' said I. 'But I wouldn't if I were He.'

She did not answer me, but stood very still; and though my hands were trembling, I was so resolved to be deft that I think they could have been trusted to set a watch. Be that as it may, I had my way with the 'bobbles' in half the time it had taken to put them into their loops, and I never once touched her skin or, so far as I know, snapped a thread of the most inconvenient confection that ever a woman put on.

'That's that,' said I. 'Will you go to bed first? Or shall I?'

She drank her water and put the glass back on the tray.

'As I'm half undressed,' she said, 'I'm afraid I must ask you to wait.'

'Very good,' said I. 'Sing out when you're through with the bathroom, and I'll start in.'

She shrugged her dress on to her shoulders and left the room, and I flung myself into a chair and covered my eyes.

I confess that I felt sick of life.

A sudden storm had arisen out of a halcyon day—a savage, senseless squall that had carried us whither it listed and left us leagues apart. All my dreams had been shattered within twelve hours, and my very pleasant fortune replaced by as grim a prospect as anyone could have devised. Once a relation is soured, the only thing to do is to sever it out of hand: but we could not sever our relation; we had to work together—perhaps for months. To spend your life with someone with whom you are in love, who does not love you, can only be a bitter-sweet business, when all has been said and done: but to spend your life with someone with whom you are in love *and* on very bad terms—well, if such an outlook appalled me, I think I may be excused. It must, of course, be remembered that Lady Audrey Nuneham was a very exceptional girl. She was undeniably lovely, her charm was very potent, her spirit was very high—and, when she was out of humour, her tongue was a sharp sword.

A quarter of an hour went by before she lifted her voice.

Then—

'All clear,' she cried, and, before I could make any answer, I heard the slam of her door.

Though I knew that I should not sleep, it seemed best to retire. I did so heavily—to find my bed unready and the coverlet still in its place. I stripped it in some impatience, but when I could find no pyjamas, no slippers, no dressing-gown, then it dawned upon me that the servants had naturally expected that I should spend the night in the other room. My things were there, of course—and the door was shut.

The discovery did me good. For Audrey must have seen them and have purposely let them lie—to put to inconvenience the man with whom she was cross. And that was not the way of a great heart; that was the way of a jade.

I took out clean pyjamas, performed my usual toilet and went to bed. What is more, I went to sleep. My wounds had been salved by the thought that my idol had feet of clay.

* * *

I do not know how long I slept, but I know that something woke me and I started up on an elbow and sought for the switch.

'It's all right,' breathed Audrey. 'It's me. Don't put on the light.' I gave up my search for the switch and lay very still. 'I waited such ages for you to come for your things, and then I realized that you must have done without them and gone to bed. So I had to come to you. I mean, you see, we couldn't have parted like that.'

I propped myself on an elbow and felt very much ashamed. But, whilst I was searching for words, a warm arm slid round my neck and her cheek came to rest against mine.

'Why did we quarrel, St John?'

'I don't know,' I said. 'I'm sorry. It's—the last thing I wanted to do.'

'Or I, my dear. I'd been so happy with you.'

I found her fingers and put them up to my lips.

'I'm afraid I broke down,' I said. 'I'm not a very good actor, and actors who can't really act sometimes get carried away. And when they realize that—well, then they break down.'

'You silly St John,' said Audrey. 'If you could act at all, I shouldn't be here.'

'I don't understand,' said I.

'I know. Never mind. But always be natural with me. I'll tell you where to get off. And please forgive what I said. I said it to make you angry, and I take every syllable back.'

I held her fingers tight.

'I—I wasn't too charming,' I said.

'You were simply odious,' said Audrey. 'You can be, you know. But only when you're acting—so please give it up.'

'But——'

'Whoever wakes first calls the other. Good night, St John.'

As she moved, I turned my head quickly, and brushed her face with my lips.

'Good night, Audrey—my darling.' She caught her breath. 'I thought there was no one like you, and now I know.'

'Sleep well, St John.'

And then she was gone, and only her perfume was left.

CHAPTER 5

Close Quarters

When English people drive to the *Gare du Nord* and take a train which is going to one of the Channel ports, it may be fairly assumed that they are about to return to the country which gave them birth. But some such trains stop at Amiens. . . .

Audrey and I reached the city before midday.

We put our luggage into the cloakroom, inquired the way to the cathedral and left the station on foot. After a few minutes' walk, we entered the famous shrine. For a quarter of an hour we examined the treasures of glass and stone—to say nothing of those of wood, which, honestly, I liked better than anything else. I never saw anything finer than the carved-oak stalls of the choir, and when I learned from some book that the men who made this magic were paid three-halfpence a day, I perceived that the progress of which mankind is so proud, may well be known to the gods by another name.

Then we came out of the church—by another door, to see that four cars had been berthed a little way off. One was a business-like coupé, painted an elephant gray, and Bell was standing by this, with a hand on its door.

A moment later we three were within the car, and Bell was picking his way up a crowded street.

'No news, Bell?' said Audrey.

'Not at the moment, my lady—from London, I mean. But everything's all right here. I've found a nice little villa—it's nothing much to look at, but inside it's very clean. And it's got a very good garage, that takes two cars.'

'What about the cooking?' said Audrey.

'I have a cook-general, my lady. She's very willing and quiet and I don't think she'll talk. I've followed her twice to market, but she doesn't seem to have any friends. She buys what she wants, but she never stops to gossip, as most of them do.'

'Isn't he marvellous?' said Audrey. 'Bell, I'd love to have seen you stalking the cook.' Bell, who was very reserved, permitted himself to smile. 'And now for the burning question. What have you said about us?'

'I've called you "*Madame*," my lady, from first to last. I said that "*Monsieur and Madame*" were coming today. But she never asks no questions: she's not that sort.'

'Good for you,' said Audrey. 'But you mustn't call me "my lady," or that'll tear everything up.'

'Very good, madam,' said Bell.

'You mentioned two cars,' said I.

'This and another, sir. The other's the best of the two. This one'll do all you ask, and do it well. But—well, the other's a Lowland.'

'Oh, I can't believe it,' said Audrey.

'Mr Chandos' orders, madam. In fact, he arranged it all, and I only did as he said.'

Audrey, sitting between us, returned to me.

'Have you driven a Lowland, John?'

'Never,' said I. 'But I've heard they're terribly good.'

'A Lowland,' said Audrey, 'is alive. Whatever action you take, a Lowland's response is so swift that sometimes it actually seems as though the car must have known what you wanted to do.'

'Poor Mr Plato,' said I. 'He's not going to have a look-in.'

'There are times when I hate you,' said Audrey, and left it there.

The villa was very well placed, for it stood at the end of a road on the skirts of the town, and a lane, which was little used, ran down by its side. The principal entrance, of course, was facing the road, but doors from the stable-yard gave into the lane. The latter led into the country without any check, and since, within two miles, it met a main road, was affording a way of approach which suited us down to the ground. The garden was walled and the villa itself was low, and indeed I sometimes think that the fellow for whom it was built must have been about some business which he wished to keep to himself. In a word, it was just what was wanted—by someone without the law.

The house looked ramshackle, and, frankly I should not have cared to winter beneath its roof; but within it was very pleasant and though there was only one bathroom, this had been recently made and fully deserved its name.

For some reason best known to himself, Bell had made up his bed in the harness-room: but I think the truth is that, though he waited upon us from morning to night, during the hours of darkness he liked to be near the cars, for on the Vane and the Lowland our enterprise hung. Had anything happened to them, we should have been awkwardly placed, for they were both picked cars, and to get them into the country had not only taken time, but had cost eight hundred pounds. Both cars could have come in for nothing on any day in the week, if Chandos had been content for them to bear English numbers and G.B. plates: but such things distinguish a car in a foreign land, and Richard William Chandos did nothing by halves.

Like master, like man. No matter what it cost him, Bell would leave nothing to chance. I have shown that he was efficient as very few servants are: as I shall show, his sense of duty was high: but a rarer quality still was his *amour propre*.

After luncheon I took the Vane and drove along to the station to take our luggage away. And while Audrey unpacked her clothes and Bell was dealing with mine, I studied the large-scale maps of the country which we were to learn.

At the first blush, our task looked monstrous. An irregular network of roads sprawled without rhyme or reason wherever I gazed, and it must, it seemed, take a lifetime to learn one tenth of the number we hoped to know. Then I saw that the first step to take was to get by heart two things which I could have from the maps without going out of doors, for that these two things were, so to speak, master keys, which would unlock every gate to which we might come. And one of the two was distance; and the other, direction.

If I always knew how far I was from, say, Rouen, and always knew exactly where Rouen lay, though I had seen it but once, the district between me and Rouen would take rough shape in my mind, and I should know where a road led to because I knew the country which it had been made to serve.

And then I saw the value of landmarks. If the country was as flat as it seemed, one good landmark might serve me for twenty miles—signpost and milestone in one, whose legend I could read, however far off I might be.

And so I arrived at the truth that, if we were to make good, the country was what I must study, and not the roads. The rivers and hills and forests would all give me information which I could trust, but, unless it was posted, a road would tell me nothing and, if I depended upon it, would certainly let me down.

Once I had realized this, the orderless system of ways which had shocked me so much, sank to its true proportion for good and all, and though, from this time on, I used a map a great deal, I was never again dismayed by such a labyrinth.

Here Audrey appeared—in tweeds and a white silk shirt.

'Dear God, St John, aren't you ready? Bell's starting the Lowland up.'

'Sit down,' said I, 'and I'll teach you to read a map.'

'You go and change,' said she, 'and I'll teach you to drive a car.'

Though he knew it to be out of order, Mansel himself, I think, would have done as she said, for her big, brown eyes were alight and her eager face was aglow, and the man who could have put out such radiance must first have put off his manhood—or else have been blind from birth.

She let me choose the way, so we went to Dunkirk by St Omer, and back by Boulogne. That was a run of well over two hundred miles; but it seemed a great deal less, for the Lowland was very smooth and went like the wind, and Audrey drove as though she was a part of the car.

By her especial desire, I drove for half an hour.

'Go on. I want you to. It isn't fair that I should have all the fun.'

In fact, I was something reluctant to take the wheel, for she was a far better driver than I shall ever be, and to suffer the weaker vessel was not her way.

As I let in the clutch—

'Have you ever watched,' I said, 'a fool untying a knot?'

She looked straight ahead.

'I've often been sorry for that. But I didn't know you then.'

'Audrey,' said I, 'you have one most remarkable gift.'

'Only one, St John?'

'All the others are graces,' said I. 'But this is a gift.'

'Very quick,' said Audrey. 'Go on.'

'You can inflict the very hell of a wound: but you can heal it so gently that your victim treasures the scar.'

'I see. But the scar remains.'

'Oh, damn the girl,' said I. 'She's got it the wrong way round.'

A hand came to rest on my sleeve.

'No, she hasn't, St John. But she doesn't like the word "scar." '

'Scar be damned. "Sweet and twenty" has kissed it and made it well.'

With the tail of my eye I saw her chin go up.

'Fall out, the officers,' she commanded.

'I'm not on parade,' said I, and let the Lowland go.

* * *

As a rule, Bell stayed at the villa, for, to keep in touch with Mansel, one of us had to be there from nine to ten in the morning and from seven to eight at night. (This, of course, in case of a telephone-call. In case such a call was urgent, whoever was out in the car would always ring up the villa about midday—an inconvenient duty, which we were sorely tempted but never dared to omit.) But once a week I sent him abroad with Audrey, and once a week my lady would 'hold the fort.'

Every day, rain or shine, either the Vane or the Lowland would be on the road by six, but we always came back to the villa before night fell. This seemed the wisest plan, for though it meant a long run before we could enter the region that lay about Havre, at the villa we could relax as we could never have done at any hotel: and that was everything, for there were times when we were too tired to eat, and once, I remember, Audrey fell asleep at the table and never opened her eyes, though I picked her up in my arms and carried her up the stairs.

So long as the weather was fair—and it very seldom rained—our work was about as pleasant as work can be, and after a very few days we, so to speak, found our feet and began to 'sense' direction and to pick up the lie of the land with astonishing speed. I never would have believed that with so little practice I could have told what was coming before it came into my view, but the study proved to me that a countryside is just like a living volume which very few of us have ever been trained to read. I have spent so much of my life in the open air that I was more fitted than some for such an exercise, but to learn to read was so simple and the legends, when read, were so clear that I think any man could do it, who cared to try. Best of all, the roads, from being our masters, became our humble servants to carry us where we liked. We knew where they must lead us, because we knew the country through which they ran, and, though sometimes, of course, they turned upon us and bit us, as serpents do, our confidence was not shaken, because we had come to treat them as they deserved.

Since the Lowland's head could be dropped, we were free of the sun and the wind from morning to night, and though for most of the time we had to sit still, I think we grew harder and fitter every day. The hot weather coming on, Audrey took to a singlet and well-cut shorts—and lent a grace to an outfit which not every woman can wear. Her form was so slim, and her legs were so clean and so straight that to see her stand up on some knoll, with an early sunshine about her and the sparkle of the dew at her feet, remembered the tales of the classics which I had learned as a child: she always went bare-headed, and when she shook back her curls and shaded her eyes to scan some stretch of country which could not be seen from the car, she might have strayed out of some idyll, such as Theocritus wrote.

I do not think we attracted lasting attention, because, perhaps, the ground which we had to cover was spread so wide: then, again, the French number-plates were a very great help, for they made the car one of a thousand, instead of one of a score: and I must confess that Audrey's barbarous spectacles did their share, for they dimmed—for passers-by—the light of her countenance.

Either Mansel or Chandos wrote to us three times a week. Their letters were very cheerful and did us good; but only one, which came on the tenth of June, let fall any sort of hint that the man for whom we were waiting was thinking of making a move.

When the time comes, *it said*, Rowley will join you somehow, as best he can. You two will stick to the Lowland, and he and Bell to the Vane: and the four of you, working together, will, I am sure, be able to bring it off. But don't forget that, until you report your progress, we two shall have to sit still—for the simple reason that we shall not know where you are: so warn the cook that Carson is coming to take Bell's place, and ring him up at the villa as soon as ever you can.

But, though the days went by, the telephone-bell never rang, and Audrey began to get fretful and to flirt with the mutinous theory that we were wasting our time.

I did my best with her, but, when all was said and done, I had a very poor case, for to draw a bow at a venture costs little enough, but we were intensively training for an action which might never take place.

* * *

We were seven miles from the coast, when I touched my companion's arm and pointed up at a coppice which rose on our right.

'Take me there, will you, Audrey? On the other side of that wood, I think there's a bluff. If I'm right, I believe that from there a man with a pair of glasses can see the crossroads at Cerf.'

'But Cerf's over there—the other side of those hills.'

'I know, but a valley runs east. Less than a valley—a groove. And I think that that bluff commands it. I can't be sure.'

'Ridge upon ridge in your way. Can you see through chalk?'

'That wood stands high,' said I. 'It's worth trying, anyway. I've dreamed about those crossroads. They're a perfect place for Plato to give us the slip.'

Audrey shrugged her shoulders and let in her clutch.

'I'll honour your whim,' she said: 'but only because that wood looks nice and cool and I want my lunch. I'm sick of this "girl guide" business, and that's a fact.'

'Sorry,' said I. 'I forgot it was Ascot week.'

'Ascot be damned,' said Audrey. 'I'd rather be here than there. But I want to do something worth while. In the last two months I've drunk enough speculation to float a fleet. And I never did like soft drinks.'

'I'll fight you on your own ground. What else can we do? It's no good calling Barabbas to come and be killed.'

She made no answer to that, and two minutes later, perhaps, we came to the end of the track above which the coppice stood.

As I had done so often, I took our lunch and her cushion out of the boot: then I climbed, with her behind me, until I came to the trees.

Almost at once I found an agreeable spot, where the ground rose very sharply and then fell flat, to make a natural landing some four yards square. The sun was so hot that only to stand in the shade was refreshing enough; but when I turned—to survey the rolling country, spread out like a map, and, beyond, the glitter of the Channel and, above, the elegant flash that argued an aeroplane, then I saw that, whim or no, I had not wasted our time, because I had brought us both to a perfect dining-room.

But though I piped to my lady, she would not dance.

She laid her glasses aside and she ate and drank; but she made no effort to talk, and the scornful look I dreaded was back in her face.

At length I threw in my hand, picked my binocular up and began to rake the country which I had come to know; while she lay supine beside me, her slender ankles crossed and her fingers laced together behind her head, searching the maze of canopies hanging above and watching the higher lattices sway to each idle breeze.

So for perhaps ten minutes. Then I lowered my glasses and got to my feet.

'I shan't be long,' I said. 'I'm going on through the wood to the head of the bluff.'

'To make perfectly sure that the crossroads at Cerf haven't moved.'

'The answer to that,' said I, 'is extremely short. I don't propose to make it, because it's extremely rude. But——'

'Don't be so damned conscientious.'

'Audrey Nuneham,' said I, 'you've got me wrong. I've set my heart on doing a certain thing. Some people might call it murder, but that's neither here nor there. Now I don't know how to go about it, except by the way I've been shown. It's a damnably roundabout way—I'll give you that. But as I know no other, and I want what I want so much, my common sense—not my conscience—is keeping me up to the bit.'

'Very beautiful,' said Audrey. 'There is no god but Mansel, and John Bagot is his prophet.'

I leaned against a tree and fingered my chin.

'You're a difficult girl,' I said. 'I can bear the naked truth; but you serve the damsel up in her underclothes. And that's embarrassing.'

'Then you stop trotting her out in an angel's kit—one bare foot and a face and a shapeless robe.'

'I was nicely brought up,' said I.

'God knows you were,' said Audrey. 'And God knows what it must cost you to muck in with me like this. Your bishop will never believe it was all O.K.'

'He would,' said I, 'if he saw that look on your face.'

'What d'you expect—darling? We're not on parade.'

I sighed.

'At times like this,' said I, 'I could wish we were.'

'Only at times like this? I'm much obliged.'

'All the time,' said I. 'Scratch the curate, you know, and you find the man.'

'How nice for you,' said Audrey. 'And what about me?' She sat up and smacked the turf. 'Don't be so damned self-centred.'

'That's rather hard,' said I. 'You wring the truth out of me: and then, when you've got it, you rub my nose in it.'

Audrey expired.

'Will you try, for one boring moment, to look at this show with my eyes? My aim is the same as yours—to put Barabbas to death. Like you, I am offered a very roundabout way. I think there are better ways; but, because I was born a woman, I cannot take them alone. And, as no one will take them with me, I have to do as I'm told and go by the roundabout way.

'Now "roundabout" is your word. No doubt you chose it because it means "merry-go-round." But I don't see it that way. I'm very fond of the country—I always was. But the countryside is your *job*. And you can get all worked up about some blasted contour that I only pretend to see in order to keep you quiet. And so there are many times when what is a joy-ride to you makes me want to scream. And that, my little friend, is only one side of the coin.'

'I know the other, my dear.' With my eyes on hers, I sat down on the turf at her feet. 'You showed it to me in Paris. And please believe that I've done my very best——'

'You don't know this. On the 'plane you met at Le Bourget were a couple of women I knew.'

'Oh, my God,' said I, and put a hand to my head.

'Don't think I care,' flamed Audrey. 'The game's the thing. But when you prate about duty——'

'I don't. I haven't. But, oh, my dear, I'm so sorry. I wouldn't have——'

'You set the pace,' said Audrey: 'and what the hell can I do? If I don't keep up, I'm keeping the good man down. Fourteen hours a day! I want to let up sometimes. But, if I do, I'm letting the old side down. Side? Troupe. If Plato could only see us, he'd laugh till he couldn't stand up.'

'Be fair,' I pleaded. 'Be fair. I've taken things for granted, but that's because I'm a fool. I've had my eyes on the job, when I ought to have had them on you. But that's not all my fault. If ever I've tried to spare you, you've always caught my arm.'

'I don't want charity. I'm ready to do my bit. But can't you possibly see that if you'd let up sometimes, it'd give a girl a chance?'

I swallowed.

"My dear,' I said, 'aren't you setting a pace of your own? There is no earthly reason why you should run level with me. After all, I'm the tougher vessel, because of my sex. Let Bell come out with me every other day.'

'Whilst I sit still at the villa—and wait for the telephone-bell? What a truly shining prospect! Can't you get this, John Bagot? *I want to relax*. Not to be left in the kennel to shift for myself.'

'Then, go on leave,' said I. 'God knows you've done your bit. No woman on earth could have—'

'How do you know? You know as much of women as you do of the Khyber Pass.'

'I've learned a bit,' said I, 'in the last six weeks. But that's by the way. Why shouldn't you go on leave? There's nothing the matter with Paris; and you could be back in three hours.'

'Dear God,' said Audrey. And then, 'Do I look that sort? The bachelor-girl on the loose?' She looked me up and down. 'You know, if ever you marry, you'll have to have police protection within the week. Or else your wife will break down and go out of her mind. No, no, dear friend, don't send me to Paris alone. I mean, if I could have Bell—I'm sure he's been nicely brought up. Of course that would let the side down, and I should forfeit my right to the old school tie. But, perhaps, "the tougher vessel" would carry on. Out and about in the morning, just to see that the B in Boulogne is still in its place. Then home to lunch, in case the scout-master rings up—to say that Plato's chauffeur's been washing his car. Then out again, to—'

'Leave it there,' said I. 'You've whipped me enough. I'm sorry to be such a fool, but I'm made that way. I was shown the road to take, and I've just been blinding along and thinking of nothing else. I've been thankful to have you with me——'

'Thankful?'

'Proud and thankful and happy—and more than that. But now I see that I haven't been fair to you. I'll write to Mansel tonight and tell him we're getting stale and so we're going to Paris for two or three days.'

'I don't have to go to Paris. I only want to let up. Breakfast at ten—for a change. And sometimes, when we go out, to go as we please and think about something besides the lie of the land. Since my reputation is dead, we might have a wake at Dieppe—dine and dance, or something, and see the dawn come up from the other end of the day.'

'It shall be done,' said I, and got to my feet. 'As we're here, I'll check up on those crossroads, and then I'll knock off.'

Audrey sat very still.

'Can you play backgammon?' she said.

'My favourite game,' said I, but I did not say where I had learned it. I had played with George at Peerless, on many a winter's night.

'There's a board in the car,' said Audrey.

'What a girl,' said I. 'Above all, what an English girl. Bang in the great tradition. Fancy throwing dice on a hill-top, somewhere in France.' I glanced at my wrist. 'Give me ten minutes' grace, my lady. I'll run all the way.' And, with that, I picked up my glasses and took to my heels.

The wood was thicker through than I had believed, but, as I was certain it would, it came to a sudden end at the head of a bluff.

Looking west, I could see down my gully, as I had hoped; but from where I stood I could only see Cerf itself, and not the crossroads, which lay to the south of the village by forty or fifty yards.

At once I began to move along the edge of the trees, and after perhaps twenty paces, the junction for which I was looking came into my sight. This, to my great relief, for, folly or no, I had added a valuable viewpoint to those I had. The coppice was easy to reach and the view which it offered was clear: and when you are watching someone who must not suspect your game, it is very much wiser to do it from four miles off.

I made my way back to our aerie in very good cue, for if we were to take our ease for the rest of the day—and I must confess I liked the idea very well—at least we had ended our work on a very high note.

I went so fast that I had no time to reflect—to be perfectly honest I did not want to reflect—upon a postprandial communion I had not at all enjoyed. The storm was over, and that was enough for me. My lady had been out of humour, and now was appeased.

But when I came to where I had left her, she was not there: and when I looked down for the Lowland, the car was gone.

And then I saw a page from my note-book, lying where I had been standing, at the foot of a tree.

Its legend went straight to the point.

You had been warned.

* * *

If I cannot defend my lady, I cannot defend myself. A man with the sense of a louse would have played backgammon first, and afterwards walked to the bluff to look at the view. But, because I had no such sense, I had let her wait upon a business of which I knew she was sick. And that was the straw which had broken the camel's back.

It was true—I had been warned. But having no ears to hear, I had not heard the warning—with this result.

Audrey was gone . . . with the car. And the nearest town was Dieppe, some seven miles off.

I did not at all mind walking the seven miles—for, though there were villages nearer, Dieppe was the nearest place at which I could charter a car. But I could not cover the distance in very much less than two hours, and I did not like the idea of Audrey's driving alone on the open road. I hoped and prayed she had had the good sense to go home. But out of her present mood God only knew what folly might not arise. And she was far too attractive and far too attractively dressed to leave the car unescorted by some cavalier.

Once this pregnant reflection had entered my head, I began to imagine vain things and to picture my darling beset by somebody stronger than she, whilst I was out of her ken and so unable to help her in her adversity. This brought the sweat on to my face, and when I put up my glasses to search what roads I could see, my hands were trembling so much that I had to lie down on the ground and hold the binocular steady against the root of a tree. But labour and time were lost, for I saw no sign of the car, so I got to my feet and put the glasses away and then struck out for Dieppe as fast as I could. I went, of course, across country, as being the quickest way, aiming to strike the main road at a point three miles from the coppice, where four ways met. In the ordinary way, this would have been a profitable exercise, but I had no eyes for the country or for the roads I crossed, for all I could think of was Audrey and Audrey's lovable ways.

I felt no resentment at all for what she had done. I could only remember how sweet and how splendid she was and what it must have cost her, on that afternoon at Le Bourget, to play to such perfection the part she had promised to take. And then, for more than a month, she had laboured early and late with all her might—and that at an enterprise of which nine men out of ten would have tired in less than a week. She had put her hand to the plough—a hand by no means fitted for such an implement: and until this afternoon she had never looked back. She had never spared herself: and I, who should have spared her, had taken all she gave as a matter of course. Look at it how you will, she had been in my charge; and I had made no allowance for the time-honoured way of a maid.

Looking back, I think the truth is that, though I scourged myself as I stumbled across the fields, I was not so much to blame as I then assumed. I had kept my eyes upon the duty which I had been set and had favoured a discipline which Audrey had come to observe. But this I had done not only for duty's sake. Placed as I was, I had been afraid to 'let up.'

I was in love with Audrey, and Audrey was at my disposal from morning to night. I had her all to myself for the whole of each day—a privilege, I think, for which a great many rich men would have given as much as they had. We were living on intimate terms and our quarters were very close, and we were posing as lovers—

for such as had eyes to observe. Yet, I was not her lover. And though, perhaps, some men would have tried their luck, opportunism so flagrant was more than I could digest.

So something had to be done.

By keeping my nose to the grindstone, I left myself no time to think about love. At least, that was the idea—the method in my madness, a word I can fairly use. For I was mad about Audrey: and that is the downright truth.

* * *

I had struck the highway within a very short distance of where I had meant to arrive and was pelting along the tarmac as hard as ever I could, when I breasted a sudden hillock to see the Lowland before me, a quarter of a mile away. The car was standing still by the side of the road.

My first emotion was one of intense relief: but, as I drew near, I saw that the car was empty, and when I came up at a run, there was no sign of Audrey and nothing whatever to tell me which way she had gone.

With this, my worst apprehensions came back in a flood, and I went about the car in a frenzy, searching for traces of a struggle within and without. But, though I could find no such signs, I was not comforted, for to my disordered mind this only went to show that the scene of my darling's abduction was somewhere else.

I wiped the sweat from my face and threw a frantic look round.

The road, of course, was empty: there was, I knew, no turning for two or three hundred yards: and, though for the most part the highway itself was open, at this particular spot tall banks were hiding the country on either side.

Unable to stand such blindness, I flung myself at the bank beside which the car was berthed; and a moment later I was overlooking a meadow of very fair grass. This was studded by several magnificent trees and, since the herbage was green and the sunshine was very bright, the patches of shade which they threw made what was a pretty picture into a striking scene. As though to humour some painter, a number of good-looking Jerseys were leisurely eating their fill, while, sunk in the trees in the distance, I saw the gleam of a farm. A dog and two little children were clearly in charge of the herd, but, since the meadow was fenced, their duties were light: this in a way was as well, for the three were sitting down with their backs to the cows and their six eyes fast upon Audrey, who I afterwards found was telling a fairy-tale.

The dog was the first to see me, and told the others by growling that I was there. Then Audrey looked round and saw me—and put up a hand and waved.

As I drew near, she spoke.

'Are you terribly cross, St John?'

'I'm too much relieved,' I said.

'But why "relieved," St John?'

'You don't deserve it,' said I, 'but—to find you safe.'

Audrey addressed the children, speaking in French.

'I told you,' she said, 'that he was the sweetest thing.'

With that, she introduced us.

Jeanne Marie was five, and her brother was six: and both were very clean and very polite: and both, I am sure, believed that I was Audrey's husband—or if they did not, then it was not Audrey's fault.

She patted the ground by her side.

'Sit down, my darling. We're on parade, you know. So take a leaf out of my book and don't let the side down.'

As I took my seat, she turned to the children again.

'Monsieur,' she said, 'is more clever than any dog. I left him four miles from here, and I never said where I was going, and he never saw me go. Yet, you see he has found me within the hour.'

Jeanne Marie regarded me, finger to lip.

'That,' she said, 'is because he loves Madame so much.'

'I never thought of that,' said Audrey. She threw me a dazzling smile. 'Is that how you did it, St John?'

'I like to think so,' said I, with the blood in my face.

Audrey addressed my tell-tale.

'You're perfectly right,' she said. 'I think I'm very lucky, don't you?'

Jeanne Marie smiled at me and then looked down at her feet.

'It is not for me to say.'

'Oh, you home-wrecker,' said Audrey. 'And what does Edouard think?'

The boy regarded me straightly: then he returned to Audrey, who plainly had all his heart.

'I think Monsieur is luckier still.'

Audrey shook her head.

'You're wrong,' she said. 'He's very much nicer than me—and I ought to know.'

'Audrey,' I said, 'have a heart. When you talk like that, I want to burst into tears.'

With the tenderest look, she put out her hand for mine. Then she returned to the children and told them what I had said.

They nodded approvingly.

'It does not surprise me,' said Edouard.

Jeanne Marie went further.

'That,' she said, 'is quite right. It shows that Monsieur loves Madame more than himself.'

'Can't we change the subject?' said I. 'That child's too old for her age.'

Audrey strove not to laugh.

'Play up, m-my darling,' she quavered. 'Don't let the side down.'

I took a sudden decision.

'It's time we were going,' I said, and, with that, I got to my feet and put out my hands for hers.

She gave them me, and I pulled her up to her feet. But I did not let her hands go. So we stood very close together, face to face.

'I'm very sorry,' I said. 'I've been all sorts of a fool. But I'm wiser now. And I was so thankful to find you—my darling girl.'

Then I drew her to me and kissed her—to Jeanne Marie's great delight, for she came to me, all smiling, and asked me to kiss her, too.

But Edouard regarded me gravely. And when I took him aside to give him a hundred francs, he would not take it from me: so Audrey had to come and put it into his hand.

* * *

We spent two hours in Rouen, before going home that day: and since, though I did not know it, she had a skirt in the car, we were able to berth the Lowland and prove the city on foot. To say I enjoyed myself means nothing at all, for Audrey was at the very top of her bent; and the pleasure she had of, surely, as simple an outing as ever two people took, made me still more ashamed that she should have waited so long for such a holiday. But when I told her as much, she only took my arm and entered a jeweller's shop and, selecting a silver lighter, ordered this to be engraved with the initials 'St J.'

'When will it be ready?' she said.

'At midday tomorrow, Madame.'

'Thank you,' said I. 'We'll pick it up after lunch.'

I spoke more truly than I knew.

It had been in my mind for us to lunch at Rouen and dine and dance at Dieppe; but when, some two hours later, we entered our stable-yard, Bell was there to greet us—with a telephone-slip in his hand.

'Excuse me, sir,' he said, 'but I think we're off.'

Audrey and I together pored over the precious words.

Stand by for Dieppe. Meet Rowley Rouen Cathedral tomorrow midday.

CHAPTER 6

The Kingdom of Heaven

Forty-eight hours had gone by, and Audrey, pencil in hand, was watching my face as I dealt with the telephone. Behind her, Bell stood like a statue, betraying no sort of emotion, not seeming to breathe: and Rowley, keen-eyed and smiling, was standing beyond him again, with the tray which he had been using still in his hand.

And then I heard Mansel's voice.

'I rather think that'll be John.'

'It is,' said I. 'I'm here.'

'Good,' said Mansel. 'I thought you'd like to know that all is O.K. The car in question was shipped twenty minutes ago. Ring up tomorrow somehow, to say where you are.'

'I will,' said I.

'Take care of your lady friend and give her my love.'

'I will.'

'Till then—goodbye and good luck.'

'Goodbye,' said I, and he put his receiver back.

I put mine back and looked round.

'The curtain's up,' I said. 'His car was put aboard twenty minutes ago.'

I think everybody relaxed.

'What else did he say?' said Audrey.

'He only sent you his love and wished us good luck.'

Audrey glanced at her wrist.

'How soon do we start?' she said.

'At midnight, please,' said I. 'His boat will come in at two: and I think we ought to be there by half past one.'

'I'll see the cook right away, and then I shall go and lie down. Why don't you do the same? Bell or Rowley will call us at a quarter to twelve.'

'Perhaps I will,' said I. 'Is everything packed?'

'All but the food, sir,' said Bell. 'I'll see that's put in the cars the very last thing.'

'Well, take it easy, then, for the next two hours. And Rowley, too, of course. It might make a difference tomorrow—you never know.'

'Very good, sir.'

I got to my feet.

'Before we break up,' I said, 'there's one thing I'd like to say. I've shown you the line which I think we should try to take. But I haven't consulted Plato: and Plato may not agree. At a moment's notice, therefore, we may have to scrap it all and to take some sudden action for which we are not prepared. We shall have no time to think, much less to consult; for if we hesitate, our man will be lost. Now if this should happen to me, I shall act on my own: and everyone else must do exactly the same—and ring this villa up as soon as he possibly can. We're going to get home tomorrow—no doubt about that. But we're going to get home on instinct, and nothing else. Of that I'm perfectly sure. And instinct's a damned good horse: but you've got to give him his head.'

'Very good, sir,' said Audrey, before Bell or Rowley could speak.

And then she was gone, and the three of us were laughing because we could do nothing else.

* * *

Though we left the villa at midnight, we might, as things turned out, have stayed there till six o'clock, for Plato remained aboard until half past eight.

I had feared that he might do this—in fact, to tell the truth, I was pretty certain he would: but he could, had he pleased, have landed at two o'clock, and so we had to be ready in case he did.

Had he disembarked at two, he could have taken the road a long time before it was light; but though the darkness would have helped him to get away, it would also have stood a pursuer in very good stead. Indeed, I should have been thankful if he had taken this course, for he could never have driven without any lights: but this we could have done, because we knew the country so well: so he could never have seen us, although we were close behind, and we could never have lost him, because of the light he shed.

But if I could see this, so could Plato. So Plato took it easy and never left the steamer till half past eight. But we spent a wretched night, for, as though to make it still harder, the Customs' landing hours were not only two and eight-thirty, but also half past five: so we had no rest at all, but had to stand to three times, when once would have done.

Still, the weather was fine and warm, and, thanks, of course, to Bell, we were able to bathe and breakfast in somebody's private flat in the heart of the town. I strongly suspect that the owner was never aware of the flying visit we paid, for the caretaker spoke in whispers and seemed immensely relieved when we took our leave: but we were too thankful to ask any awkward questions and made our way back to the Lowland like giants refreshed.

I shall never forget one moment of all that day, but for some strange reason I seem to remember most clearly the 'shining morning face' of the town of Dieppe. It was by no means lovely, and its toilet was very slight, but the sunlight made it look cheerful and the rapid change of its expression from that of a sluggard to that of a business man must, I think, have arrested the most preoccupied mind. The streets, from being silent, became in a short twenty minutes the very abode of uproar of every kind, and where there had been no movement, something approaching tumult seemed to prevail. I think it was the bustle and racket which stamped those particular moments so deeply upon my brain, for I had been accustomed to working in peace and quiet, and I found the hubbub distracting—now that I needed my wits as never before.

Of one thing I was quite sure—that Plato's vigilance would be, so to speak, at the flood, when first his car began to move off from the quay. Every being he saw would be suspect, and if any car behind him appeared to be going his way, he would simply pull into the pavement and let it go by. As like as not, he would make a tour of Dieppe, his chauffeur driving and he looking out of the window at the back of the car: and if he chose to do that, we were either bound to lose him or bound to betray our interest in his excursion. And so we had decided to let him go as he pleased until he drove out of the town, and then—but not before—to fall in behind; for by that time, I hoped, the edge of his suspicion would have been taken off.

Here I should say that six roads run out of Dieppe. But that, from our point of view, was not so bad as it sounds, for the six fall into two groups, and three run out to the east and three to the south. Again, as luck will have it, each group of three has a common starting-point, where if a man will stand, he can see, without moving, which road any vehicle takes.

These starting-points were at opposite ends of the town, and though to man them both was simple enough, the line of communication between the two was far too long to be kept by a force like ours. Yet, for obvious reasons, touch had to be maintained, and Plato's passage signalled the moment he had gone by. Indeed, if this were not done, half our force would not only be left at the post, but be out of the race.

At half past eight that morning, the Lowland was in a side street, commanding the shapeless nave from which, as so many spokes, ran the south-bound roads: Audrey was in the Lowland, whose hood was up: and I was sitting outside a café, some forty or fifty yards off, pretending to read a paper, but really regarding the Lowland with all my might. A taxi was awaiting my pleasure, the width of the pavement away, and its driver knew where to go and was ready to move.

Disposed in just the same way as were Audrey and I, Bell and Rowley were watching the east-bound roads. This meant that Rowley and I were much further apart than I liked, and I would have given the world for a proper connecting-file: but beggars cannot be choosers—we were but four: and if our arrangements were clumsy, they were the best I could think of, and that is the honest truth.

So the four of us sat and waited—for a Swindon 'sports saloon,' bearing an English number and G.B. plate. Rowley, of course, had described it from bottom to top, but in fact we all knew it by sight, for, one by one, that morning we had viewed it where it was standing upon the quay.

Now why Plato kept us waiting, we never shall know: but he did not leave Dieppe till a quarter past nine. At that hour, with the tail of my eye, I saw the Swindon slide into and out of my view.

As I got to my feet, Audrey's near-side direction-indicator rose and fell—rose and fell twice over . . . to say that the Swindon had taken the Rouen road.

As the Lowland pulled out to follow, I flung myself into my taxi and cried to the driver in English to go like hell. But I think that he understood—or perhaps he saw the hundred-franc notes in my hand.

Now that I had to do it, it sent me half out of my mind to drive *away* from the chase: but somehow or other Bell and Rowley had to be fetched, and, as I have said, I had thought of no other way.

I must confess that my driver wasted no time, but fought his way through the traffic, as few would have dared to do, swinging and swerving and darting, as though he were out to win some obstacle race: for all that, it seemed an age before we took some corner, I think, upon only two wheels, and there was Rowley standing a hundred yards off. He saw me before I saw him, and had paid his taxi off before we were by. Then he turned to run for the Vane, beside which my taxi drew up . . .

And then we were both in the Vane, and Bell was driving like fury the way I had come.

The hunt was up.

* * *

Now it was of the utmost importance that I should take my place in the Lowland as soon as ever I could, for the Lowland was our first string, and Audrey at present was doing a double duty which Mansel himself, I think, would have sought to evade. In a word, she was observing and driving, too: and though that is easy enough when you are up in the air, it is very much harder to do when you are down on the road. But before I could take my place, we had to come up with the Lowland—and Audrey and Plato had had about six minutes' start.

One terror, at least, I was spared—that, without our knowing it, they might have turned off the main road: but of that we had no fear, for Audrey had by her side a basket of phials of red paint, and it had been arranged between us that if she left the main road, she should drop a phial on to the surface to tell us where she had turned.

So we whipped up the Rouen road at eighty-five, Bell with his eyes on the distance and Rowley and I observing the mouths of the by-roads and straining our eyes for a tell-tale splash of red paint.

Then—

'There she is, sir,' said Bell. 'Just the other side of that lorry. I saw her turn in.'

Half a mile ahead a lorry, going our way, was approaching a rise, and, as I looked, the Lowland rose up beyond it and into our view.

I heaved a sigh of relief.

'Well done, indeed,' said I. 'And now there's a switchback coming. Let's try and run alongside in one of the dips.'

'Very good, sir.'

'When I'm gone, keep your eye on us. If I want you to pass, I'll say so. If you lose us, make straight for Rouen and try the main roads out. But there's not much fear of that, if you shift like this.'

'We didn't ought to, sir; but you never know.'

As we left the lorry standing—

'I don't see him yet, sir,' said Rowley.

'You will in a second,' said I. 'He's down in a dip.'

And so he was.

As the Lowland sank into the first of the switchback's dales, the Swindon rose out of the last, six furlongs ahead.

Audrey had seen us coming.

As the Lowland sailed out of its dale, her hand went out, and when we had breasted the first of the switchback's hills, there was the Lowland at rest in the second dale.

Bell ran alongside, and Rowley opened the doors.

I was out and in in a flash.

'Goodbye, you two.'

'Good luck, sir.'

Audrey let in her clutch.

'Well done, my beauty,' said I.

'And you, St John. But listen. I think he's going to turn off. He hesitated just now, but he didn't like the look of the road.'

'Just in time,' said I. 'If you're right, he'll turn at Paletot, a mile ahead. Not too fast round that bend: we can see it from there.'

We took the bend at thirty, to see the Swindon approaching the four crossroads.

Sure enough, the car slowed down and then turned to the right.

'Let her go,' said I, and signalled to Bell to stop.

'Let him see us go by. We needn't follow him there.'

We overran the crossroads by a hundred and fifty yards.

As I flung out of the car—

'Tell the Vane to stand by,' I said, 'but to keep out of sight. He's got to take one of two roads—if he values his springs. But be ready in case he doubles, before I've time to get back.'

Two hundred yards away, a ruinous ivy-clad tower was commanding the stretch of country through which the Swindon must pass. I had proved it two or three times, and I knew it would serve my turn.

As Audrey backed into a farm-yard, to go about, I vaulted over a gate and ran for my precious viewpoint as hard as I could. Then I climbed its crumbling stair and settled myself at what was once an embrasure and now was a gap.

My binocular showed me the Swindon—approaching a sturdy plantation which grew upon rising ground. Though I could not see the road, I knew that, just short of the wood, the Swindon would have to turn to the right or the left: and once she had made her choice, I knew where she must come to and where we could pick her up.

I watched her comfortably. Except for a tumbril, the road behind her was bare. If Plato had had suspicions, they ought to be fading away.

The nearer she drew to the junction, the slower she went. Then she turned to the right very slowly and came to rest. A quarter of a minute later, the chauffeur's head came out. Then the Swindon began to move back—past the mouth of the road she had left. And then she had switched to the right and was on her way back. . . .

I was down the stair in a flash and was racing over the sward: but I need have had no concern, for when I came up to the gate, the Lowland was not to be seen, but Audrey was watching the crossroads from the opposite side of a wall.

'He's coming back,' I panted. 'You get back to the Lowland. I'll take your place.'

I dared not show my head as the Swindon went by, but, as I was sure she would, she turned to the right—that is to say, she headed once more for Rouen, and that, without hesitation, after the way of a horse who means to go home.

I watched her swing round a bend. . . .

Then Audrey drove out of the farm-yard, and twenty seconds later the Vane drew up alongside.

'Rouen for a monkey,' I said. 'And Rouen will give him a chance of twisting our tail. When you see me take a taxi, pass the Lowland and don't let me out of your sight.'

I saw Rowley touch his hat, and we were away.

Audrey drove like the wind till we sighted the Swindon again.

Then—

'I wish,' she said, 'you wouldn't give me these shocks.'

'Sorry,' said I. 'What shocks?'

'Wasting time talking like that. Supposing the swine had turned off.'

'Across country?' said I. 'A Swindon's an automobile—not a whippet tank.'

'You took a risk,' said Audrey. 'You know you did. I'll admit you're doing wonders, but don't be too clever by half.'

'I love you,' I said, 'when you put your chin in the air. Never mind. Not quite so fast. We're a shade too close. And now let's get this straight. You talk of my taking risks: you might as well blame me for breathing fast when I run. This show is the purest gamble. Whenever we take a corner, we take a risk. And all we can hope to do is to choose the lesser evil or, if you like it better, to pick the right risk to take.'

'I reserve the right to say if I think you're wrong.'

'Of course—if we've time to argue. Close up a little, will you? And fall in behind that van. I'll be able to see him all right, but he won't see us.' As she did as I said, 'I wish I knew Rouen better,' I added, thinking aloud.

'That's not my fault,' murmured Audrey.

I set my teeth.

'We're both on edge,' said I. 'And who wouldn't be, by God? But don't let's throw any stones. It'll break my heart if we lose him, but you shall have the pieces—to jump on and grind to dust.'

She made no answer to that, and we covered two miles in silence, using the van as a screen. But every mile was taking us nearer to

Rouen, and I knew that if Plato meant business and his chauffeur knew how to drive, that ancient city would help him to shake us off. As I saw it, my only chance was to pick up a taxi at once and to follow the Swindon in that. But if no taxi was waiting, or if the driver was dull . . .

I wiped the sweat from my face and asked Audrey to pass the van.

'He's stepping on it,' I said. 'I wish I knew why. If it's a ruse, he'll stop round one of these bends. If he does, we shall have to go by, but I'll try and stop Bell.'

But though that fear rode us both and made each bend a nightmare from that time on, the Swindon held on its way till it came to a road on the left that would take it to Neufchatel.

A coppice was masking this corner in such a way that, once a car had turned it, that car could not be seen from the road we were on—unless you stood still at the junction and so gave your business away. For that reason, no doubt, it found favour in Plato's eyes, and the Swindon slowed up to take it, as if the man who was driving was sure of his way.

I gave my covert signal to Bell to stop, and, as before, we went by, without slackening speed.

As Audrey lifted her foot, some instinct showed me something I could not see.

'Go on,' I cried, with my eyes on the road behind. 'Put your foot right down. As like as not, it's a plant.'

I felt the Lowland leap forward. . . .

Then I saw a man's figure appear from the mouth of the Neufchatel road. He was looking after us—I could see the white of his face. Then he turned to look back towards Bell, and I found myself praying that the Vane was not to be seen. And then we dropped down a descent and out of his view.

'Stop her now,' I said.

Audrey pulled up all standing, and I flung out of the car.

'Stand by to turn round,' I cried, and ran for the crest of the hill.

The figure was gone now, but I had no means of knowing whether the Swindon would turn or would go on to Neufchatel. I hurled myself at the bank by the side of the road. . . . And then I was in a hayfield which had been recently mown and was rising up to a ridge some fifty yards off.

Keeping an eye on the corner, I ran for the ridge as hard as ever I could. I reached it just in time. As I breasted the rise, I saw the Swindon below me heading for Neufchatel. Then she rounded an easy bend and passed out of my sight.

I waved to Audrey to turn and stumbled back to the road.

As I took my seat by her side—

'Neufchatel,' I said. 'Hang at the corner a moment, for me to signal to Bell.'

But Bell had not waited for me. Rowley had done as I had. In fact he had climbed a tree—and so had seen the Swindon stealing a march. So, though I did not know it, I made my signal in vain, for Bell and Rowley were leading, and we were behind.

More than a minute went by before I saw them ahead. And when I did, I could hardly believe my eyes, because I had supposed that they were following us.

I think perhaps this may show how very hard was the thing we were trying to do, for Bell and Rowley had done as I had told them to do and had acted without instructions, rather than let our quarry make good his escape. Yet, by taking that action, they were running between my legs and very nearly upset the plan I had made.

I stifled an oath. Then—

'It's not their fault,' I said, 'but they're going to tear everything up. Catch them somehow, Audrey. We're going to turn off in a mile.'

My lady let the car go. . . .

Then one of them saw us coming, and Bell slowed up to give way.

As we went by in silence—

'Slow right down,' I said, 'and then take the first to the right.'

'He's not turned off,' said Audrey, lifting her foot.

'I know,' said I. 'But the road he's on comes round in another twelve hundred yards. This is the old road, lady. We can watch him all the way and pick him up, if we like, just short of the town. But what I want to do is to get there first.'

'I see. Please tell me one thing. Was it a plant?'

'At the corner? Yes. The chauffeur walked back and took a careful look round. I'm sorry. I ought to have told you. But what with——'

' "Don't speak to the man at the wheel" is a very good rule.'

'So,' said I, 'is "Necessity knows no law." Slow down at that poplar, will you? I want to check up.'

Almost at once, I saw the Swindon below. To my relief, she was not moving very fast, and I shall always believe that the fox had thought he was being followed, but now believed he had given the hounds the slip.

'All's well,' said I. 'And now let her go, my beauty. If we're to be there before him, we've got to shift.'

Then I signalled to Bell to close up, and away we went.

(The signals I made to Bell were as easy to make as to read, for I had five left-hand gloves, the palms of which we had painted different colours, as vivid as we could find. Since they were gardening gloves, it took no more than an instant to slip one on. Then all that I had to do was to drop my arm over the door and open my hand, keeping its back to the Swindon and showing its palm to the Vane.)

For the first time since leaving Dieppe I now had five or six minutes in which to survey the position and look ahead, and though to devote them to Audrey would have done me more good than her, I dared not squander the respite which Chance had thrown into my lap.

At once I saw that if, as I believed, Plato had left the main road to throw any car that was trailing him off the scent, it might be taken for granted that he was making for Rouen, but going by Neufchatel. In other words, he was simply fetching a compass which would carry him into the city from the north, instead of the west.

And something else I saw: and that was that if Plato believed that he had made good his escape, it was of the utmost importance that we should give him no reason to change his mind. Though we managed to hold him in Rouen, soon after leaving that city, we should almost certainly enter a country we did not know, and if Plato were then to resume his endeavours to shake us off, either they must be successful or else he would know for certain that we were following him.

Revolving these two conclusions, I decided, with great reluctance, to split our party in two and to send Bell and Rowley ahead; for unless, when we came to Rouen, a taxi was ready and waiting to take up the chase, we should have to close on the Swindon, to keep it in view, and that, of course, would set Plato thinking again: but if, when we came to Rouen, Rowley was in a taxi whose driver was only waiting to do as he said, and the taxi was lying in wait where the road from Neufchatel ran into the city's streets, then the Vane could follow the taxi and we could follow the Vane, and Plato, with any luck, would see no cause for alarm.

Now all this was very well, but we were up against Time. We must be at Neufchatel before Plato arrived—if for no other reason, because the Vane must be gone before the Swindon came up. 'Out of sight, out of mind,' says the proverb, and a very true saying that is. Yet I had to give my instructions to Rowley and Bell: and that would take two full minutes—far more than we could afford.

With my eyes on the sunlit road, I savaged my underlip, racking my brain for some way of doing what could not be done.

And then I saw the solution, clear as the dawn.

The Lowland must go on ahead, instead of the Vane, and Rowley must drive with Audrey, and I with Bell.

I could give my instructions to Audrey, here and now: then Rowley and I could change places—a matter of seconds only, if we were quick: and the Lowland could go on to Rouen, instead of the Vane.

My lady did not like it, but neither did I. There was no time to argue: and, what I found ten times worse, there was no time to explain.

As she brought the Lowland to rest and the Vane ran up alongside—

'Change places with me, Rowley.'

I was standing beside her window, before he had taken his seat.

'Good luck, my darling. Till Rouen.'

But Audrey looked straight ahead and let in her clutch. . . .

We ran into Neufchatel with sixty seconds to spare: but when the Swindon appeared, the Lowland was gone, the Vane was in a blind alley behind a cart, and I was across the street inside a small greengrocer's shop.

For one unforgettable moment, it looked as though the Swindon was going to take a turning which led to the Beauvais road—a hideous gesture, which took a month from my life. Then the chauffeur saw his mistake, or his master put him right, and I watched him pull his car round with the sweat running down my face.

And then he was bound for Rouen, and I was out on the pavement, and Bell was bringing the Vane from her hiding-place—

and a most insistent old lady was forcing upon me six pounds of good-looking potatoes and the change from a fifty-franc note.

The arrangements which I had made for Plato's reception at Rouen seemed to me to warrant a much less pressing pursuit; so, though we were careful to keep the pace which the Swindon set, we stayed a good distance behind her and only came up rather closer when she was approaching crossroads. Though I cannot honestly say that Bell could drive as could Audrey, I very soon found that he knew every trick of the trade, and the way in which he used other traffic as cover from view showed me not only how much I had yet to learn, but that this was not the first time that he had shadowed a car. Indeed, it was very soon clear that until we came to Rouen, I should have little to do and could, so to speak, put up my feet, if I felt that way.

It seems a small thing now, but it seemed a great thing then that the only time that day when I could at all relax should have had to be spent by me away from Audrey, with whom I was so anxious to put things straight. It is easy enough to say that she ought to have understood—should not have taken it ill that I left her out of my counsels and made no more of her than I did of Rowley and Bell. But there was no reason at all why she should have understood: and it was very natural that she should have taken my change of behaviour ill. For more than a month, we had made ready *together* for what was happening now. Day after day we had roved this very country, and I had made her free of my hopes and fears. From dawn to dusk we had worked and consulted together, weighing this contingency, measuring that. And now when the day had come to put into practice the theories which she and I had composed, I treated her as a hired chauffeur—whose job was to take my orders and hold his tongue. Little wonder she felt aggrieved; and that though she did her duty as well as it could have been done, such treatment bore very hard on as proud a spirit as dwelled in a woman's flesh. That I, who worshipped her footsteps, should have had no choice but to use her in this despiteful way was, when I had time to think, a very depressing thought: but the present realization that now, having sent her on, I had thrown away a fair chance of setting the matter to rights made me vow such vengeance on Plato and all his works as would, I think, have found favour in Satan's exacting sight.

However, there was nothing to be done. So, with trembling

fingers, I lighted a cigarette and began to picture the country which lay south and east of Rouen and to try to make up my mind whereabouts to drop our pilot, the taxi, and take up the running again.

Then the short thirty miles were over, and the suburbs of Rouen were there, and the city was hanging below us, astride of a bend of the Seine.

I was watching the Swindon slow up, to let a waggon go by before passing a furniture van, when a taxi fell in behind her and a moment later the Lowland slipped out of a builder's yard.

At once Bell closed on the Lowland, and so the procession took shape: but though all had started so well, when I saw the first of the traffic, the palms of my hands grew hot, for I knew in my heart that we only needed one check to turn our cake back into dough.

I will not set out the dance which the Swindon led us, because I shall always believe it was undesigned: but to follow a man who must not know you are there, who rates too high what sense of direction he has—and this, through the streets of a city which might have been built to mislead. . . . I can only say this—that till then I had thought I could drive: but when I saw Audrey's performance, let alone Bell's, then I knew that handling a car may be raised from a game of skill to one of the finer arts.

Be that as it may, after thirteen dreadful minutes, which seemed more like forty-five, the Swindon entered the *place* which lies like a little apron before the Cathedral's door. And there her chauffeur had 'parked' her before we could think, leaving us stuck in a street which was inconveniently narrow and overfull.

Enter the *place* we dared not, for the *place* was so very small that we should have been parading before our gentleman's eyes: there was no room to turn round, and, because of the traffic behind, we could not retreat: yet Bell and Audrey escaped—by taking a turning which they had already gone by.

I cannot tell how they did it, for I had gone on to a café on the opposite side of the *place*, from where I could watch the Swindon—and her chauffeur, standing beside her, *inspecting every car that came into his view*. And I must confess that I had a very bad time, until Rowley pushed his way past me and murmured that all was well.

At once I paid for my liquor and followed him into a shop; and there he said that the taxi and both the cars were berthed in a little alley not more than a hundred yards off, and that if I would move to a café some thirty yards east, I should still be able to have the Swindon in view, yet could myself be seen from where he proposed to stand as connecting-file.

Two minutes later, these dispositions were made.

I was sitting beneath an awning, beside a small screen of privet, growing in tubs, surveying the busy *place* and watching the Swindon's chauffeur tighten some nut: and Rowley, guide-book in hand, was standing upon a pavement some fifty yards off, apparently conning his surroundings, after the way of a tourist determined to call back Time.

Now Plato had disappeared before I had entered the *place*, but it seemed pretty clear that he was within the Cathedral—a something disturbing thought. Indeed, had I dared, I would have entered myself, in case he was using the church as we had made bold to use it two days before. But there again we were held, because our force was so small; for to search such a shrine would have needed three or four men, and since there was more than one door, to leave my post would have been to stake on a shadow what little substance we had. For all that, when ten minutes had passed, but Plato had not reappeared, I began to get so uneasy that I could hardly sit still, for if indeed Barabbas were in the Cathedral, by sitting outside we were throwing victory away. And then, to my great relief, I saw Plato came out—and the moment I saw him I knew that my fears had been vain. The man was but playing a part, and playing it devilish well.

He was wearing clerical clothes—of course to publish the fact that he was a man of God: and there can, I think, be no doubt that his visit to the Cathedral was paid to adorn this truth, for he came forth as though refreshed, fairly breathing goodwill and wearing his cloth as though it were levee dress. He beamed upon English tourists, saluted and was saluted by cassocked priests; but he never looked at his chauffeur, standing beside the Swindon and smoking a cigarette. The latter watched his progress across the *place*, and a hand went up to his mouth, as though to conceal a smile: and I think he may be forgiven, for Plato's performance was really masterly, and nobody could have doubted that he was a man who was used to devote his life to the glory of God and the health of his fellow men.

(Here perhaps I should say that, as I was later to learn, Plato was known among thieves as 'The Kingdom of Heaven'—a trenchant sobriquet. To his face he was always called 'Kingdom,' by such as were high enough up to be so familiar.)

He took a street which led to a decent hotel, and since it was now past twelve, I had little doubt that he was proposing to lunch. If I had had time, I would have summoned Rowley and sent him off in his wake, for I did not like the idea of the man's being out of our ken: but the start which he had was too long, so I turned again to the Swindon and hoped for the best.

Could we have been sure that Plato had gone to his lunch, we could have taken things easy, if only for half an hour: but here the proof of the pudding was in the eating alone, and though I did leave my table to wash my hands, I was back within thirty seconds—in case of accidents.

Of such is the luck of the game, and we had no cause for complaint: but we had been up all night, while Plato had not, and it was extremely provoking to imagine him taking his ease, whilst we, who were far more weary, were waiting upon his pleasure, because we could do nothing else.

I should not have minded so much if I could have been with Audrey, or at least have visited her, to tell her what was happening and see that she rested a little and broke her fast; for, when all was said and done, she was only a girl and had now been doing duty for more than twelve hours on end.

I remember I was picturing her, as I had seen her so often, making the pace, her steady gaze fixed upon the distance, her eager lips just parted, and her very beautiful profile as still as that of some statue set up in a hall, when Plato's chauffeur looked round and then began to walk slowly across the *place*.

To my disquietude, he seemed to be making directly for where I sat, but, as he approached, he began to bear to the left, and two or three moments later he entered a newspaper shop. But though I was greatly relieved, my relief was short-lived, for when he came out, he looked again at the Swindon and then walked into my café and called for some beer.

While this was being brought, he looked about for a seat from which he could view his car and finally sat himself down at the very next table to mine, with his back to my face.

Whether he studied me, I have no idea, for I was staring over the privet, with my elbow upon the table and my chin in the palm of my hand, and all I had seen of him I had seen with the tail of my eye: but my feelings may be imagined, because the last thing I desired was that either he or his master should get to know me by sight.

Now my impulse was to be gone as soon as ever I could, but I had the sense to perceive that any withdrawal must be most casually done, for, because of his occupation, the fellow was on the alert and was bound to remark any movement which anyone close to him made: and if such a movement should seem in any way strange, he would measure the man who made it, for future reference.

So, without more ado, I proceeded to drink up my beer, of which, as luck would have it, my glass was three-quarters full. But I dared not drink it right off, so I drank it leisurely, looking about for a waiter whom I could ask for my bill.

Meanwhile my friend settled down to the paper which he had bought—a well-known English paper, which had been published that day.

He opened it wide, I remember, and scrutinized some item low down on a page: I rather think he was reading the racing news. But his action displayed to me the whole of the opposite page, and though I was not at all minded to read the paper just then, I could not help seeing the headlines which graced that particular sheet.

And then the name 'St Omer' hit me between the eyes.

George's Will had been proved, and its contents were out.

I think I shall see the headline as long as I live.

FORTUNE FOR HUNTING CRONY.

And there was my photograph . . . a very excellent likeness, as I could see for myself.

CHAPTER 7

The Toll of the Road

There was only one thing to be done, and I did it at once.

I poured what was left of my beer into the tub at my side, got to my feet somehow and walked uncertainly into the café itself.

My waiter was not to be seen, and so I went up to the bar and laid down a five-franc piece.

A man who was polishing glasses lifted his head.

'Good morning, sir,' he said. 'And what have you had?'

'By God, you're English,' I said.

'That's right, sir. I own this place.'

I leaned over the bar towards him and spoke very low.

'Look here,' I said. 'Have you got a door at the back? There's a wallah sitting out there, and I'd rather he didn't see me before his time.'

The other raised his eyebrows.

'So?' he breathed. 'Well, we get all sorts in this town. Come this way, sir,' he added, and made for a door on his right.

A moment later he let me into a street.

'I'm much obliged,' said I, and put out my hand.

The Englishman took it in his.

'That's all right, sir,' he said. 'That chauffeur bloke?'

'That's him. But for God's sake mind your step, or he'll get ideas.'

'Not from me, sir, he won't. Goodbye.'

A sudden thought entered my head.

'D'you own this house?' said I.

'I live upstairs, sir,' he said, 'if that's what you mean.'

'Will you lend me a first-floor window for half an hour? If you will, I'll send one of my men to take my place.'

My friend was plainly impressed.

'Send him along, sir, and tell him to come this way.'

'In two minutes' time,' said I. 'Goodbye, again.'

Three minutes later, I was standing on the pavement, studying Rowley's book, and Rowley was leaning against the jamb of a window, directly above the awning beneath which the chauffeur sat.

'All's well, that ends well,' says the proverb, and so perhaps it is. But, now that I had time to reflect, I found myself weak at the knees. It had been a very near thing. More. From this time on, neither his chauffeur nor Plato must see my face. So far they had not seen it—at least, that was my belief. But now they had been warned against me: and that, by Fortune herself. *Behold the man to beware of—St Omer's friend*. One glimpse of me in the car would be more than enough to cancel all we had done and bring to nothing all we had hoped to do.

It was no good cursing our luck, but I must confess I felt sore that now on this day of all days we should be forced to carry this extra weight. As it was, the odds against us were heavy enough. Hitherto I had done what I could to keep Bell well in the background in case either Plato or his chauffeur knew him by sight: but from now on I myself, who was leading our enterprise, must take the greatest care on no account to be seen, for master and man alike would have my face fresh in their minds. Indeed, I can say with truth that I know exactly how those unfortunates feel who have a price on their heads, who see their photographs staring out of the public prints.

I had told Rowley that when he saw the chauffeur go back to his car, he was to come downstairs and sit by the privet hedge, and that when the Swindon moved off he must somehow rejoin the taxi, which would, of course, take the lead. It would have been very much simpler for me to do this, but now I dared not do it, because I feared to travel so close to the Swindon's tail. Thanks to this decision, which may have been bad, we very nearly lost Plato for good and all, for soon after two o'clock, the Swindon swung out of her berth and turned to the left and then passed Rowley and me—with my face to the wall.

This meant that Rowley must cover a hundred yards—and the taxi wait while he did so, before taking up the pursuit: but though he was running like a madman, the Swindon was now well away, and, as she must turn any moment, I let out a roar for Audrey to take the lead.

She was by my side in a flash: but the Swindon was gone.

As I opened the door—

'The first to your right,' I cried, 'as quick as you can. Hang on the corner, for the others to see where we go.'

With storming gears, the Lowland sped to the corner—just in time.

As Audrey slowed up, I saw the Swindon swing out and turn to the left.

'They're coming,' said Audrey. 'They see us.'

'Then let her go.'

We were down the street in a flash.

As we came up to the turning, the taxi appeared behind us some eighty or ninety yards off.

Right and left again . . . keeping the Swindon in sight by the skin of our teeth . . . and playing connecting-file at thirty-five miles an hour. . . .

And then we were all on the quay, and the Swindon was travelling west.

'Paris or Chartres,' said I, and gave the signal to Rowley to pass us as soon as he could.

A moment later the taxi raved on its way, and I sank back into my corner and breathed again.

'These towns,' I said. 'Never mind. I'm so glad to be with you again. You did have some lunch, didn't you?'

'I did very well,' said Audrey. 'And you, St John?'

'You are sweet, aren't you?' said I. 'You've——'

'Did you have some lunch?'

'I did not—by the grace of God. You can pour beer into a tub, but you can't get rid of an omelet as easy as that.'

'Whatever d'you mean?'

I told her what had occurred.

'Dear God,' said Audrey. And then, 'I'll try and make up.'

Before I could ask what she meant, the Swindon switched to the right—for Pont de l'Arche.

We were out of the city now and I told her to put on her lights.

'Just for a moment, my lady. That's the signal to Rowley to be ready to drop the pilot and pay him off.'

The street we were in was turning into a road, and half a mile ahead I saw a convenient bend.

'As the Swindon rounds that bend, I want you to touch your horn. And when the taxi pulls up, please stop alongside.'

'Don't say "please" any more, my dear. It makes me feel so ashamed, and—I'm all right now.'

As she spoke, she put out her left hand, and I caught it in mine and kissed it and let it go.

'Now?' said Audrey.

'Yes—now.'

The moment she touched her horn, the taxi pulled in, and as it came to a standstill, we ran alongside.

Rowley was out in the road, with a note in his hand.

'Listen,' I cried. 'We're going to pass the Swindon any time now. But you are to stay behind and take no notice of us.'

'Very good, sir.'

'Put her along, my darling. You heard what I said.'

As the Lowland leapt forward—

'You see,' I said, 'it's like this. I'm almost sure he's making for Pont de l'Arche. And that is a danger-spot. A long bridge over the river . . . in and out of the town . . . and slap up to four crossroads about twice life-size. Well, that's quite bad enough, for you've got to be right on his tail to be certain which way he goes. But say that he takes the Chartres road—as I have a feeling he will. That is a punishing hill—a punishing hill, *dead straight* for a couple of miles or more: and a man in a car that climbs it can see those crossroads below him until he is out of sight. But we can't wait until then, for we can't give him three minutes' start—in country we hardly know.'

Audrey nodded.

'I'm there,' she said. 'Just when and where shall I pass?'

'Not just yet,' said I. 'Let her down a little: he's just in front of that car.'

I made quite sure he was making for Pont de l'Arche. Then we followed him up a hill and bore to the right. And then I told Audrey to pass him—and go like hell.

The road was broad and empty and looked like a racing-track. And as such, indeed, we used it, for because it was so inviting, the chauffeur had chosen this moment to let the Swindon go.

God knows at what pace we passed her, for Audrey's foot was right down—and my head was between my knees; but when I ventured to lift it, the Swindon was not to be seen.

'They can't have seen much,' said Audrey, and fell down another hill.

So we came to the River Seine and Pont de l'Arche.

Over the bridge we went, and in and out of the town. Then into the forest and up the punishing hill . . .

With my eyes on the crossroads, I waited until I could see them no more. And then I told Audrey to stop, snatched my binocular, flung out of the Lowland and ran the way we had come.

It was very nearly two minutes before the Swindon appeared. With my heart in my mouth, I watched her come up to the crossroads. . . .

And then she came on, as we had, to tackle the punishing hill.

As she started to climb, I saw what I thought was the Vane emerge from a cobbled street.

I ran for the Lowland, exultant.

'O.K.,' I cried. 'He's coming. Put her along. As it's worked all right, I guess we'll do it again.'

As Audrey let in her clutch—

'Just what d'you mean, St John?'

'We'll try and lead him, sweetheart. Follow him with the glasses, but always keeping ahead. If he lets us down, Bell's got him: and all we've got to do is to catch him up. But I don't think he'll twist our tail: I believe he's through with his tricks and he's going for Chartres.'

* * *

I will not set out in detail the rest of the journey we made on that blazing afternoon: indeed, if I did, I think it would fill up a book, for the way was long and every bend was a hazard—and every town was a nightmare, because a miss was so much worse than a mile.

Louviers, Evreux, Dreux—somehow we survived them all: and by hook and crook we led the Swindon to Chartres. And when I say 'led,' I mean it. For the whole of those sixty-odd miles, she was never once out of my sight for as much as two minutes of time.

It took a lot of doing, and that is the truth.

Between the towns, we did little but spurt and stop and I continually left and re-entered the car: we proceeded, so to speak, by short rushes, as infantry used to do—a very exhausting business as well for Audrey as me.

Down, full tilt, to some valley and up the opposite side, to stop just over the crest and so out of sight: back on foot, to take cover behind some wayside tree: and then, when the Swindon appeared, back again to the Lowland and off, full tilt again, for the nearest bend: more slowly then, because of a road on the right, and coming to rest in a hollow a drive and a chip ahead: out of the car again, and ten steps back: and then off again, like fury, to gain our proper distance before the Swindon appeared.

On the level, our task was less wearing and yet more difficult, for we had to keep further ahead and I had to kneel on the seat and look through the window behind, continually turning my head to see what country was coming and how the road itself ran: then again, we could seldom stop, but could only play with our pace, losing ground when obscured by some lorry, and things like that.

But the open country was nothing compared with the towns.

Luckily these were well posted and Audrey's sense of direction was very fine: her eye being very quick, she managed to pick her way through them without going wrong, but we had to make up our minds to let the Swindon come up uncomfortably close and to aim at keeping no more than a street ahead. And that was the devil and all, for we were not the only stuff on the road. At times the traffic stopped Plato, and more than once it stopped us—to bring the Swindon so close that, though by that time I was kneeling down on the floor-boards with my head as low as the seat, the sweat of apprehension was running upon my chest.

From what I have said, it will be manifest not only that Plato had seen us again and again—that is to say, seen the Lowland and Audrey sitting inside—but that we had made no attempt to keep out of his ken. This may have been a mistake: but, if it was, it was mine, for Audrey had no say in the line which I took. But, for what it is worth, this is the way I saw it that nerve-racking afternoon.

If a man is afraid of being followed, he will pay no attention at all to a car which is moving ahead—and that, for the very good reason that *followers stay behind*: and though a car is persistently leading his own, he will at the most assume that it is carrying someone whose way is his: his interest may be excited—faintly enough, but so long as that car behaves in a rational way, he will attach no importance to the something ding-dong business of alternately losing distance and gaining ground. But a car which stays behind him is doing as followers do, and so becomes more and more suspect with every mile.

The risks which we ran, by leading, are so very obvious that I will not point them out: but no man can have it both ways, and since we were running through country which I had never set eyes on, which Audrey had seen but once, I felt any risk was better than that of arousing suspicions which I believed to be dead. I was, of course, terribly worried about the Vane and wished a thousand times that I had told Rowley to fall rather further behind: still, I was ready to swear that, until he was this side of Rouen, Plato was unaware that there was such a car on his road; and that and the thought of the cunning which Bell would certainly show did something to combat misgivings which were, of course, as futile as they were importunate.

Looking back, I sometimes wonder if we should have done any better if I had had time to think: but I do not believe that we should, for the business was such a gamble from first to last that the instinct on which I relied served us as well as or better than could have circumspection itself.

Of level-crossings I went in the greatest fear, for had we come to one closed, we must have stood still while the Swindon came up to our tail—and, as like as not, Plato descended, to walk about the Lowland and look at her points: but this ordeal we were spared, though once we escaped it by seconds, and Plato was left behind. But though we thanked our stars, in a sense we had passed from the frying-pan into the fire, for the check which he thus received was more than enough to let us swim out of his ken; yet we had to let him catch up—yet not let him think we had loitered, to gain this end. Whilst I was racking my brain for some way out of this pass, I saw a filling station three furlongs ahead, and though we needed no petrol—for Bell had somehow or other replenished both tanks at Rouen—I told my lady to make for the apron of concrete and bring the Lowland to rest by one of the pumps.

Since the train had not yet gone by, we took in a gallon of petrol for the good of the house, and then, whilst I watched the road, she held the attendant in talk until the Swindon appeared. When I was sure they could see us, I gave her the order to go, and we took up our old position, as though by accident.

That was but one of the narrow escapes which we had, for though I must frankly admit that Plato played into our hands, we dared take nothing for granted and had to work just as hard and to think as fast as we had done that morning when first we had left Dieppe. I shall always believe that we actually guided the Swindon through more than one town, but though, from this distance of time, I am able to focus the humour of this absurdity, I never felt less like laughing than when it in fact took place.

I never can say how wonderful Audrey was. The whole of that afternoon, she not only never failed me, but picked up the cues I tossed her as though she had read my mind. More than once she had served my turn before I had said what it was, and she actually made me eat, getting the sandwiches ready, whilst she was sitting still, and handing them, whilst she was driving, with such a casual air that I took and began to eat them without thinking what I did. In fact, though I never spared her, she did her best to spare me—and she comforted me in the most understanding of ways, if ever I gave her to think that I was in some distress.

There, perhaps, I am giving myself away, for I never saw Mansel or Chandos show any sign of strain. But I know there were times that day when I drifted from speaking to her into thinking aloud, and my thoughts were not always as cheerful as I could have wished. Each *contretemps* that we met with rammed home the brutal fact that luck alone had brought us to where we had come, and seemed designed to argue the manifold changes and chances of such a venture as ours. One error of judgment could put us out of the running: one guess that was wrong could sink us for good and all. And France is a pretty big country: and more than two thirds of her acres lie south of Chartres.

* * *

For some extraordinary reason, for which I can never account, both Audrey and I were quite certain that Plato would spend that night at the city of Chartres.

But whether he did or did not, he would have, she said, to enter the *Place des Epars*, for there stood the best hotels and from that oval the principal roads ran forth.

'He must see us stop, too,' said I. 'If you circle the *place* can he see us? I don't want him up too close.'

'From what I remember, it's spacious: with a very good view all round.'

'Then go round slowly,' said I, 'as if you were taking stock. Where's that hotel you lunched at?'

'*Le Grand Monarque*? On the right—on the side we come in.'

'Steady. I don't see him yet.' The Lowland slowed down. 'Yes. There he is. Carry on. I hope to God the Vane isn't right on his heels. And yet I don't know. If she isn't, she'll go right on, not knowing he's stopped. I've got to this—that I don't know what to hope for . . . except an earthquake or something, to slow things up.'

'Poor St John. You must be so frightfully tired.'

'It's the pace that kills,' said I. 'I only want time to think. A little faster, my beauty: he's coming up.'

'We'll be in the *place* in a minute, and that'll give you a chance.'

A moment later, we entered the *Place des Epars*, and glancing over my shoulder, I saw the truth of her words. The place was a great arena, the whole of which could be seen from wherever you took your stand.

We passed *Le Grand Monarque* and swung to the left. Then we circled slowly, to see what the Swindon did.

With the width of the oval between us, we saw her extremely well.

She passed *Le Grand Monarque*, but she did not swing to the left.

She took the Vendôme road—and passed out of our sight.

★ ★ ★

As things turned out, I think our dismay was misplaced, for Plato must have seen us turn off to the left, and to stop for a drink at Chartres was natural on such a day. In his eyes, therefore, we did as a tourist does; and though we overtook him some twelve miles on, I doubt if he saw more in this than a friendly rivalry. Then, again, I was able to intercept Rowley and Bell—and to tell them to take any risk but that of arousing suspicion by keeping too close. But I had been so certain that Plato would stop at Chartres that I felt I could never again rely on what instinct I had. And I could have spared that feeling at that particular time, for all we had was my instinct to get us home.

I sent on Bell and Rowley the way the Swindon had gone. Then I waited for two more minutes—to colour the illusion that Audrey had stopped for refreshment and taken her time. And then we swung out of the *place* for the Vendôme road.

★ ★ ★

Châteaudun . . . Vendôme . . . Tours . . .

There are times when I dream of that stretch—eighty-six miles long.

For seventy-four of those miles we ran in front of the Swindon, as we had done to Chartres.

Three times we thought we had lost her, and twice the tears were running on Audrey's cheeks.

As she brushed them away—

'Sorry, St John. These women. But take no notice, my dear. It's only my safety-valve.'

I put my arm about her and held her close. Then I called upon her again, as one calls on a thoroughbred: and she responded at once, as a thoroughbred does.

And so we came to Tours—at twenty-five minutes past six.

And there the Swindon stopped—at the best hotel.

I saw Plato enter the house: and his chauffeur drive round to the garage and put the Swindon away.

And when I saw this happen, I very near wept myself—and that, out of sheer relief, for to ask any more of Audrey was more than I could have done, and I was so much exhausted that I could hardly stand up.

* * *

By seven o'clock that evening, we had, in a manner of speaking, consolidated our gains.

We were, all four, installed at a little hotel.

Audrey, too tired to bathe, was lying full length on her bed, with her shoes and stockings off and her beautiful arms stretched out: Bell was going over the cars in the yard below: three hundred yards away, Rowley was watching the garage in which the Swindon was lodged: and I was speaking to Mansel, two hundred and thirty miles off.

'Tours? I can't believe it. By God, John Bagot, you've lighted a candle this day. And you're at the *Panier d'Or.* Well, don't let up, old fellow. Chandos and I are coming, and then you shall take your rest.'

I was glad to hear him say that. I had made what arrangements I could: but if Plato saw fit to go on, we were not fit to follow—and that is the truth.

Audrey was out of the running—until she had had some rest. The drive itself was nothing—many a day we had covered far more than three hundred miles; but it must be remembered that she had been up all night, and the constant stopping and starting and changing gear, the spurting and slowing down, the effort of picking her way through towns which she did not know, above all, the ceaseless strain of being ever ready to do whatever I said and sharing with me a burden which was not hers—these things had conspired together to wear her resistance down. In fact, they had failed of their purpose. But now she had surrendered, because the danger was past.

The duty was, therefore, divided between the servants and me. One must watch the garage in which the Swindon stood—and be ready to run for his life to the *Panier d'Or*: one must be with the Vane, all ready to leave the yard and resume the chase: and the third could be off duty, taking his ease. Four hours on and two off seemed the obvious way. Two hours by the Swindon's garage: two in the yard with the Vane: and two at the *Panier d'Or*.

I took my two hours off until nine o'clock. I bathed and I changed my clothes and I broke my fast—and I sat in a chair beside Audrey, now fast asleep. And then I got up, feeling better, and went to see Bell.

Bell had sent for petrol and filled the tank of each car, and he had been over them both, oiling and greasing and wiping and making sure all was well.

I told him that Audrey was sleeping and asked him to stay within call in case she woke up, and in any event to wake her at ten o'clock and to do his best to persuade her to take some food.

And then I went on to Rowley.

He showed me Plato's chauffeur, dining in style at a café, not thirty yards off, and he said he had entered the garage and talked with its keeper within. The latter had told him the orders which he had received—to wash and polish the Swindon and have her ready by nine o'clock the next day.

This was most comforting news: but though I was very much tempted to return with Rowley forthwith to the *Panier d'Or*, I knew that, if I did so, I should not be able to rest, because we were not keeping the watch which ought to be kept. So I sent him back to relieve his faithful companion—who was himself due to relieve me in two hours' time.

The light was failing now, because we had come so far south, and since I was moving in the shadows, I had no fear of the chauffeur's seeing my face: but I could see the man well, for he sat without the café, and a light was hanging directly above his head. But so long as he kept his distance, I was not concerned with him: I was concerned with the garage in which the Swindon was lodged. So I strolled up and down with my eyes on its narrow entry, thankful for the cool of the evening and wondering how long it would be before Mansel arrived.

And then I got the shock of my life, for a car came out of the garage with both its headlights on, and I could not see what it was, because its surroundings were dark, but its lights were full in my eyes. It had entered the stream of traffic, before I had time to think, and since this was moving fast, was away in a flash, and I only saw its number by the skin of my teeth.

In fact, it was not the Swindon, although it was very much like her in several ways: but the incident showed me that I must cross the street and stand quite close to the entry, if I was to do any good—or else must watch the chauffeur and let the Swindon go.

After a moment's reflection, I decided to cross the street . . .

The entry which served the garage was really more of a tunnel than anything else: and that is why, no doubt, the drivers of cars which used it employed their lights: and the garage itself was very dimly lighted, although it was very spacious and seemed to be full of cars.

It was I think this condition which showed me that I should do better to enter the garage itself, for out on the pavement I had no cover at all and if the chauffeur appeared, he might very easily see me before I saw him; but in the garage itself a troop of men could have lurked without being seen.

And so I walked into the garage, slipped between two of the cars and began to look round.

At the far end lights were burning, but they were round some corner and so in fact out of sight. But the light which they threw illumined indirectly the rest of the place. This illumination was naturally very faint, and I saw at once that I had done well to come in, for that here I could go as I pleased without being seen.

Out of sight, where the lights were burning, some man was washing a car—I could hear the hiss of the jet and the sudden snarl of the water striking the wings. I assumed that this was the watchman, for I could see no one at all.

Carefully moving forward, towards the light, I presently found the Swindon, standing in line.

With an eye on the narrow entry, I stole round about the car—my shoes, which were soled with rubber, making no sound. All the windows were down, and I looked inside.

And then I noticed something.

The luggage was still in the car.

The cushions which made the back seat had been taken away,

and suitcases—four, I think—had been stacked in their place—a wise enough proceeding, for though the floor was empty, the weight of the baggage was lying above the back axle and so must help to hold the wheels down on the road.

And then I heard a voice raised—and almost jumped out of my skin.

'Hi, you there,' someone shouted. And then again, 'Hi!'

Of course I knew it was Plato; and of course I knew that he was addressing me: and my knees were loose, as I turned to saunter away.

Once, as I thought, out of sight, I darted behind a car, to peer in that direction from which Plato's voice had come. And then I saw that he was not addressing me, but was trying to make himself heard by the man who was washing the car.

I saw him plainly now, standing framed in some doorway which afforded a private entrance to the hotel, and he had a small case in his hands and a hat on his head.

The noise of the water had ceased, and the washer was shambling forward towards where the other stood.

'Where's my chauffeur?' cried Plato—and spoke such very bad French that even I could understand what he said.

I do not know what the man answered, but he pointed towards the entry, and Plato looked that way and then walked into the garage and met the man in its aisle.

Now I ought to have left there and then. I had seen and heard quite enough. But, while I hesitated, the chance was lost: for the two of them turned together, to walk towards the entry and so cut off my escape.

And then I saw that I ought to have had the Vane waiting—*not three hundred yards away, but somewhere just round the corner*, as we had done at Rouen and Neufchatel. I had employed half measures: and half measures never pay.

With two minutes' start *in the darkness*, the Swindon was going to vanish, as though she had been swallowed up.

Mansel told me later that, had he been in my place, he would have unscrewed a valve and let the air run out of one of the Swindon's tires, but such was my state of mind that I never thought of that.

Instead, my tired brain offered a truly desperate shift: and since it was that or nothing, and I had not a moment to lose, I entered the back of the Swindon, shut the door behind me and then went down on my knees.

It was a very tight fit, for I am not a little man; but, so long as the darkness held, I could see no reason why Plato should know I was there—always provided, of course, that neither he nor his chauffeur looked into the back of the car.

My position was that of a Moslem, saying his prayers, and since the floor was flat and the carpet was thick, I was not uncomfortable. But such was the slam of my heart, I began to think that that must give me away. Then I noticed the sound of my breathing, and when I endeavoured to curb it, I thought I was going to sneeze. . . .

In fact, to tell the truth, I was halfway to regretting what I had done—when something happened to kick me the rest of the way.

It was, in a way, a query.

I had entered the car unseen: *but how was I going to get out? The next time that Plato stopped, he would stop for the night . . . and the luggage would have to come out . . . and, to get the luggage out, the chauffeur would open the doors which gave to the back of the car.*

At once I felt for a handle, to let myself out.

And then I heard Plato's voice.

'I told you half past nine: and it's nearly twenty to ten.'

I let the handle go.

It was too late now.

CHAPTER 8

The Stolen March

I shall never forget how I felt when Plato flung open his door and flounced into his bucket seat. No doubt because the space we were in was confined, his presence was overwhelming, and all he did was, so to speak, magnified.

He was breathing hard through his nose, as an angry man: he settled himself in impatience—*against my back*: and when he cried to the chauffeur to ask if the tank was full, he seemed to speak in my ear.

Indeed, at that moment I gave myself up for lost, for it seemed impossible that he could be so close, yet stay unaware of my presence within the car; and I waited, as one may wait for the chime of a clock which is slow, for the sudden, abrupt exclamation which would tell me that I had been seen.

Yet this did not come.

The chauffeur took his seat and started the car. Then the doors were slammed and the Swindon began to move.

It was as we passed out of the garage that Plato let fly. The control which his cloth had insisted that he must display had, I am sure, inflamed him as nothing else, for the violence with which he rent the chauffeur was quite unprintable. No ordinary servant would have endured such abuse, but the other only waited till his master paused to take breath and then advised him curtly to 'whip behind.'

'When we're clear of the town,' growled Plato. 'It's no good yet. And anyway, what's the odds? We're going to settle it later for good an' all.'

'It's settled already,' said the chauffeur, 'if you ask me. I had a 'unt round just now—that's why I was late.'

'Hunt round be ——,' said Plato. 'A man that can tail you for close on two hundred miles is not going to wait round the corner while you have tea.'

'Imagination,' said the chauffeur. 'That's what it is. Look at the Vanes on the road. The wonder is——'

'I'm taking no risks,' said Plato. 'Either there's nothing in it, or else that —— has tailed a car before. Well, we'll know the answer tonight: and if I don't like its shape, we're going straight home.'

There was a little silence, of which I was more than glad.

My sudden admission to the counsels which I had sought to divine, the blunt confirmation of my particular fear, and the blinding revelation that had I done as I had planned and run for the Vane, we must have walked into the trap which Plato was going to set—these things were a gift from the gods, *if I could only escape*. Then I saw that, before I escaped, I must learn where Plato was going—at any cost. And then I saw that I should never escape. . . .

In such disorder of mind, I knelt as flat as I could with my cheek pressed tight against the carpet and my knees and my insteps already beginning to ache, while the Swindon whipped over the *pavé* at a pace which I reckoned as thirty-five miles to the hour.

Now when we had left the garage, I felt the car swing to the left: since then we had not turned nor so much as slowed down, and as, by the grace of God, I had studied the plan of Tours at the *Panier d'Or*, I knew the way we were taking out of the town.

The main highway runs straight as a ruler through Tours, slicing the city in two from north to south. As luck will have it, the garage stood in this street, so that when we had swung to the left I knew we were going south. Once it is clear of the city, the highway splits into four—as a family tree: and each of its offspring is heading a different way.

And that was as much as I knew.

Plato extended my knowledge almost at once.

'Straight as you can,' he said. 'Chatellerault's the name.'

'I thought you said Poitiers.'

'Chatellerault first,' said Plato. 'Look out for that.'

We had left the *pavé* now, which meant we were clear of the town. Then we whipped under some bridge: and then we bent to the right and back to the left.

'Chatellerault,' muttered the chauffeur, as though he were reading some sign.

'And now,' said Plato—and brought my heart into my mouth.

The man had turned in his seat, to look out of the window behind—and was speaking across my body, twelve inches below his chin.

'Faster,' he added, shortly. 'Let her out all you know.'

Very soon we were doing sixty—or so I judged.

'Anythin' doin'?' said the chauffeur.

'Not yet,' said Plato, turning. 'They may be afraid of their lights.'

'If you ask me,' said the chauffeur. . . .

'You're here to drive,' said Plato. 'Put her along.'

We were fairly flying now, and I remember hoping the Swindon's light were good.

After a little the chauffeur re-opened his mouth.

'Funny seeing that piece in the paper. It give me a turn.'

'Funny be ——,' snapped Plato. 'I wish I'd known it before. If Bagot's in Mansel's pocket, he's gone as he —— well pleased.'

'An' wot can he do?' said the other. 'I've seen these " 'untin' cronies." They're all backside.'

'St Omer, for instance?' sneered Plato. 'You blind —— fool, this Bagot was jam for Mansel. I'll lay a monkey he's spread him all over the place. An' that's why you're going back.'

'Me goin' back?'

'Tonight. From Poitiers. There's a train that leaves for Paris at twelve o'clock.'

'But——'

'Don't argue with me. You're going straight back to London and you're going to put Bogy on. He's got to run down Bagot at any price. I don't care where he is. He's got to be found.' I heard him expire. 'These blasted Willies. You never know where you are.'

'You're seein' things,' said the other. 'What with the Vane an' Bagot——'

'I've eyes to see,' spat Plato. 'That Vane was being driven by someone who knew his job.' Again he slewed himself round, to look back at the road behind. 'An' Mansel's been lying too low. I thought it was queer—the two of them sitting so still.'

'Queer?' said the chauffeur. 'They're windy. That accident made them think. An' windy or no, they're stuck. They don't know where to begin.'

As though he were thinking aloud—

'This Bagot fits,' said Plato. 'You can't get away from that. He's just what Mansel needed—a Willie we didn't know.'

'Easy, Kingdom, easy. He'll be in the Vane in a minute—talking like this. This Bagot's a "huntin' crony." What does he know about snooping? If he started to watch a tea shop, the coppers 'd move him on.'

'Maybe,' said Plato, 'maybe. But Mansel's no sucking Holmes, and the —— fits. I've got to know where he is before I go on. You'll be in London tomorrow, and Bogy's to get right down. The moment he's placed him he wires me where Bagot is. Poste Restante, Poitiers. I'm sitting tight as hell till I get that news.'

'Code or clear?' said the chauffeur.

'Clear,' said Plato. 'Signed "Arthur." And no —— guess-work, either. He's got to be sure.'

'I see. Am I comin' back?'

'I guess I'll do without you.'

'I guess you will,' said the chauffeur, and let out a laugh. 'You don't trust no one, do you? Last time I got down at Tours.'

'What a memory,' said Plato, slowly—and if ever DANGER was signalled, it showed itself in his tone. 'Do you remember The Mule?'

'I should say so,' said the other. 'I'd like to see him again.'

'You will—one day.' said Plato. '*He had a memory . . . too.*'

I despair of describing the manner in which he spoke those words. I can only say that he lent them a significance so dreadful that all my body tingled and the hair rose up from my head. His voice was not cold or brutal, but quiet and clear; and his meaning stood out as some doom written up on a wall.

In fact, he nearly ended all three of our lives, for the Swindon swerved to glory and Plato himself cried out. Then the car slowed up, and the wretched chauffeur was pleading and Plato was shouting him down and using most hideous imprecations because he had slackened speed. Twice I heard him strike him, but the man only whimpered back, and very soon we were moving as fast as before.

As he whipped through some sleeping village—

'You're all the same,' said Plato. 'You can't stand corn. I let you talk to me because this is a two-man job. Result—you think you're promoted: and there you're wrong. I'm using you—that's all. I hang my thoughts on you, to see how they look. And because you sit by my side, you needn't climb on to my knee. Get that and hold it, buddy. You'll find it better than Bovril for keeping you fit.'

'All right, Kingdom,' gulped the chauffeur. 'You—you needn't keep on.'

'And not so much of the "Kingdom," you green-faced rat.'

'No—no offence,' quavered the chauffeur. 'I didn't mean nothing wrong.'

Plato spat out of his window.

Then—

'Put her along,' he said.

I now had but one idea—to get out of that car.

Though Plato talked for an hour, I had no more to learn. But what I had learned was vital. Unless we could act upon it, the game was up.

And I had another reason for wishing to leave that car.

I had seen a side of Plato I did not like. And I knew that if I was discovered, my life, like that of The Mule, would come to an end.

I mean, the thing was too easy. Night, in France, in the depths of the countryside . . . two desperate men to one—*whose legs were already so cramped that their power was gone* . . . and that man the very man whose activities Plato suspected, not to say feared . . .

If the situation was ugly, my state was miserable.

I was not so much bent double as folded in three: I was jammed between the two seats: and, worst of all, I was choking for want of air, for the night was very warm and, though the windows were open, the breeze passed over my body and never approached my face. My knee-caps seemed to be splitting: the agony in my insteps will hardly go into words: the springs of sweat had broken, and all my flesh was creeping with wandering rivulets. I would have given a fortune to have been able to shift. But I dared not move a muscle in case the movement was heard.

I was, of course, quite frantic to save the game—in other words, to escape without being seen. The news I had won was so precious that I could not bear the thought of having to let it go. And yet I had little hope of a triumph so great as that. Indeed, what concerned me most was the bitter reflection that if it came to a fight, I could not do myself justice because of the cramp in my legs. This was a serious matter. Had I been lifted out, I could not have stood.

So mile after mile went by, and still the chauffeur maintained a very high speed. Now and again we slowed down—I rather fancy, because of somebody's lights: but the traffic must have been slight, for such checks were few. Sometimes Plato would turn, to look out behind: but I think he saw nothing suspicious, or if he did, he never reported the fact. Indeed, for a very long time, he never opened his mouth—as though to ram home the fact that the chauffeur had gone too far. I found the silence more trying than any speech, for speech is an occupation, and I did not like Plato beside me with nothing to do.

It was, as I afterwards found, about twenty minutes past ten when I began to feel faint.

Now I had never fainted since I was a little boy at my private school, but I knew the symptoms at once and they gave me the shock of my life.

There can, I think, be no doubt that it was the lack of fresh air that brought this condition about; but my powers of resistance were low, because I was very tired and in great discomfort and pain. Be that as it may, I now knew that, unless I could breathe some fresh air, my senses were bound to leave me before very long and that though I could fight off the faintness for, possibly, several miles, the time would come when I must raise myself up or else lose consciousness.

That anything was better than fainting was very clear, but to raise my head to a level at which I could catch the breeze would be to put that member into the lion's mouth. Though he did not see my movement with the tail of his eye, once my head was lifted, Plato had only to turn to perceive me twelve inches away.

I think I can fairly say that I know what it means to have your back to the wall. . . .

With a frightful effort, I pulled myself together and tried to focus the facts with which I was faced.

How far Poitiers was, I had no idea. All I knew—and that from what Plato had said—was that Poitiers was beyond Chatellerault. And we had not even come to Chatellerault yet. Of that, though I could not see, there could be no doubt: villages we could rush, but we could not take a town in our stride.

An embryo problem bewildered my failing wits. If Poitiers was as far from Chatellerault as Chatellerault was from Tours . . .

My head was going round, when Plato opened his mouth—to lug me back from the brink.

'Chatellerault twelve,' he quoted. 'That's just over seven miles. Slow when you come to the streets: we're going to turn off. Just off the main road—that's all: we're going to lie up. *I'll see if I'm being followed.* And if I'm not, we'll go on—at eleven-fifteen. Poitiers is only a matter of twenty-one miles.'

Had he given me a cup of cold water, he could not have done me more good. If Plato turned off the main road, he could not watch the main road without getting out of the car. That meant that in seven more miles my chance would come. Not, perhaps, my chance of escaping—the two might be standing too close: but at least, my chance of breathing, of filling my lungs with the blessed, life-giving air.

Seven more miles . . .

Reducing miles to minutes, I made the answer nine.

Nine more minutes . . . and then my release would come.

I remember that I tried to keep going by counting the seconds away: but the faintness began to return, and I had to fight like a madman to beat off its subtle attack. By the time the mists had cleared, I had, of course, lost my reckoning for good and all, and so was deprived of that chance of cheering my struggling wits. And then I found that Plato was talking again . . . And then, to my horror, I found that his voice seemed a great way off—which told me what I had not known, that my senses were unobtrusively stealing away.

This discovery, strangely enough, was my salvation. In a word, it shocked me so much to find that the battle was lost, that before I knew where I was, the battle was won. I was startled out of my faintness—and that is the simple truth. Something seemed to surge in my temples—it may have been blood: then once again the mists rolled back and away.

(Here perhaps I should say that I sometimes think that in fact I was unconscious for two or more miles, for, try as I will to remember the last of that drive, there is a clear hiatus for which I cannot account.)

'Steady now,' Plato was saying. The car had slowed down. 'I don't want to get too far in.' I heard him turn round in his seat. 'All clear behind—for the moment. D'you see a street on your left?'

'There's one comin' now,' said the chauffeur, and set a foot on the brake.

'Take it,' said Plato. 'And stop—about forty yards down.'

Almost at once I felt the car swing to the left, and two or three moments later the chauffeur brought her to rest.

'Switch off your lights and your engine an' follow me.'

As Plato gave that order, he opened his door . . .

The chauffeur was quick to obey. His door was slammed but a moment later than Plato's. I heard their footfalls retreating the way we had come.

And then somehow I was clinging to the sill of a window, conscious of a pain like a sword in the small of my back and drinking great draughts of an air that seemed cooler and sweeter than any I ever encountered before or since.

* * *

A very few moments sufficed to make me myself again, and almost at once I began to prepare to escape.

Through the window at the back of the car, I could see the main road or main street, out of which we had turned: but I could see no one standing—at the corner or anywhere else. Straining my ears, I could hear no footfalls or voices. It looked as if, for the moment, I had the side street to myself.

To this day I do not know how I managed to turn myself round without crying out, for my legs were as though paralysed and their slightest movement caused me the sharpest pain: but by holding on to the back of the driver's seat I dragged myself up and, propped between that and the luggage, I dragged myself round, and then once more I subsided on to the floor, with my legs stuck out before me instead of folded beneath. Then I set to work to massage them back into life.

I was, of course, terribly tempted to open the door behind me and drag myself out of the car: but, though I may have been wrong, I felt that it would have been folly to leave my cover before I could trust my feet. So I sat, in fear and trembling lest Plato or his man should come back, and worked upon my legs like a madman, plucking and pinching and slapping the helpless flesh.

Those two or three minutes were almost the worst I passed, for, the pain apart, I could keep no sort of look-out, and if someone had come to the car, he must have heard my movements before I so much as heard his. Still, after what seemed an age, the pain began to grow less and at last when I called upon an ankle, it haltingly did as I said.

That was enough for me.

At once I raised myself up and looked out of the window again: and since I could see no being, I ventured to open a door.

My legs were still so faithless and I was trembling so much that I very nearly fell down when I stepped into the street: but I steadied myself by holding fast to the door, and after a moment I felt my strength coming back.

It was my actual emergence that made me well. The blessed knowledge that I was clear of the trap uplifted my heart and drove the blood through my veins. I no longer hoped to be saved. I intended to win the rubber—and put the blackguard enemy where he belonged.

As though I had an hour to myself, I held that door into its frame and then released its tongue by sixteenths of an inch. Then I pulled its handle towards me and found it locked. And then, with uncertain steps, I padded away . . . away from the corner and Plato and all his works . . . exalted by the knowledge that I had escaped unseen and that Plato would never know that he had given John Bagot the lift of his life.

* * *

I took a street on the right and glanced at my watch.

Twenty-five minutes to eleven. And Plato was not proposing to leave until eleven-fifteen.

At once I saw that I must report to Tours, and then, if I could, beat Plato to Poitiers Station, from there to follow the fellow and see where he meant to lie.

Unless I reported to Tours, God only knew what action the others would take. When Bell found the Swindon gone, as he would at eleven o'clock, he would instantly give the alarm. My own disappearance would have a sinister look: and, as Audrey was sure to take charge, as like as not both cars would be manned forthwith to go different ways—with Audrey, unfit to drive, at the Lowland's wheel. And unless I went on to Poitiers, I could not be sure that Plato had done as he said: and in any event I should not know where he was staying—in fact, I should lose the fox with which I had managed to stay for two hundred and fifty miles. But of course *I must precede* him. I must be at Poitiers before him, because if I came behind him, the man would never rest till he saw my face.

It seemed pretty clear that the street which I was using led into the heart of the town, but since there was no one to ask, for the place seemed dead, I began to run along it as fast as I could. And then I saw a station . . . and two or three taxis waiting . . . and an omnibus bearing the name of the Grand Hotel.

I chose the best-looking taxi, and two minutes later I entered that kindly house. . . .

I tremble to think what I looked like—hatless, coatless, tieless and stained with travel and sweat: but I could not have been better served had I been a millionaire. Maybe they thought I was, for before I did anything else I made the porter a present of two hundred francs and showed him another two hundred which might be his.

Then I bade him bring someone who spoke English.

He not only did as I said, but he raised the house.

By the time he was back, with a nice-looking lad of eighteen, waiters and maids and a valet were smiling and bowing about me and asking me how I did, while the lady who owned the hotel was standing at the top of some staircase, commending various cordials which she considered could usefully serve my need.

As I presently found, the nice-looking boy was a guest—or, rather, the son of a doctor who lived next door: and the English he spoke was nearly as good as mine.

In two minutes' time I had a room with a bath, a waiter was pouring me beer, a maid was running water and a valet was cleaning my shoes: downstairs, the porter, abetted, of course, by his mistress and half the staff, was alternately calling on God and commanding an obstructive exchange to 'give me Tours . . . *Hôtel Le Panier d'Or* . . . *Milady* Audrey Nuneham . . . on a matter of life and death.' And the nice-looking lad had gone off to a garage near by, *to get his own Bugatti to drive me to Poitiers.*

For all this precious attention, I very near missed the tide, for I never got through to Tours till past eleven o'clock. Indeed, I was writing my message and the doctor's son was translating it into French, when at last the telephone went and I snatched the receiver up.

'Is that you, Audrey?' I cried.

'Mansel speaking,' said Mansel. 'Is that you, John?'

I could hardly believe my ears. Four hours ago he had been at Amiens. And now he was speaking from Tours. And from Amiens to Tours is two hundred and thirty miles.

'Listen,' I said. 'Where's Audrey?'

'She's here—by my side.'

'Thank God for that,' said I. 'And now—all's well. Meet me at Poitiers Station—but not before one o'clock. Don't enter the town before one, whatever you do. *And Audrey is not to drive.*'

'She shan't,' said Mansel. 'I promise. Anything else?'

'Keep the Vane in the background,' said I.

'I understand.'

'Goodbye,' said I.

'Goodbye.'

I paid my debts and fairly ran out of the house.

And then I was in the Bugatti, and René de Boulon was streaking out of the town.

* * *

Poitiers was not very far—as Plato had said, 'a matter of twenty-one miles.' Indeed, I had time to burn, for René covered the distance in twenty-two minutes dead.

Had I allowed him to do so, he would have stayed on; but I thought he had learned quite enough, so I took his address and did my best to thank him and told him that, for what it was worth, that night he had made four friends.

And then I watched him drive off the way he had come, and heard the professional stammer of his exhaust ripping the mantle of silence for nearly a league.

I found a hut in the shadows by the side of the station-yard: and in its mouth I sat down, to wait until Plato should come.

The man was as good as his word.

Precisely at a quarter to midnight, the Swindon swept into the yard. There master and man got out: and when they had entered the station, I left my hut for the road.

There I stopped a taxi, which was coming to meet the train, gave the driver a note and bade him draw up in the shadows some fifty yards off. But I stood still where I was, by the mouth of the station-yard.

The Paris train came in, a few minutes later: but Plato was taking no risks: not until the train had departed did he come back to his car.

To my surprise, he did not enter the Swindon, but walked to the nearest taxi and spoke to the man at its wheel. And then I saw that he was engaging a pilot . . .

Yet, there again I was wrong, for the taxi followed the Swindon out of the yard.

At once I turned to run for my waiting taxi—for they had turned to the left, but I had told my driver to wait to the right. But after two or three paces I stopped in my tracks, for the taxi which I had taken was not to be seen. With my fifty francs in his pocket, its driver had let me down and gone to his bed.

Feeling like murder, I turned to run after the Swindon as hard as I could, when to my surprise and relief I saw its satellite taxi slow down by the side of a garage a hundred yards off.

I had noticed the garage when I had gone past it with René some thirty-five minutes before, because it was open and lighted and seemed to be almost as busy as are such places by day. And I shall always believe that Plato, as he had gone past it, had noticed it, too, and had seen with half an eye that that was the very place in which to bestow his car.

For that was what the man did.

From a little way off, I watched him drive into the garage: and from very much closer I watched him come out on foot, a mechanic walking behind him, with a suit-case in either hand.

For what it was worth, I had taken his taxi's number, but once again that night the Kingdom of Heaven played into my grateful hands.

He addressed the mechanic—in his atrocious French.

'The Hotel Crystal, you said? Are you sure it is quiet?'

I think the other said it was quiet and clean.

'And it's not in the fashionable quarter? I don't want that.'

'No, no. It stands by a church: and its rooms look over the park at the end of the town.'

Plato addressed his driver.

'The Hotel Crystal,' he said.

Then he gave the mechanic some money and followed his suit-cases into the quivering cab.

Lying beneath a lorry, I watched his driver turn round.

And then he drove off past the station, making more noise with his gears than the train he had met.

* * *

I suppose it was the realization that now my duty was done that brought to my notice the truth that I was as good as worn out. This was scarcely surprising, for though I am very strong and was used to long stretches of work, I had been up and doing for more than twenty-four hours and more than once, during that period, Chance, so to speak, had driven me pretty hard. Be that as it may, as Plato drove off in his taxi, my energy seemed to fail, and, but for my appointment with Mansel, I think I should have lain where I was and have given way to the slumber of which I stood in such need. Because this need was so strong, I dared not lie still; but as I crawled backwards from under the lorry's bulk, I wondered how on earth I had managed to occupy a post so hard of access with such rapidity.

Indeed, I was now so heavy that, as I stumbled back to the station, much of what had recently happened seemed to belong to some dream, and for the life of me I could not remember the name 'Chatellerault'—a detail which did not matter, but for some ridiculous reason caused me the gravest concern. When I entered the yard, I stood looking round for the Swindon and I remember crying, 'My God, she's gone': but the very shock of this absurd discovery was just what was needed to rally my wandering wits.

Something ashamed of myself, I made my way back to my hut and once again sat down in its dingy mouth . . . and the next thing that I remember was Audrey's voice and a grateful stream of iced water trickling over my brow.

I shook myself and sat up, with a hand to my head.

'Are you all right, dear?' said Audrey.

'I've been asleep,' I said. 'He promised you shouldn't drive.'

'I know. I didn't. I came in the Rolls with him. But tell me—are you all right?'

The moon was up now, and I stared at her kneeling beside me and sitting back on her heels. I inspected her bare, brown knees and the sponge on a cloth by her side. And I gazed at her parted lips and the eager light in her eyes.

'Yes, I'm all right,' I said slowly. I put out a hand, and she took it in both of hers. 'Oh, Audrey, I'm so glad it's you. I've got him, my darling. I know where he is—and the Swindon: the chauffeur's gone. But I wanted to tell you first—before anyone else.' I dropped my head and brought her hands up to my lips. 'You see, when you're mad about someone, you want to lay down at their feet what you happen to win.'

I looked up to see her smiling.

'St John the Gallant,' she said swiftly. Then she looked over my shoulder. 'He's all right now.'

'Good God,' said I—and Carson helped me to rise.

As in a dream, I watched Mansel hand Audrey up to her feet.

My head became painfully clear.

'And Bell and Rowley?' said I. 'Why did you let me begin before they'd arrived?'

'Carson'll tell them,' said Mansel, and the four of us laughed.

And then we went back to the road, and there was Richard Chandos, sitting on a step of the Lowland, smoking a pipe.

* * *

Then we drove back out of the city and into a country road, and there the Vane was waiting, with Rowley and Bell.

And while the servants kept watch, I told my tale. But I must confess I was thankful that Mansel and Chandos were there.

For I was too tired to give orders or even to think for myself.

Indeed, I have no recollection of how, a little later, I came to be in a nice bedroom, which gave to a little bathroom, all hung with blue and white tiles: but there was Rowley, laying my sleeping things out, so I asked him only one question—and ripped my shirt over my head.

'Next door, sir,' said Rowley, and stooped to unlace my shoes.

CHAPTER 9

Audrey's Way

Swathed in a silk dressing-gown, Audrey was standing, smiling, at the foot of my bed.

'I'm so sorry to wake you, my dear.' I propped myself on an elbow and rubbed my eyes. 'But Jonah wants to see you at half past nine.' I sat up and looked at my watch. 'It's all right—he's coming here. But he said I was to have you clear-headed before he came. So I've run your bath all ready . . . I should put on a shirt and trousers and shave when he's gone.'

'And you? Have you had your breakfast?'

She shook her excellent head.

'I'm going to have it with you.'

Before I could protest, she was gone—by a door which I had not noticed, which gave to her room.

I was able to bathe and shave before Rowley knocked at the door.

Then he ushered in Mansel and Chandos—and Audrey opened her door and asked if she could come in.

'Of course,' said Mansel. 'Rowley, stand outside: and knock as usual, if anyone comes too close.'

'Very good, sir.'

Then the two doors were shut, and the four of us took our seats.

Mansel went straight to the point.

'John Bagot,' he said, 'I've one or two questions to ask which you were not fit to answer eight hours ago. The first is this. Did Plato say in your hearing how soon he expected the wire from Bogy to come?'

'No,' said I. 'He didn't. His words were these: "You'll be in London tomorrow, and Bogy's to get right down." '

'Did he seem really uneasy? Or was this mission invented to get the chauffeur away?'

'He was definitely uneasy. He said I was just what you wanted—"a Willie *they* didn't know." '

'But the chauffeur didn't agree with his point of view?'

'No,' said I. 'He didn't. He told Plato plainly that he was imagining things.'

'Did he think it was just an excuse to get him out of the way?'

'I'm inclined to think he did.'

'Let me put it like this. Plato has told him to take a certain precaution. He believes the precaution to be superfluous and suspects that Plato's true object is to get him out of the way.'

'Exactly.'

'But Plato is really killing two birds with one stone?'

'Yes.'

'And he really will wait for that wire, before going on?'

' "Wait"?' said I. 'He'll haunt the Poste Restante—unless I've got him all wrong.'

'Good,' said Mansel. 'That's all I wanted to know. And now that the air is clear, I just want to say this.' He looked from me to Audrey, sitting on the arm of a chair. 'The show you two have put up is one of the very best that I've ever seen. We know that Plato never suspected the Lowland—and yet you were round his neck for over two hundred miles. Well, that was a great achievement: and if you hadn't done it, I'd have said that it couldn't be done. John Bagot's epilogue belongs to another class. That was an exploit. He had the courage to take a tremendous risk: and, together, that wit and that courage have saved the game.'

Chandos looked up and smiled.

'No doubt about that,' he said. 'Friend Bogy's wire would have blown our endeavours to bits.'

' "Would have"?' said I. 'But how on earth can we stop it?'

'We can't,' said Mansel. 'But we can forestall it—and that's what we're going to do. The chauffeur should be in London by half past three today. A wire will be sent from London at half past four. It won't be sent by Bogy, but Plato will not know that. It will be signed "Arthur" and will say that you are at home. Bogy's own wire will come later—I hope and believe. But Plato will never see it, *because he will think that he's had it*—you see what I mean?'

'Yes, I see that,' said I: 'but why don't you want him to see the wire which Bogy will send? My people at Shepherd's Market don't know I'm in France.'

'Because, my dear John, the good Bogy won't wire about you. All he wants at this moment is Plato's address. And the instant he gets it he'll wire him some far more important news—*that Mansel and Chandos and Carson are somewhere in France*.'

'God Almighty,' said I, and Audrey cried out.

'So you see how vital it is that Plato should get our wire before Bogy's arrives. From what you've told me this morning, I think he will; for while his impatience will send him to the Post Office early, the chauffeur away in London will take his time. Anyway, we must hope for the best. I dare not have our wire sent before half past four: otherwise, it will be obvious that Bogy has not had time to find out where you are. Oh, and Carson is watching the Crystal—I don't think there's anything else. But a day off will do us all good—including our clerical friend. If everything goes as we wish, he'll get our wire tonight and leave tomorrow morning—a giant refreshed. And as we're now seven to one, I don't much care where he goes.'

'I don't wonder,' said Audrey, 'that he is afraid of you.'

'He isn't,' said Mansel, swiftly. 'But he knows that we are worth watching, because if we get a chance, we're not going to throw it away. He has an instinct, Plato. To suspect the Vane was natural: but his instinct, like some familiar, is making him look at John. I know how he feels—exactly. His common sense declares that his instinct is wrong: but he has such faith in his instinct that Bogy must *prove* it wrong before he will budge.' Here he glanced at his wristwatch and got to his feet. 'And now I must get on to London about that misleading wire. After that, William and I are going to have a look at the country—with a view to tomorrow's run. You two shall give us some lunch about half past one: till then, please stay in these rooms—I don't think it's very likely, but Plato might go for a stroll.'

'Supposing,' said Audrey, 'just supposing he did a flit?'

Mansel wrinkled his brow.

'Bell's seen to that,' he said. 'The Swindon's all washed and ready, but one of her tires is flat. It happens like that sometimes. You pick up a nail one day, but the tire doesn't die on you for twenty-four hours.'

* * *

Glad as I was to have nothing to do that day, there were times when I thought that the sun would never have run his course. Though neither Mansel nor Chandos betrayed concern, they must have been just as uneasy as Audrey and I, for there was no blinking the fact that, once Mansel had spoken to London, the matter was out of our hands and we could do nothing whatever but hope for the best.

To make things worse, it was, of course, painfully clear that, before the chauffeur had left him, Plato might well have varied the rough and ready instructions which I had heard him give: and then, though our telegram came before that which Bogy dispatched, it would declare itself spurious because it was not worded as Plato had said.

However, as I have said, there was nothing to do but wait: but the hours went by very slowly, while Fortune considered the verdict she meant to return.

Plato rose about ten and went for a stroll in the gardens before he took lunch: but at half past two he was still within his hotel, so Mansel sent Audrey and me for a drive in the Rolls.

'You're sick of moving,' he said, 'so I shouldn't go far. Would you like to sit down in a meadow and look at a stream?'

'That's about all I'm fit for,' said Audrey. 'How did you know?'

Mansel smiled.

'It's very refreshing,' he said. 'I've done it a good many times, and it's done me a great deal of good. I marked a good place this morning, and Carson shall take you there.'

So it came that, at three o'clock, Audrey and I were at ease in a blowing meadow by the side of a lazy stream, and a nightingale was singing in a thicket, and a peasant was cheering his oxen some two or three acres away. Now and again a fish would leap out of the water and now and again we could hear the drone of a distant car, but movement and sound were not those of a work-a-day world and only served to commend the wisdom of Æsop, who must have written his fables in just such a pretty place.

Audrey laid back her head and stared at the cloudless sky.

'Jonah,' she said, 'is a very remarkable man. He marked this place this morning, because he knew that to come here would do us good. Well, he's perfectly right, as usual. I feel miles better already for lying here. . . . And yet he's absurdly modest. He honours Plato's instinct—you heard what he said today: but Jonah's instinct is almost like second sight. Look at the bricks he's made without any straw. From Sermon Square to Poitiers. I mean, if we get no further that's not too bad.'

'Supposing,' I said, 'supposing things go wrong, and Plato goes home.'

Audrey looked at me sharply, and then sat up. Then a slim hand shot out and caught hold of my wrist.

'Listen, John dear. Jonah and Richard are terribly nice to us: they treat us just as their equals in every way: but in fact, compared with them, you and I are like two children—for all we've done. And though I'm younger than you and though, as the boy, you properly take the lead, because I'm a girl I can sometimes see a bit further—get things you can't. Besides, you see, I was in on the Blanche Mains show. . . .'

'I'll say you're right, my beauty. But why have you chosen this moment to point it out?'

'Listen. You said just now, "Supposing things go wrong and Plato goes home." '

'So I did,' said I. 'And what about that?'

'This,' said Audrey quietly. 'Plato will never go home.' In spite of myself, I started, and I felt her fingers tighten about my wrist. 'The moment he landed in France, his race was run. If things go wrong today, he'll die a day or two sooner—that's all. If things go right, he'll lead us up to Barabbas: and then, having served our turn, he will lose his life.'

There was a little silence.

Then—

'I give you best,' said I. 'You're wiser than me. But, now that you've shown me, of course it sticks out a mile. Once he was under his hand, Mansel would never spare Barabbas' *chargé d'affaires*.' I hesitated. Then—'And I'm not surprised his instinct's pointing at me. I've been his evil genius, from first to last.'

'Perhaps. But remember this. We are all, including Plato, without the law. Supposing he'd seen you last night—when you were crouching there, just under his nose.'

'He'd have bumped me off,' said I. 'I realized that.'

'And have thought rather less about it than of running over a hen.' She drew in her breath. 'Oh, John, how could you do it? It was the maddest venture. I know it came off—because you're here, by my side: but it was as good as throwing your life away.'

'I'd really no choice,' said I. 'It was that or losing the swine. Besides, when I saw what I'd done, I did try to get out.'

'Yes, but not to save yourself: you thought you'd made a mistake and you wanted to save the game.'

'Look here,' said I. 'To be honest, I'm not as brave as I look.'

'I'm not trying to make you out brave. But what would you say if I'd done a thing like that?'

'Don't be indecent,' said I. 'It's not the same thing at all.'

'Wouldn't it shake you up?'

'My lady,' said I, 'it shakes me up to conceive it. But if you had actually done it—well, last night, for instance, I should have slept in your room.'

'Thank you, my dear,' said Audrey. 'That's just what I did.'

'Audrey!'

'Don't worry—I straightened things up, before I was called. But what I want you to see is that when you do that sort of thing, it does upset your—your girlfriend. . . . I mean, I think that's natural. You can't muck in with someone as I have mucked in with you, without becoming anxious that they shall come to no harm. Then again, St John, you've been very sweet to me, and I've had the squarest deal that ever a woman had.'

I sat very still—with my eyes on the sunlit water, stealing between its banks.

'You know that I love you,' I said.

'Yes, my dear.'

'And that when I say that I love you, I'm putting it very low.'

'Yes.'

I turned and looked at her.

'But you don't love me, my darling—tell me the truth.'

She did not look at me, but she put out a little hand and I took it in both of mine.

'I don't know, dear,' she said gently. 'I'm terribly fond of you, and when you make love to me, I wish you would never stop. But I've never felt about you as I felt about George. I know I'm being unkind—and, perhaps, I'm showing bad form, but, to tell you the truth, you do deserve a square deal. You see, my darling, it would be quite all right if you didn't—love me so much. But you do care so much, that I've simply got to care back. And I'm not quite sure that I do.'

'That's good enough,' I said hoarsely.

'For me: but not for you. I'm not going to let you down.'

'You couldn't do that,' I sighed. 'But you'll never feel about me as you did about George. He and I were out of two different moulds.'

'That's nothing to do with it.' She took her hand away and laced her fingers about an elegant knee. 'When first I met you that night—that terrible night, I was glad you were there. I knew all about you, of course, though I never let on. George had told me about you so many times. And so we had something in common—we had both of us worshipped George. We have that in common now. I think we shall always have it, as long as we live.

'Of course I turned to no one—I'm not that kind. I must work out my own salvation, without any help. But when you had to ring up, I was thankful to hear your voice. And then . . . you met me in Paris . . . and upset everything.

'You see, my dear, I was acting; but you were not. I saw that instantly: and it hit me over the heart. It was—so damned unfair. And so I tried to be nice. . . . And then, all at once, I found that I wasn't trying—that I was just happy with you.

'We went to Amiens. If I thought at all, I thought that I was in charge. And then I found that you had taken charge—that you were just as efficient as I was out of my depth. That put me in my place. I saw that, if I was to see you, I'd got to look up—not down. . . .

'And so I came to respect the man who had made me happy, who obviously loved me so much.

'You made the rest so easy . . . so very easy, St John. Day after day, you've served me, stood up to me, led me: but you have never used me. In a way, I've been at your mercy—sometimes, more at your mercy than you might think. Sometimes I've tried to prove you—piped to you just to see if you wouldn't dance . . . and been all wild with you because you put me to shame. But that's a woman for you. We're built like that.'

I put a hand to my head.

'As I've told you before,' I said, 'I'm not much good at women. But——'

'And I am afraid,' said Audrey, 'I'm not much good at men. I've told one the truth today. And that is a thing no woman should ever do.'

I was on my knees by her side.

'My pretty darling,' I breathed, 'you are unlike any woman I've ever seen. And when you say things like that, I want to stand up and shout. I am so proud of you—so terribly, terribly proud. I know where I am with you. And that's a thing no man can say of a woman—and yet it's true. . . . I'm sorry that you don't love me, but let me tell you this—I'd rather go on as we are till the day of my death than have the finest harem the world has ever seen.'

Audrey kneeled up and took my face in her hands.

'My blessed, honest St John—whoever but you would put up with a girl like me? You give, and give, and give: and I pick, and choose, and take. But you never complain, and you never take advantage, and you never pick up and throw back the stones which I throw at you.'

'I have my own ammunition.'

'I know. But it never hurts. And because of all this, I cannot help loving you. If anyone harmed you, I'd do my best to kill him. That's how I feel—the tigress defending her young. But—I—am—not—mad about you, my darling boy. Not mad about you, as you are mad about me. There, you see—I've said it. I've spoken the naked truth. And I cannot give myself to you—even to you, St John—until—that—comes.' She let me go, and her beautiful head went down. 'I'll tell you something, though. If I don't take you, I'll never take anyone else. I could never stand the touch of them . . . after the brush of your lips.'

I put my hand under her chin and tilted her rosy face.

'Oh, Madonna,' I faltered, 'will you let me kiss your mouth?'

The stars leaped into her eyes and the rarest smile swept into her countenance.

'Why, yes, my blessed,' she whispered. 'With all my heart.'

As I kissed her lips, her arm went about my neck.

* * *

Plato was pensive.

At half past six that evening I saw him come out of the Post Office, head in air, to stand on the pavement without, with a hand to his chin. I saw him raise his eyebrows and purse his lips: and then he turned on his heel and strolled slowly away.

Another man came out—a dirty-looking fellow, in filthy overalls and a cap too big for his head. As he turned to follow Plato, I saw him put up a hand and scratch the back of his neck.

'Nothing yet,' breathed Chandos. 'And that's not true. The wire we sent is certainly lying upstairs. But nobody wants to go down, so there it will stay.'

'We must get it down,' said Mansel, 'before he comes back. If we don't, Bogy's wire will arrive, and he'll get the two together—and then we're sunk.'

'Half an hour,' said Chandos. 'Ten to one he'll be back at seven o'clock.'

'Rowley,' said Mansel.

'Sir.'

'Mr Bagot and I are going across to the Post Office right away. Cover us up to the door and use your eyes. If you see Plato coming, enter at once and then get out of the way.'

'Very good, sir.'

We left the room together—a little, ramshackle bedroom, which Mansel had somehow procured: and I must confess that I was taken aback by the swiftness of his decision to dip his hand, so to speak, in Plato's particular dish. I had great faith in Mansel and all he did, but it seemed to me sheer madness to sail so close to the wind.

As we crossed over the street—

'I shall talk,' said Mansel, 'and you will keep an eye on the door. If Rowley comes in, say, "Coming" and stand by to do as I say.'

A moment later we entered the airless hall . . .

Although I was watching the door, I heard all that Mansel said and was conscious of all that he did.

I heard him ask for the letters for 'Mr Mason' and I saw him produce some letter, to show that that was his name.

Of course there were none.

Then he asked for 'the' telegram. . . .

Again, of course, there was none: but Mansel declined to accept that obvious fact.

As ducks to water, the French to argument: and when a man is as pleasant as Mansel was, irrelevance is a virtue and trouble beside the point.

Before two minutes were past, three assistants were listening to all he said, and a fourth had gone toiling upstairs to the telegraph-room.

Whilst he was gone, Mansel was telling some story which made the other three laugh, and though the fourth reappeared, *with a telegram in his hand*, Mansel never faltered, but only put out his hand and went on with his tale.

As this came to an end—

'There is nothing for Mason, Monsieur. I told you so.'

'Let me look,' said Mansel.

'This is for Plato,' said the fellow, holding the telegram up. 'There is another coming, but that is for Plato, too.'

'My friends neglect me,' said Mansel. 'Well, well, it can't be helped.'

Then he thanked them and touched his hat and said that he would return—and I followed him out of the place, with a feeling in the pit of my stomach that made me want to sit down.

As we left the building, Mansel turned sharp to the right.

'We're going upstairs,' he said, 'to the telegraph-room. Reconnaisance, John, is a very valuable thing. I got up early this morning to have a look round this place.'

'B-but what can you do?' I stammered.

'Get hold of that wire,' said Mansel, 'before it goes down. It's not a very big risk—and there's no other way.'

We entered a small side-door, by which there was some notice I did not read: then we climbed a flight of stone stairs, and a moment later we stood in the telegraph-room.

It was not what I had expected.

One or two machines were ticking, and over some low partitions I saw the heads of two or three men at work: but the atmosphere was not busy, but rather that of careless occupation of which the men engaged were heartily sick.

As we came to a kind of counter, a man looked up from a desk and then returned to some matter of scissors and paste.

'Come on, look alive,' snapped Mansel. I saw the man jump. 'They tell me downstairs there's a telegram here for me. "Plato, Poste Restante." ' He drew a large envelope out and slapped it down on the wood. 'There's my name, and I want that telegram now. Why you can't send it down, I don't know: but it seems, if I want it, I've got to come up and get it. . . . Come on, look sharp. Time's money to me, you know, if it isn't to you.'

(The envelope bore Plato's name and address. It contained the Swindon's papers—which Plato had left in the car and Carson had found and had taken that afternoon.)

A man came forward, with a cigarette in his mouth and a sullen look on his face. He glanced at the envelope and pitched a telegram down.

'There you are,' he said. 'It has this moment arrived. If you had been content to show patience, you need not have walked upstairs.'

'Yes, I know that one,' said Mansel.

He picked the telegram up and left a coin in its place. Then he ripped the telegram open, glanced at its contents and put it into my hand.

'What did I say?' he said.

I read it with bolting eyes.

Plato Poste Restante Poitiers France
Return immediately
Arthur

Had I been able to speak, I should have had nothing to say. But I managed to shrug my shoulders and hand it back.

Mansel picked up the Swindon's papers and led the way out of the room.

Rowley was in the side street and he followed us into an archway a hundred yards off.

Mansel wasted no words.

'Give Mr Chandos this wire: ask him to wait for Plato and then to come and join us at Lady Audrey's hotel. Do the same yourself: but first give these papers to Carson and tell him to put them back.'

Then we turned to the left and Rowley turned to the right, and ten minutes later I knocked upon Audrey's door. . . .

So, though I saw Plato pensive, I did not see him blithe: but Chandos later reported that all was well and that though, when he entered the Post Office, he wore an uneasy look, he emerged a moment later 'with his tail right over his back.'

* * *

'A near thing—yes,' said Mansel, stifling a yawn. 'It was a near thing. But the risk was nothing like as big as it looked. And nothing will happen now. The French don't keep cross-entries. A wire arrived for Plato, and someone who said he was Plato took it away. If anyone should suspect that something is wrong, his one and only idea will be to cover it up.'

'But when Plato came to the desk and was given our wire, that assistant was well aware that there was another wire waiting, which hadn't come down.'

'Of course he was,' said Mansel. 'But if he had told Plato so, he'd have had to go up and get it—don't forget that.'

'My God,' said I, weakly—and Audrey and Chandos laughed.

The former laid a hand on my arm.

'Never argue with Jonah, St John. Somehow he does the trick—which no one but he could have done. But if you ask him about it, he will immediately prove that only a drivelling idiot could have done anything else.'

'She's not far out,' said Chandos.

'*Et tu, Brute?*' sighed Mansel. 'I really thought you knew me better than that. And now let's get down to business. Give me that map.'

CHAPTER 10

The Château of Midian

Twenty-four hours had gone by, and Audrey and I were sitting on a step of the Lowland, and the Lowland was standing in a lane on the outskirts of Dax.

We had done nothing all day but follow the Rolls. Indeed, as Mansel observed, the day had been Chandos' day, for he had 'covered' the Swindon for over two hundred miles. But not with the Vane. The Vane had been left at Poitiers—in case of accidents. Chandos had done his work with the help of two nondescript vans—small, delivery vans, as unobtrusive as swift. One he had driven himself, with Bell by his side: and Carson had driven the other, with Rowley by his. On these two vans Chandos had rung the changes the whole of the way: and he actually altered their appearance from hour to hour—by adding a flapping tarpaulin, or letting a tail-board fall, or lashing a battered bicycle on to a roof. Since he himself was disguised and the servants looked very much as van-drivers usually look, Plato can hardly be blamed for noticing nothing wrong, and Mansel himself confessed that more than once he nearly overran the *cortège*, through failing to recognize some change which Chandos had made.

So Plato had brought us to Dax by seven o'clock, and there it seemed that he was proposing to stop; for, upon some signal from Chandos, Mansel had left the Rolls just short of the town and Audrey, quick as a flash, had taken his place. Two minutes later Rowley had come running back to tell us to berth both cars just off the main road: then he took his stand at the corner, to see and be seen by Mansel whenever the latter should come.

And now half an hour had gone by, but we were still without news.

'Tired, my darling?'

'I am a little, St John. But I'm not all in. This time two days ago . . .' She drew in her breath. 'And you were more tired than I was, and yet you went on.'

'As I've said before,' I said, 'it's the pace that kills. You mustn't make a mistake, yet you never have time to think. That was what got me down—that terrible day.'

'It was terrible, wasn't it?' said Audrey. 'No one but you and I will ever know what we suffered—from Chartres to Tours.'

'I never spared you, did I?'

'How could you spare me, St John? All the same, you went to keep watch, and left me asleep. And you couldn't stand up, yourself. And then, dead beat as you were, you took your life in your hands and got into that car. . . . I'll never forget when Bell came back that night to the *Panier d'Or* and said that the Swindon had gone and you weren't to be seen. He'd run so fast he could hardly get the words out: and I was so dazed I could hardly take them in. I don't know what I said, but I made for my shoes: and then I sat down on the bed, whilst he put them on. I remember him looking up, with one of my feet in his hands, and saying, 'Don't worry, my lady. Mr Bagot's safe as a house—but he'll never let go.' And then I looked up to see Jonah, standing still in the doorway, with one of his hands on the jamb . . . and then, a moment later, the telephone went. . . .'

'Sheer melodrama,' said I. 'And that is exactly where Mansel and Chandos excel. They're never melodramatic.'

'*Cherchez la femme*,' said Audrey. 'It's all my fault. The play is a straight enough play when I am not on.'

'Rot, Madonna,' said I. 'Of course you provide the love interest, but . . .'

And there I saw Rowley move.

In a flash we had taken our seats, and both cars were ready to leave, when Mansel came round the corner, as though he were nearing the end of an evening stroll.

So Rowley took over the Lowland, and I got into the Rolls, and Audrey, by Mansel's direction, began to compass the town.

'And now I'll surprise you,' said Mansel. 'He's staying here for the night, and tomorrow at six in the morning he's taking the train. He drove straight to the station here, before he did anything else—and Bell walked in behind him to see what he did. He bought a ticket for Orthez—that's twenty-six miles from here—and he registered all his baggage for Orthez, too. And that's where our luck comes in, for I happen to know the town: and, what is better still, I know the country about; for nobody lives at Orthez—it's only a market-town and a good rail-head.'

'Oh, Jonah, what luck! And then?'

'Then he went and bestowed the Swindon: and then he went to put up at the best hotel.'

'But what's the idea?' said Audrey.

'I think it's twofold,' said Mansel. 'For one thing, the car is a link—between Virginia Water and where Barabbas lives: and Plato is snapping that link by leaving the Swindon at Dax. Secondly, the train he is taking here connects with the Paris express, by which a guest from England would normally come: his arrival, therefore, will attract as little attention as any arrival can—in other words, Plato's conforming to what he knows is the rule.'

'The rule?' said Audrey. 'D'you mean to say that Barabbas——'

'My dear,' said Mansel, 'Barabbas mayn't be in *Who's Who*; but I'll lay you any money he knows how to live.'

* * *

Now that, as children say, we were growing warm, we took more care than ever to make assurance sure, for we all of us knew that the prize was within our reach and the thought of losing it now was quite unbearable.

We were all of us up at dawn, for the Paris express was due at a quarter to six. Rowley was chosen to travel by Plato's train: Chandos and Bell and Carson followed him down to the station at half past five: and Audrey and Mansel and I watched the train move off. Then we left for Orthez by road—some twenty-six miles.

We were there a full forty minutes before the train, for the latter went slowly and took a roundabout course: and this enabled Mansel to make his dispositions without any fuss.

I will not set these down beyond saying this—that Chandos alone was to follow the car which took Plato away, Mansel himself was to be in Orthez on foot, and the rest were to watch the roads which ran out of the town. Whoever saw Plato go by was to watch him as far as he could and was then to report to Mansel with all dispatch.

We were all in position by seven, although the train was not due till a quarter past, 'for,' said Mansel, 'if the fellow is to be met, some car will enter Orthez before the train, and we need not present its driver with our identity.'

The lot fell upon Audrey and me.

We were watching the road to the south, that is to say to the foothills which ushered the Pyrénées. At about ten minutes past seven we saw a car approaching and travelling north. Two or three moments later, a handsome *coupé de ville* went by very fast, with two liveried chauffeurs in front and a cipher on one of its doors. And though there was nothing to say so, I knew as well as did Audrey that that was Barabbas' car.

The sight of it made me more angry than anything Plato had done. I do not know what I had expected, but it seemed to me so monstrous that the man who had cut off St Omer should be living in such a style. I remembered George's old car—in which he had met his death . . . the servants' quarters at Peerless—in which he had lived . . . the man and his wife who provided the only service he had . . . All this, because he was faithful—upright and honest and faithful as the man who had slain him was vile. George could have had his chauffeurs, his *coupé de ville*: but if he had, then Peerless would have suffered, and tenants faithful to Peerless would have fallen on evil days. So George had denied himself—and had lost his race: and the man who had made him lose it was living in pride and splendour on the proceeds of stolen goods.

How long I stood peering after, I do not know, but Audrey's

hand stole into mine, and when I looked round I saw the tears on her face.

'I know how you feel, St John; I know how you feel. But please don't look like that—it makes me afraid.'

'What of?' I said thickly. 'Barabbas? You needn't fear. I'm not going to spoil my chances by rushing in. I'll play the —— serpent—I promise you that. But before I kill him, I'll tell him——'

'No, no. Don't talk like that.' She had hold of my arm. 'Jonah and Richard are here, and you've got to do as they say.'

'Up to a point, I will. They're wiser than me. But I have the right to do it and *I am going to do it* . . . at any cost.'

Her hands were upon my shoulders and her face was four inches from mine.

'You said you loved me,' she said.

'And you know it's true.'

'Then give me your word——'

'Not on your life,' said I. 'Turn me down here and now—but my hands have got to be free.'

'I'm only asking you——'

'—to leave it to them?' I said.

'—to do as they say. That's all. If they say "yes," well and good. But they may want to wait awhile, or they may even——'

'What's the matter with you?' I said, frowning. 'This isn't like Audrey Nuneham.'

'Never mind what's the matter with me. I make that request.'

'But two months ago——'

'Two months ago be damned. I'm asking you now.'

'To swear away my right, as George's best friend?'

'They knew him almost as well.'

'They never knew him as I did. They've never set eyes on Peerless—where I used to share his life.'

'And what about me? Haven't I any say in this show?'

'Up to a point,' said I. 'And so have Mansel and Chandos. But the right to deal with Barabbas is mine alone.'

'I don't say it isn't. But they are older than you and all I ask you to promise——'

'And what would you think of me if I gave you my word?'

Her eyes left mine.

'I should be—very grateful, St John.'

'I didn't ask you that.'

Audrey hesitated.

Then—

'I should think that you loved me enough to do as I wished.'

'Look in my eyes,' I said quietly.

She did as I said—for a moment. Then her arms went about my neck, and she hid her face in my shirt.

'You're always right, aren't you, St John? If it—comes your way, you must do it. Only—don't go after it, darling. Not by yourself. You see, you're not up to his weight—and . . . I don't want to lose you, too.'

* * *

Plato was duly met by the *coupé de ville* and was driven to the Château of Midian some miles to the south: and since that same afternoon I surveyed the place from a distance, I will here and now describe it as best I can.

The house was by no means a castle, but rather a country mansion of a considerable size, and it stood surrounded by meadows on three of its sides: but the fourth or south side was close to the edge of a cliff, which rose straight up from a river—a deep and troubled water, some eighty feet wide. Such trees as grew in the meadows were young and slight and had been planted apart, so that all the domain was open and anyone trespassing there could be immediately seen. North-west of the house stood the stables, about a three-sided courtyard: but these had been converted, partly into a garage and partly into quarters for some of the staff. And when I say 'garage,' I mean it. A private petrol-pump stood up in the stable-yard, and a lift had been installed in a coach-house, to raise a car of four tons. Except for the stables, there were no outbuildings.

Now though three sides of the house could be more or less inspected by such as went by on the road, the fourth or south side was as private as any recluse could desire. And this was the side that mattered to such as dwelled in that place, for here a magnificent terrace aproned the length of the house, with an elegant, stone balustrade on the very edge of the cliff. On to this hanging pleasance, both ends of which were screened by a six-foot wall, a man could step from any of the principal rooms—to find himself free of a mighty belvedere, with the magic of the sunlight about him and the song of the river below and, before him, as lovely a distance as ever rejoiced his heart. The cliff beyond the river was thickly wooded with beech, and, above and beyond again, a very riot of forest rose up to the weathered flanks of the Pyrénées. These very charming mountains stretched like some glorious backcloth for miles upon either side, their summits smoking with haze against the blue of the sky; and the picture would have become the page of some fairy-tale, for when I saw it first, it seemed too good to be true.

Such then was Barabbas' domain—a very lovely stronghold, a very luxurious fort. I do not mean that it was armoured: but it could not be privily approached. Even to observe it in secret was very hard—and almost impossible from any side but the south. But from that side it could be done: and it was from there that we did it, as I shall presently show.

The first thing that Mansel did was to send Bell off to Poitiers to get the Vane. He told him to take the Rolls—to my great surprise: for such an exchange was almost robbery—and, on his way back, to stay the night at Dax and to berth the Vane in the garage in which the Swindon stood. The result of this visit would be that, if Plato returned to Dax, he would find his battery dead and would have to stay where it was until it was charged: so that though he might have left Midian before we knew he had gone, we should have a very good chance of catching him up.

Then he took his seat by Chandos and drove clean round the estate, 'for we must do this,' he said, 'to get the lie of the land.' Whilst they were gone, the rest of us broke our fast—a fact of which, I may say, I was something ashamed, for Mansel and Chandos and Bell had had nothing to eat: but I very soon found that, when they were 'on the job,' food and rest to them meant nothing at all, and that though they could not ignore such physical needs, they were able, far more than are most, to make them await their convenience without any ill result.

Mansel was back in an hour, and ten minutes later Chandos and I set out—to search the woods and forests of which I have spoken above, and to find some point of vantage from which we could measure the house. It went, of course, without saying that such a post would have to be well concealed, yet it must be of such a kind that observation therefrom could be more or less comfortably kept by more than one man at a time; for a sole observer must leave his post to report—or else must postpone some report which ought to be made.

We took the Lowland—and Carson, to drive her back, for whilst we were at work, we should have no need of a car and, what was more to the point, we did not want to leave a car berthed near Midian, until we had found some harbour which nobody would suspect.

(Here, once for all, let me say that if I seem to labour some detail or to place upon record some unimportant fact, it is because I am seeking not only to set down what happened, but to reproduce our outlook at that particular time: for when all is said and done, we were more or less ordinary people, like anyone else, who were rightly or wrongly determined to take the law into their hands.)

By Chandos' direction, we drove to the east of Midian and then, when we were beyond it, turned to the west: so, after nearly an hour, we found ourselves on a very inferior road, which may have been pretty good once, but had, since then, been used for hauling timber and so had been badly broken and never repaired. Though, of course, I could guess where we were, I could see no distance at all, for the road was sunk in a forest, whose curtains of living green were quite impenetrable. Still, that we were on the side of some mountain was very clear, and the road was really a shelf, for the ground rose as sharp on our left as it fell away on our right.

That the surface was so shocking was just as well, for no doubt because of this, we met no more than a labouring bullock-cart, and when, after four or five minutes, the Lowland came slowly to rest, the silence was such that we might have had the world to ourselves.

'I make it about here,' said Chandos. 'If I'm right, there's a torrent below; but it's some way down.'

We left the car and looked round. We could neither see nor hear water, but only, now and again, the flutter or pipe of a bird.

Perhaps thirty paces ahead, the road curled round to the left, and I walked down that way to see what I could. As I rounded the bend, I saw before and below me a sudden dell, where a tumbling rill was threading a little pasture—about half an acre of meadow, shaped like the bowl of a spoon. Long years ago, no doubt, some enterprising peasant had cleared the site of timber because of its shape, but at once I saw that it might be of use to us, for, because the dell was projecting away from the road, where it came to an end the curtain of leaves must be thinner and the fall of the ground more abrupt.

And so it proved.

Lying on the brink of the dell, we were ourselves projected some way from the mountainside, and there, below, we could see the torrent we wanted, to which the rill was hastening by leaps and bounds. But, though, between the boughs, we could see odd fragments of country some six or eight miles away, we could not see anything nearer—much less the château we sought.

'Never mind,' said Chandos. 'At least, we now know where we are—to within half a mile. And in country like this, that's something.' He rose and stood looking round. 'Funny thing, you know. I've used this road once today, but I never noticed that dell.'

'You were driving the van, sir,' said Carson.

'So I was,' said Chandos, and seemed very much relieved.

Then he saw my face and laughed.

'I should have seen the dell, but I didn't. Now how was that?'

'Damn it,' said I, 'one can't see everything.'

'I like to think,' said Chandos, 'that the answer is this—that the van has a left-hand drive: so the dell was out of my view.' He turned, still smiling, to Carson. 'And now you get back to Orthez. Go on this way till you come to a village called Salt: and there turn sharp to the right and go as straight as you can. And tell Captain Mansel that we shall be here at sundown, whatever we know.'

A moment later, Carson went by in the Lowland, and we had begun to climb by the side of the rill.

I have made it very clear that we could not see the landscape we knew was there, because it was summertime and the trees were in leaf. As is always the way, the leafage was thickest above, and it was not the trees round about us which spoiled our view, but those which grew lower down on the mountainside. If, therefore, we climbed up the mountain directly above the dell, we should presently come to a spot from which we could see, for the trees which had grown in the dell were no longer there, and so there would be no tree-tops to get in our way.

In fact, as Chandos said, a clearing upon a slope argues a viewpoint of sorts higher up on the hill: and after ten minutes' labour we had our reward.

That the gap was much smaller than the clearing is really beside the point, for it gave us a first-class prospect of several miles, and though we could not see Midian, Chandos was able to tell where the property lay.

'I've overrun it,' he said. 'No doubt about that. And now let's get back, till I think we're in front of the house. And then we'll go down to the water and see if I'm right.'

I learned a great deal of Chandos that hot afternoon. Though I was far less heavy, he climbed far better than I, and he never fell once, though I fell time and again. He always had his bearings, though I was hopelessly lost. He recognized traces of man and bird and beast: and he always knew in a moment which was the line to take and which was treacherous ground. But though I was out of my depth, he would never allow the impression that he was the better man, but always explained his knowledge by saying that Mansel had told him in days gone by or that once he had made some blunder—far worse, of course, than mine—and that that had taught him a lesson which only a fool could forget.

So we returned to the road, walked back the way we had come and then went down to the water we could not see.

Before we had gone very far, we could hear the music it made, but as we drew nearer, the undergrowth grew very thick and the slope, which was steep enough, became precipitous. Indeed, it soon became clear that we had reached the level at which the water had run many ages ago, but now must descend a side of its personal bed—that is to say, the bed it had made for itself, by wearing away the rock over which it ran down.

This was no easy matter, because, whatever else happened, we simply must not be seen from the opposite side: for, though at this time, we did not know of the terrace of which I have spoken above, we knew that the house was not far from the edge of the cliff.

At length, however, we managed to reach a ledge some twelve feet above the torrent, which now was declaring its might, and, parting the leaves of a beech which seemed to have its roots in the rock, we looked across the water, to see a bare cliff standing up on the other side. At first we could see nothing to tell if the house was there: then Chandos craned his neck and looked upstream to the right.

For a moment he stood like a statue, then his fingers closed on my arm and I looked over his shoulder to follow his gaze.

And then for the first time I saw the long balustrade on the edge of the crag—*and two men leaning upon it, as though contemplating the view.* As I saw them they lifted their elbows and turned and passed out of our sight, but I think we both knew that they were Barabbas and Plato, as surely as if their names had been painted on the face of the cliff.

We had now contrived to 'place' Midian, in spite of the woods that veiled it against our eyes, and, before we did anything else, we took care to mark its position—for future reference. But not on the map, for the scale was far too small.

First we regained the woods which lay between us and the road and then we began to climb sideways along the slope, until, as Chandos judged, we should be abreast of the parapet which we had seen. To make sure, we descended again—this time to within six feet of the water's edge, to find that his judgment was good and that now we were actually facing the length of the balustrade.

This time we saw no movement and, because we were down so low, we could not see so much as the roof of the house, but we did see a slice of some awning of red and white stripes which proved that the place was a terrace, and more than a belvedere.

Once more we climbed back to the woods, and Chandos marked the spot by jamming a moss-covered boulder between the roots of a beech. From there we climbed up to the road in a dead straight line, and Chandos marked the spot where we reached the road—by setting another boulder by the side of the way: but this time a stone of such size as no one would have believed that a man could move by himself. Yet he would not let me help him, but only bade me keep watch.

Then we found a little gully and sat down to take some rest, and when we had drunk from a little, leaping rill, Chandos produced a parcel of bread and cheese. Though this was very little, he took out his knife and divided it into two parts; and he seemed very much concerned when I said that I was not hungry, because I had eaten at Orthez an hour or so back. Though I think he must have been starving, he wrapped up my half again and stowed it away, and then devoured what was left—surely as sorry a ration as ever a giant consumed.

Then we sat and smoked for perhaps a quarter of an hour: and then we began the search which we had come out to make.

Since our labour resembled the labour which I have tried to describe, I will not set out in detail the efforts we made: but we scoured that difficult country for nearly four hours and a half, before at last we stumbled upon success.

Foliage can keep a secret as can nothing else. And now I think I know why the tellers of fairy-tales so often enfolded their castles in glancing woods, where wit and courage were useless and magic alone could prevail. For woods and forests confound and bewilder a man, denying him all those aids which he always takes for granted when he is seeking his way. And that, of course, was our trouble that afternoon. We were not only looking for something which we were not sure was there, but we spent two-thirds of our time defeating the confusion and blindness with which we were ceaselessly plagued. The sun was our compass and so our most valuable friend, and, since he knew the region, Chandos could put such friendship to excellent use: but soon after half past four this present help was withdrawn, for some clouds rose out of the west to promise a storm.

It was nearly six o'clock, and we were descending the mountain, to verify our position by viewing the road, when we came to the sudden brink of a miniature precipice. This was not very high and had been made by some landslip in years gone by, but it was too steep to go down if we could go round, so we bore away to the right, and hoped for the best.

Now had we borne to the left, instead of the right, we should, as we afterwards found, have come to the end of the precipice almost at once: but, by bearing to the right, we were moving along its length, and so were taken considerably out of our way. This was bad enough, but when, after five or six minutes, the precipice seemed to grow deeper and, what was still more provoking, to bear to the right itself, Chandos called a halt and looked back the way we had come.

'I think we've come round,' he said. 'I know we were facing due north: but I think we've come round.'

And with his words the sunlight began to come back.

Chandos glanced at his watch and then stood waiting until the sun was full out.

Then—

'I thought so,' he said. 'We're facing not quite due west, and we're on the flank of some spur.'

Now how he perceived this truth, I cannot divine, for though I know a spur when I see it as well as anyone else, I cannot recognize features which are buried beneath a quilt some sixty feet thick: yet Chandos was right, for we *were* on the side of a spur—or of what had once been a spur, for now its lower part had fallen away.

Just as a spur-rest juts out from the line of the back of a boot, a mass of soil-covered rock was jutting out from the line of the mountainside. And we had climbed on to its flank, without knowing what we did.

Chandos led the way up. . . .

After a minute or two the foliage seemed to fall back, and I saw far more of the heaven than I had seen for hours: but we were not clear of the tree-tops by any means, and though we were not yet up, I could see with half an eye that our view would still be prevented, because the spur was not as tall as the trees.

But I had not looked behind me—as Chandos had. . . .

It made the prettiest picture, framed in a dainty oval of trembling green. I could see the length of the terrace and all of the house beyond. And when I had taken my glasses and trained them on to the place, I saw that Plato was laughing with a lady whose hair was as fair as her lips were red, while two other fairies in shorts were doing a song and dance—I think, to the gramophone.

'I wonder where he got them,' said Chandos. 'They're devilish good.'

'He' was sitting on a couch which was slung beneath the awning a slice of which we had seen from the river's bed—a great, big bull of a man, all dressed in white. His nose was hooked, his eyes were like two black beads and his mouth was as brutal as any I ever saw. His hair was an iron gray, and his face was red, and his jaw stuck out as though he were underhung. Even from where I sat I could see the drive that had won him the place he held, that strange, relentless force that made the others look puppets and him a puppet-master that knew no law.

'Now Barabbas was a robber.'

Perhaps he was. But this was a robber-chief.

CHAPTER 11

My Lady's Chamber

There are many lonely barns in the Pyrénées—sturdy, stone-built aeries, to house the sweet-smelling hay which the mountain meadows yield. Sometimes, if the ground is convenient, they cover a byre, but they are part of no homestead and often stand five miles from the farm they serve.

To such a barn Carson brought us at half past seven o'clock, and there we reported to Mansel and heard what he had to say.

'Having got so far,' he said, 'I should like to have waited awhile before going on. I'll tell you why. Because I've a great respect for Barabbas' brain. And I have no doubt at all that at this particular moment he has us in mind. The provisions of George's Will have most certainly made him think: and I should have preferred to let those thoughts die away, before proceeding to prove how well founded they were. But, you see, we cannot wait: for Plato won't stay very long, and if we let Plato return, when he hears what Bogy says, the fat will be burnt: and if we don't let him return—well, there just won't be any fat. And so we must go on, without any delay.

'I think it's clear that Chandos and I must lie low. We are in Barabbas' country, and we must run no risk of giving our presence away.

'Audrey complicates matters—and that is the downright truth. She cannot lie low with us, for we shall lie low in this barn: and she cannot be left to stay in some village alone. So John must take charge of her and stay with her at Castelly, where she is now.'

'How far is Castelly?' I said.

'Twenty miles from Midian,' said Mansel. 'I daren't have you nearer than that. Not that Barabbas will see you, but people talk. And Midian has many servants. . . . That's why I've laid up the Rolls: she's too conspicuous to use as a run-about.' He got to his feet and began to pace up and down. 'If you play the honeymoon couple, I think you should be all right. I'd like to give you Rowley, but honeymoon couples don't drag a chauffeur about.

'And now for tomorrow.

'I want to have a look at that cliff, so Chandos and I will survey it at break of day. And then we'll go up to the viewpoint which you have found. You may bring Audrey there—not before eleven o'clock. But you must conceal the Lowland, before you take to your feet. There's a large-scale map of these parts. Don't use the roads I've marked.'

I took it, ruefully.

Then a hand came to rest on my shoulder.

'It's all right, John,' said Chandos; 'we're not going to leave you behind.'

'It's all damned fine,' said I—and the two of them laughed.

Then—

'Look at it this way,' said Mansel. 'In view of all she has done, would you have the heart, John Bagot, to send Audrey Nuneham home?'

I shook my head.

'Very well. Since she is not to go home, would you be content, John Bagot, for anyone other than you to have her in charge?'

'No,' I said. 'I shouldn't.'

'Then that disposes of that—there's no other way. Oh, and just in case, I think you should carry a weapon from this time on.' He produced a 'life-preserver'—a slender drum-stick of whalebone, whose knob was loaded with lead. 'To be used with care,' he added. 'You can split a man's skull with that. I should carry it under your trousers, stuck into your sock.'

Then he told me how to go to Castelly and how to find the inn at which Audrey was waiting to dine: and Chandos saw me off in the Lowland and gave me what comfort he could: but I had a dreadful feeling that I was leaving the stage and from this time on I should have to watch from the wings.

* * *

'You think I've done this,' said Audrey.

'No, I don't,' said I. 'It never even entered my head.'

There was a little silence.

We had dined in our improvised salon and now had adjourned to the bedroom—which we were to share. A rough and ready bathroom—the pride of the little house—at once completed our suite and was going to save our face.

'Your heart's at the barn,' said Audrey. 'You'd rather be there than with me.'

I turned away from the window—and the mountains looming gigantic against a vesture of stars.

'All coins have two sides,' said I. 'And so, I believe, have most hearts. Mine has, anyway. And on one side of mine is your face. It will always, always be there—long after I'm dead. But I'll deal with that in a minute. Let's look at the other side first. . . .

'At dawn tomorrow they're going to get down to things. They're going right up to Midian—they say, to survey the cliff. But I shall be here—in bed. Well, that makes me want to scream. I ought to be there. I've got a right to be there. But I mayn't even be in the offing until eleven o'clock. Then I shall hear what they've done and what they are going to do. And when evening comes, I shall wish them luck and drive back here to Castelly.'

'The model dry-nurse,' said Audrey. 'You know, it's a shame about you.'

'And now we'll go back,' said I, 'to the other side of my heart.' I lighted her cigarette and took one myself. 'When I got to the barn this evening, Mansel put the cards on the table, without any mucking about. He told me that you were here and that I was to stay with you. That order I am obeying, as a matter of course. But I want you to get this, Audrey—that if he had ordered me to stay at the barn, *I should have disobeyed him* and gone to you. I knew he was with you today: but when I got to the barn and I saw you weren't there, I was like a cat on hot bricks, till he told me that you were safe. And I'll tell you this—if I had been in his place I would never have come away and left you alone.'

Audrey opened her eyes.

'For one afternoon? . . . At Castelly? . . . Why ever not?'

'I don't know. I just wouldn't have done it. You see, though nobody knows it, we're taking on Barabbas and Plato at their own game. Well, it goes without saying that that is a dangerous game. And because you are of our party, you are involved. For one thing only, you know Barabbas' secret—the secret he's taken such infinite pains to preserve. In a word, you now know who he is. And that knowledge alone has put you within the danger line. Well, that's all right so long as there's somebody with you. But——'

'The old, old story. "Women and children first." '

'That saying,' said I, 'will never apply to you. If anyone tried to apply it, Mansel and Chandos and I would all laugh in his face. But one thing you can't get away from, and that is this. If harm were to come to Mansel or Chandos or me, we should call it the luck of the game and leave it there: but if harm were to come to you, we should never forgive ourselves for the rest of our lives.'

'My dear,' said Audrey, 'what harm could come to me? I know as well as you that the nearest I'll get to Midian is the top of that spur you've found. I'm not even going to trespass. In more romantic language, I am not and am not going without the law.'

'But you're running with people who are: and, what is far more to the point, you are yourself in a position to give Barabbas away. If I'd known you were here alone——'

'I wasn't,' said Audrey. 'Jonah's as bad as you. Rowley was watching the inn, till he saw you arrive.'

'That's more like it,' said I, and felt strangely relieved.

In fact, my spirits rose, for I had been worried to think that Mansel had not taken a precaution which my instinct advised.

I stood to the window again and stared at the topless hills. But though my thoughts went back to the barn, the image of Audrey was, so to speak, superimposed. I saw her clean-cut beauty, as I had seen it tonight and so many times: I saw her waking and sleeping, and I saw her at work and at play: I saw her slim, brown hands and her slender throat—and the curls which Bell had trimmed, because 'it would take too long to go to a barber's shop': I saw the stars in her eyes and the pride of her parted lips: and I saw her smile—the light of her countenance. . . .

I never heard her move, but I found her standing beside me, looking into the night.

When she spoke, she spoke very low.

'Shall I go to London, St John? I will, if you'd like it. I don't . . . want to . . . cramp your style.'

I put my arm about her and held her against my heart.

'If you went to London,' I said, 'I should go with you: until this show is over, I cannot leave you alone.' I drew in my breath. 'I suppose I'll be able to then: I suppose, perhaps, I shall have to—though God knows how I shall do it, after these days. You see, you've become part of me—the principal part. Take you away, and what's left isn't worth having, and that's the truth. So when I take care of you, I'm taking care of myself. It's the instinct of self-preservation that makes me look after you.'

I felt her sigh.

'You give and I take—as usual. Oh, St John, shall we ever do anything else?'

'Honours are even,' said I. 'You give just as much as I do, my darling girl. What woman was ever sweeter to any man? You're not in love with me, though I am with you. Yet, to make me happy, you let me show you my love—you let me play the lover, as I am playing it now. If I liked to ask tonight, I know you'd deny me nothing, because, though you don't really love me, you'd think it would be unfair to me to refuse. That is your god—fairness: at any cost to yourself, you've got to be fair. Your sex, your beauty, your style—these things don't count with you. In your eyes, you and I are just two human beings; and since, as you seem to believe, I've been more or less fair to you, you're determined to be fair back, whatever it costs.'

Her head came to rest on my shoulder, and her hair was against my face.

'It costs me nothing, my darling. I tried to make you see that the other day. I'm being natural with you, as you're being natural with me. And I think more girls would be natural, if there were more men like you. Ten minutes ago I had my armour on—the armour I always wear with everyone—except you. But you have disarmed me—as usual. Piece by piece, St John, you've taken it off—and made me ashamed and sorry I put it on.'

There was a little silence, because, to be honest, I could not control my voice.

Then—

'All my life,' I said thickly, 'I shall remember those words. No one but Audrey Nuneham could have said such a handsome thing.'

She made no answer to that: but she lifted her head and brushed my face with her lips.

I turned her round and held her up in my arms.

'Who gives and who takes?' I said, with my eyes upon hers.

She set her hands upon my shoulders.

'That wasn't giving,' she said, with the rarest smile. 'That was an acknowledgment.'

* * *

I woke with a start the next morning at six o'clock. Then I saw Audrey asleep some four feet away, and the sight of her let recollection out of the slips.

At once I repaired to our bathroom, there to make my toilet before she should wake: but when I came out, she was sitting up 'doing' her hands—to my mind, a wanton proceeding, for Nature had 'done' them for ever, when Audrey was born.

Whilst she was rising, I got the Lowland out and had the tank filled at some pump: and then we had breakfast together, before setting out from Castelly at eight o'clock.

I fear this was earlier than Mansel had meant us to start, but I wished to approach the spur by some way other than that which Chandos and I had found: and this, of course, would take time, for I had to discover a way. The truth was I wished, if we could, to avoid that shelf-like road which Chandos and I had frequented the day before; for it was not a road which a tourist would willingly take, still less a road upon which he would waste any time, because, as I have shown, there was nothing to see. Then, again, I could remember no track, running out of that road, upon which we should have a chance of concealing the car: and that was a serious matter, for a car is not like a tank, but must have a decent surface on which to move.

All this I explained to Audrey, who fully agreed with me: and the end of it was that we took a mountain road some four miles south of the water above which Midian stood. If the map was true, this road turned north, towards Midian, before it had gone very far, and though I was rather afraid that we might have to climb some shoulder before we could get to the spur, that seemed more satisfactory than haunting the other road and trying to find some harbour which was not there.

In the night some rain had fallen, but now the sky was clear, and what with this and the very brilliant sunshine, the country looked more legendary than real. The mountains were all about us, and hanging woods and pastures neighboured the way we took: I never saw verdure so green or the detail of distance so sharp: and almost every bend would disclose some magnificent prospect, as rich and soft and peaceful as though it were tapestry. I do not think we met or passed twenty people in twenty miles, and when once or twice we stopped, to consider the map, such sounds as we heard were those of Nature alone, although the air was as still as that of a crypt.

As though for our convenience, from the moment our road turned north, it began to rise by zigzags to gain some height, and after five or six minutes we came to the gray-green saddle to which it led. From there, as was natural enough, it began to run down: but a grass-grown track ran on up, to lose itself in the trees.

In silence Audrey stopped, and I got out of the Lowland and took to the track.

This showed no signs of usage, and after ten or twelve paces the metalling disappeared and only the grass was left. And then it curled to the right and came to a sudden end, for the mountain rose up like a wall as though to arrest its course.

Not being used to mountains, I found this strange, for the track had been well made a good while ago, and yet it led to nothing and served no purpose at all. And then I saw the answer to the riddle. Years ago the track had been overwhelmed. An avalanche had fallen, to blot it out: an avalanche, so mighty that those who had made the track had thrown in their hand, preferring to lose their labour rather than fight a battle which Hercules would have shirked. And now the avalanche was part of the mountainside; and the track had become a cloister, kept by the birds and beasts.

Had we sought for a month, I am sure we could not have found a spot so safe and convenient in which to bestow the car; and before five minutes were past, the Lowland was standing silent at the foot of the mountain wall, with beeches and chestnuts about her and the bend of the track behind: and since she made no marks where she left the road, no passer-by would have dreamed that she was at hand.

'What a sweet place,' said Audrey, and so it was.

Indeed, I have often found that when Nature has taken over the work of men's hands, the result can be as charming as any which she can achieve: and here the world was so still, and the air was so cool and so fragrant, and the heaven we could not see was dispensing so gentle a light that the spot might have been the retreat of some Titania, to which she sometimes retired, to stroll instead of flitting and speak in prose instead of in poetry.

It was now a few minutes past nine, and since I knew nothing of the country which lay between us and the spur, and had but a rough idea of where that protuberance hung, I took a good look at the sun and then led the way up what remained of some path, because it seemed to be leading the way which I thought we should go.

Broken and rough as it was, it served us well, for to tread it was not so hard as to climb the mountainside, and, what was better still, it spared us the trying business of marking the way we went, because we had only to find it to know the way back to the car. And though, as a matter of fact, it took us out of our way, it brought us up to a plateau which no one could ever mistake, for there was the hollow trunk of some long-dead tree in which I shall always believe that some bear and her whelps had lodged.

The plateau was not very far from the actual top of the mountain on which we stood, and very soon after ten we gained the summit itself. Here we rested a little, whilst I surveyed the country, to find, if I could, some pointer to lead me down to the spur: and thanks to the view I had seen the day before, when I had been standing with Chandos directly above the dell, I was able to judge pretty well the line we should take.

So we began to go down and to bear to the right, and after forty minutes of by no means easy going—though Audrey did very well—I saw some movement below me, and there was Rowley waving, and making signs for us to bear to the left.

This very welcome direction brought us clean on the spur, and there was Richard Chandos talking to Bell, who was mending his master's trousers with needle and thread.

'Which is absurd,' said Audrey. 'Richard, my dear, take them off and give them to me. And while I'm doing my best, you shall give us your news.'

'But I can't do that,' said Chandos. 'I've nothing else to put on.'

'Don't be a fool,' said my lady, 'but do as I say. I'm going to look at Midian: and when I come back, those trousers have got to be ready for me to start.' She stooped to examine the tear. 'Dear God, you've torn your leg, too. How did you do this?'

'Barbed wire, my lady,' said Bell. 'And he won't have it touched.'

Audrey gave him her handkerchief.

'Find a rill,' she said. 'And soak this and bring it back.' She returned to Chandos. 'I'll give you two minutes,' she said. 'If Jenny were here, she'd have torn them off you by now.'

I took her to look at Midian, ablaze in the midday sun. Perhaps because of this, the terrace was now deserted, and though we used my glasses we saw no movement at all.

'Later, perhaps,' I said shortly, and got to my feet.

Audrey made no answer, but as she stood up, she swayed, and I had just time to catch her, before she fell.

I laid her down where she was, plucked two or three handfuls of grass, which because it grew in the shade was still very wet, and laid the blades on her temples and pushed them beneath her neck.

Then I saw that her eyes were open and fast upon me.

'Sorry, St John,' she said quietly. And then, 'I'm so glad it was you.'

I took her fingers and kissed them and felt them close upon mine.

So we stayed for a moment—she lying flat, and I on my knees by her side.

Then—

'Girls will be girls,' she said, 'but I'm all right now.'

With that, she got to her feet.

'Are you sure, my darling?' said I.

'Quite sure.' She blew me a kiss. 'And now let me get at Richard. Men will be men, I suppose, but he's got a wound in his thigh about four inches long.'

With her iodine pencil, she made a good job of the gash: then she pulled poor Bell's stitches out and fell to mending the trousers in a most professional way: and while she worked, I watched her, and Chandos told us his tale.

'As luck will have it,' he said, 'we were able to cross the water a bit higher up. It meant getting wet, but no more. Two hundred yards up-stream the water comes round in a bend, and there is a natural lasher—a horse-shoe fall. Just there the torrent's much wider: and so, of course, it's not so deep or so strong. And the pool beneath the fall is as safe as a house—smooth, straightforward water, and hardly a rock.

'Well, we got across by moonlight, and then we started down-stream on the other side. This was rather a business, for after a bit the woods gave way to the cliff. You see what I mean. For about a hundred yards we simply climbed along the face of a pretty steep slope, which was covered with trees: but then the slope got steeper with every yard, till at last it was just a cliff and there weren't any trees.

'Well, we'd got some hanks of cord, and day was beginning to break, so we took to the water again and hoped for the best. One tied a cord under one's arms and chucked the rest of it over the bough of a tree. Then Carson took hold of the line and paid it out, as though he were playing a fish. For the first ten yards or so the going was pretty rough—rocks all over the place, and the current trying to bang you against the face of the cliff: you see, you couldn't swim and you couldn't walk: you had to half float and half clamber—the sort of progress which I think a seal would enjoy. And then, without any warning, our luck came in.

'I was hanging on to some rock which I couldn't see when I lost my hold and was carried under water against the cliff. I'd just time to shove out a hand to take the bump, and the moment I touched, I knew I was up against something that wasn't pure cliff. In fact it was masonry.

'And now let's go back for a moment.

'From what I've said you will gather that the current is setting strong against the foot of the cliff above which Midian is built. That means that in course of time that cliff will be undermined, because all the force of the water is bearing upon its face. I believe the right word's "erosion." . . . Now either Barabbas or some former owner of Midian has been put wise to this, and so *beneath the water* the cliff has been reinforced. It may have been done at the end of some summer drought, when the river would be much lower than it is now. In any event, it's been done: and, what is more, the work has been done very well. They haven't just patched the cliff where the cliff was worn: they've built out beyond the cliff, the way you build your footings before you set up a wall. Which means there's a ledge under water—for all I know, the whole way along its face. Four feet below the surface: no more than that. You can walk along it keeping one hand on the cliff.

'With such a place to jump off from, the cliff is nothing at all. With five or six dogs, it'll be like walking upstairs. They're being made now, I hope: and we're going to place them tonight.'

'Dogs?' said Audrey.

'Pieces of iron,' said Chandos, 'the shape of the letter E, but without the prong. They've got a point at each end. Drive one into a cliff, and it makes you a rung. That's the best of water. If it's singing loud enough, it covers what noise you make.'

'But, once they're placed, won't anyone be able to see them?'

'I don't think so,' said Chandos. 'You see, the cliff isn't bare, and I think they'll melt into the general colour scheme. Then again they'll be jacketed with rubber—gray, rubber tubing, the same sort of shade as the cliff.'

'You don't forget anything, do you? But didn't you find that water terribly cold?'

Chandos smiled.

'It was a bit cold,' he said, 'but after a while, you know, you don't notice it much. But I was damned glad of that ledge. I can't believe Barabbas knows that it's there. I mean, with your feet upon that, you're practically home.'

'Fortune favours the bold.'

'I ran no risk,' said Chandos. 'The line was round my chest, and Carson was ready and waiting to haul me in.'

For all that, there can be no doubt that only a lion-hearted man would have entered that icy water, thereby committing himself to a mercy it did not know, and have fought and won his battle against its pace and its might. But I think it is true to say that neither Mansel nor Chandos knew any fear, or that, if they did, they had reduced that emotion to full obedience.

It may seem out of reason that danger should have been courted and efforts so bold have been made, when the terrace could have been reached by walking over some meadows and climbing a six-foot wall: but, though that way was inviting, I think we all of us knew that there was about it some 'snag'; for Barabbas was not the man to select so secure a retreat, yet not deny admittance to such as might seek to gain it without being seen or heard. And here, as we afterwards found, we were perfectly right, for Midian was girt with a system of almost invisible wire, which only had to be touched to give the alarm. But the balustrade was not wired, but was left in the charge of the cliff and the water below.

* * *

That evening Mansel went with us, to see where the Lowland lay—'not' said he, 'that I don't trust you, but because, when you've split your party, your right hand should always know what your left hand does.'

He seemed well pleased with our lair, but told us not to go back by the way we had come, but to go on over the saddle and make our way back to Castelly by using some lower roads.

'I'm looking ahead,' he said. 'If anything should happen at Midian, it is of the highest importance that no one should think about you. I don't think they will—for a moment. But peasants have eyes the same as anyone else and, as I daresay you've noticed, the cars on these roads are few.'

Audrey was very quiet.

She had looked upon Midian that morning, as I have said. But she never went back to the viewpoint, to look again. (In fact, there was little to see. Plato appeared, and Barabbas, for half an hour: but they seemed to have business within, for most of the afternoon the women whom we had seen had the sunlit flags to themselves.) Indeed, since noon she had hardly opened her mouth, although she had sat and listened to all that was said. But, as we sailed into the evening, her spirits seemed to rise, and before had come to Castelly, she was herself again.

After an early supper, she said we must go for a stroll, and we walked out into the evening, with our backs to the way we knew. Five minutes were more than enough to take us out of the village and into a countryside which belonged to another age, where sights and sounds were the stuff old days were made of and Husbandry had on the livery Thomson knew. The neat-herd's pan-pipes, the brooks, and the swaths of the hand-mown hay; the yokes of patient oxen, and the snoods that the women wore; the play of a water-wheel, and a little school of goslings, taking the air—of such was our kingdom that evening, high up in a mountain valley, from which the shrewd eye of Progress had turned aside. Young and old gave us 'Good evening,' as though they knew who we were: and I think it likely they did, for Castelly was very small, and Audrey's light was too rare for a bushel to hide it away.

* * *

Something woke me that night—or, rather, the following morning at half past three. It may well have been the moonlight, of which our bedroom was full.

At once I turned to see if Audrey was sleeping: but Audrey's bed was empty, the clothes turned back.

For one frantic moment I think that my heart stood still. . . . And then I saw her standing—a slight, pyjama-clad figure, by the side of an open window, staring into the night.

I was out of bed by now, and I stepped to her side.

'What is it, Madonna?' I breathed.

She did not turn, but she set a hand on my shoulder and held it tight.

'I couldn't sleep,' she said.

'But you mustn't stand here, my darling. This is the coldest moment of all the twenty-four hours.'

'I'm all right, St John. This silk's very thick.'

'You must go back to bed, my sweet: or else you must let me get you your dressing-gown.'

'Very well. I'll go back to bed.'

I stooped and touched her bare feet: they might have been cut out of marble, they were so cold.

'How long have you been here?' I said.

'I don't know. Perhaps twenty minutes.'

I picked her up in my arms, walked across the parquet and laid her down in my bed.

As I set the clothes about her—

'You must sleep here,' I said. 'Your sheets will be cold. Put your feet right down, and I'll make them warm.'

First I took a silk scarf I had and bound it about my waist. Then I knelt at the foot of the bed and loosened the clothes. Then I put in my hands and chafed her feet and her ankles, until they began to grow warm. Then I took the scarf, now warm, and wrapped them in that.

As I tucked the clothes back—

'Come here, St John,' said Audrey.

I went to the head of the bed.

'Listen,' said Audrey. 'They said that tonight they were going back to the cliff, to place the dogs.'

I nodded.

'Was that . . . the whole truth?'

I opened my eyes.

'Why not?'

'I'm . . . so afraid . . . they meant to do . . . *more than that*. . . .'

As some electric current, the sentence made me unable to speak or move.

Audrey continued slowly.

'You see . . . it stands to reason . . . they'd like to—get it over . . . before I knew.'

I put a hand to my head and moistened my lips.

'Yes, I see that,' I said. 'But I think you can rest assured that it hasn't been done tonight. Mansel himself arranged that we should be at the spur tomorrow—today at noon. And that he would never allow, if something had happened at Midian ten hours before.'

'We may get a message this morning to tell us to stay where we are.'

'Never,' said I, firmly. 'A message of any sort would link you up with the crime.'

Audrey considered this, with her underlip caught in her teeth. At length—

'Yes, I think that's sound,' she said. She sighed, as though with relief. 'What a comfort you are, St John. And thank you so very much for putting me in your bed and chafing my feet. I'm so nice and warm again now.' She sat up suddenly. 'And now, of course, you're all cold. And my bed is like ice.'

I made her lie down again and covered her up.

'I'm quite all right,' I said. 'Men don't get cold like women: they're differently built. And now sleep well, my beauty, and let me have to wake you at half past eight.'

I stooped to kiss her hair, but she put up her mouth.

CHAPTER 12

Cold Blood

'I think,' said Mansel, 'that our friends have gone out for the day. About half past ten this morning the women showed up for a moment, more or less smartly clothed, with bags in their hands, and I think some car went off about eleven o'clock. I imagine they've gone to Biarritz—that's only some sixty miles. But they didn't take Plato with them. He was reading some book on the terrace ten minutes ago.'

I was just in time to see him, before he left the terrace and withdrew to the cool of the house—a very natural step, for no awning could long have resisted the heat of the sun that day. Indeed, we were better off, for we lay in a little hollow on the farther side of the spur, with long, cool grass about us and a ceiling of leaves above, where a toy of a spring was welling apparently out of a rock, to lace the turf with silver and freshen the breathless air.

When I came back from the viewpoint, Audrey was sitting sideways, propping herself on an arm, and letting the lively water play with her other hand: Chandos lay flat upon his back, with an empty pipe in his mouth: and Mansel was sitting up, with a writing-pad on his knees. I never saw Carson that day, but Bell and Rowley were keeping an eye on Midian and were watching the mountain about us—in case of accidents.

I took my seat by Chandos, and asked him if all was well.

'Yes, I think so,' he said. 'The dogs are in place. I'll lay you couldn't see them, but there they are. But Mansel's the man to talk to. He was up on the terrace just before dawn.'

'Dear God,' said Audrey, 'he wasn't!'

'But he must have left traces,' I said. 'He was wet to the waist.'

Chandos smiled.

'Carson dried him,' he said, 'before he went up. He hung on the cliff below him and dried his legs. Then he shod him with socks and shoes, and he went on up.'

'An undress rehearsal,' said Mansel. He laid his writing-pad down and took out his pouch. 'The terrace, of course, was vacant, and all the shutters were shut. I expect that's a standing order: but the rooms must be hot to sleep in on nights like these. They don't shut the ground floor up till they go to bed. And that they do pretty late—it was nearly two this morning before they retired. The terrace isn't lighted, except by the moon: but the ground-floor rooms are bright, and Rowley up here with my glasses could see them playing roulette . . .'

'Servants?' said I.

'Apparently sent to bed. Barabbas himself shut the shutters: they're very well made of steel, and it's nothing to do.'

'And Plato?'

'Rowley suggests that last night he drank too much. He wasn't tight: but when he came out on the terrace, he didn't handle well.'

'In fact, it's too easy,' said Audrey.

'To be frank,' said Mansel, 'it oughtn't to be very hard. But to bump a man off never is. It's with the hue and cry that your troubles begin. And that is why we have got to mind our step.'

He filled and lighted a pipe. Then he lay back on his elbows and spoke again.

'If all works out as I hope, there will be no hue and cry. But man can only propose . . . And so we must do our best to be ready for anything.

'Now at the present moment, no one alive, except us, is aware of the information which we have won. And if all turns out as I hope, there is no earthly reason why anyone ever should know. But if anything should go wrong—well, we may as well make sure of cooking Barabbas' goose. And so I have written this letter . . . to a man I happen to know in the C.I.D.' He picked up the writing-pad and put it into my hand. 'Show it to Audrey, John, and read it yourself.'

I moved to Audrey's side, and we read the following words.

> Dear George,
>
> I have run to earth the redoubtable Number Four. He is a Mr ——, and he lives in style at his place the Château of Midian, a few miles south of Orthez, a town in the Basses Pyrénées. His London representative is the Rev Bellamy Plato, of Benning and Sheba, 22 Sermon Square.
>
> Yours,
>
> J. M.

Mansel continued slowly.

'Now that will finish Barabbas—if we haven't finished him first. They'll lay for him and they'll get him—without a shadow of doubt. And they'll send him down and they'll break him—and Plato, too. But they will not put him to death, because he will not even be charged with the murder which we know he has done.

'In a sense this letter is, therefore, our second string. If we fail, we fall back upon that: but if we succeed, that letter must be washed out. I am therefore going to send it to the Manager of my Bank, with instructions to keep it locked up until August the first, and, if I have not asked for it back before that date, to send it down by hand to Scotland Yard.

'Those orders will go tonight. I'll tell you how in a moment—a letter with such an enclosure must not be lost on the way.

'And now I want to deal with the matter of a possible hue and cry. The position is roughly this—that Audrey and John must sit tight, but we others must fade away. Our presence here is not known, and so we must disappear, like thieves in the night. That will be easy enough—we've all five done it before. But, so far from fading away, Audrey and John must be seen to be about their lawful occasions and must stay on hereabouts, until "the Midian affair" is a thing of the past.

'Now all that is common sense. We disappear, while Audrey and John sit tight. But to that proposition there is a corollary—which is that, in case of trouble, Audrey and John must have an alibi ready: and, what is more, an alibi of cast iron. In other words, if anything happens at Midian, Audrey and John must both be able to prove without any shadow of doubt that they could not have been concerned because, at the time that it happened, *they were elsewhere*.'

I did not break the silence which followed his words, because it was no use flogging a horse so palpably dead. By joining Audrey at Castelly, I had stepped out of the ring: and I could not re-enter the ring without imperilling her. The inn and the village knew us as bride and groom—a Mr and Mrs Kingscote of London Town: and if I took action at Midian and somebody saw my face . . . 'And another confidently affirmed saying, Of a truth this *girl* also was with him.' The bare thought of such a disaster brought the sweat on to my face. There was no doubt about it. If Audrey was to be saved, I must save myself.

I sometimes wonder whether Mansel had not always intended to force my hand—by cuffing me, so to speak, to my lady's wrist: for I was, after all, much younger than Chandos or he, and had had no experience whatever of dealing with life and death. Had I gone into action with them, I might have made some blunder which would have cost us all extremely dear: in fact, to put it no higher, I was a raw recruit, and so not the best material for such an enterprise. But I think the real truth is that, while he was honestly glad that I could not so much as demand to play my part, he would have let me play it, if Audrey had not been there.

Of my own feelings, I hardly know how to speak. I felt not so much sore, as ashamed. Whilst the others avenged my own familiar friend, I was going to shelter behind the skirts of a girl. Whilst they stood in the rushing water and scaled the unfriendly cliff, I should be taking pains to prove that I was not there: while the execution was done, I should be lying abed—in my lady's room: and while they were doing their best to make good their escape, I should be strutting and fretting and sitting at Audrey's feet. And yet there was nothing for it. On the evening that I drove to Castelly I had made over to Mansel my right to go up to Midian and do what was there to be done. And I could not ask for it back, for I had 'had it' one way, and no man can have it both.

Mansel was speaking again.

'And now I'll tell you two what I want you to do. This afternoon, about six, I want you to be at Bayonne. There you will post this letter—register it, of course, and get a receipt. At eight o'clock you will dine, wherever you please—at Bayonne. And will keep your bill. But when you re-enter the Lowland at half past nine, the lights will refuse to come on. Now that will be very awkward, for the garages will be closed, and you can't drive eighty miles without any lights. And so you will decide to spend the night at Bayonne. You will walk to the best hotel and explain your plight and the porter will telephone to Castelly to say that you won't be back till the following day. And then you will spend the night there . . . and leave again the next morning . . . but not before ten o'clock.

'Now that is my idea. I don't want to forcibly feed you; but *we* shall be quite all right, and it would be a great relief to know that you two—and especially Audrey—need not be worried about. If you'd rather stay at Castelly, I won't say "no." But that is too close for my liking, and your alibi won't be the same. Castelly goes to bed early. And nobody there will be able to stake their life that you didn't leave your bedroom during the night. You see, I'm being quite frank, as I always am. But for you two, neither William nor I should be here. We owe you—everything. But you cannot finish things off . . . whereas *we can*. I know that to John it's a very great disappointment—not to be in at the death. But that is nobody's fault. It's as it's worked out. Without Audrey, we should not be here. Yet this is where Audrey gets off—and she knows that as well as we. No man can rope in a girl to a show like this. And John must get off with Audrey, because they have run together, and if he was recognized, that would implicate her.'

There was another silence.

Then—

'Thanks very much,' said Audrey. 'And now let's hear Lord Justice Chandos. Or does he merely concur?'

I could hardly believe my ears. But as I stared upon Audrey, Chandos replied.

'I agree with all Mansel has said. He's perfectly right. You can cramp our style if you like, and tear everything up. But I'll lay that

John won't do that. He risked his life in the Swindon, to get us here. But, though it will break his heart, he'll walk clean out of this show and never look back. I'll tell you why. Because the game's the thing. And if he could help us to win it by holding his hand in some flame—well, I think we all of us know that he'd go off to look for a fire.'

Audrey raised her eyebrows, and turned to me.

'And now, my gentle St John.'

I moistened my lips.

'If I'm to speak out,' I said, 'I'd rather have stayed at Castelly than gone to Bayonne, for our absence tonight of all nights may make people think. But I do see Mansel's point in sending us there, for Bayonne is a business-like town and it's sixty miles from Midian instead of just over nineteen. Apart from waiters and servants, we shall have the slip and the bill and the telephone-call to Castelly to prove we were there: add the failure of the lights of the Lowland, and there is an alibi which no one can ever shake. And for that reason alone, I think that we should do it without demur. But there is another reason why we should do as he says. We may have made the pace, but Mansel and Chandos are going to do the job. Now in making the pace we ran no risk whatever—except of losing our man. But in doing the actual job, Mansel and Chandos are running a very big risk. In the first place, Barabbas and Plato will not like being bumped off, and if they can . . . prevent it, they certainly will. In the second place, if murder should be suspected, the hue and cry which is raised will not assist Mansel and Chandos to make themselves scarce. And so I think that the very least we can do is to give them no cause for worry on our account. I mean, that's how I should feel. It's how I do feel—and you know it. Why do I sleep at Castelly? Because I should be useless at Midian, if you were alone. If I thought it was safe tonight, I'd like you to sit on this spur, while I took a hand at Midian and helped to put Barabbas where he belongs . . . and flashed you the news of our progress. . . . But that's a dream.'

'I'm not a ghoul,' said Audrey.

We all looked up at that.

Audrey surveyed us squarely before she went on.

'You seem to find that statement surprising. And I don't know that I can blame you—but let that go. I needn't remind you that I have many faults. I'm impatient, unkind, unjust—to name only three. But though I know how to be brutal, I am not a ghoul. And now, Jonah, tell me this. Why have you written that letter to Scotland Yard?'

Mansel frowned.

'I've told you already,' he said. 'That letter's our second string. If anything should go wrong, that letter will smash Barabbas and Plato, too.'

'In fact, it's their death-warrant?'

'Hardly that,' said Mansel, 'because it won't cause their death. But Dartmoor after Midian will be a bit of a jar.'

'Worse than death?' said Audrey.

'To you or me,' said Mansel. 'But that type of man is deeply attached to his skin. But between you and me I don't think it will come to that.'

'Because you mean to kill them . . . to kill those two men tonight?'

'As they killed George,' said Mansel. 'That's the idea.'

There was another silence.

Then Audrey drew in her breath.

'I ask for their lives,' she said.

I started in spite of myself, but Chandos lay still as death and Mansel did no more than move his pipe to the other side of his mouth.

Audrey continued quietly.

'I know that two months ago I demanded their death—and behaved like a spoiled child, because you couldn't say "yes." I haven't changed, although you may think I have. Believe me or no, but if that letter there would send the two to the gallows, I give you my word I'd take it to London myself. But this—this Midian business is too cold-blooded for me. I mean, I'm not a fool. Because you're "without the law," you cannot afford to give those two men a run. You are going to execute them—there's no other word. And I know as well as you that you and Richard are going to make no mistake. There's no reason why you should. The terrace will be in darkness, and they won't dream that you're there. So the terrace is really a shambles—although they don't know that.

'Now I won't attempt to deny that if you like to play the butcher, that's your affair. I'm quite sure you won't enjoy it, because neither you nor Richard are built that way. *But I do not like playing the drover*: and if you go through with this, that's just what I shall have done. But for the help I gave John, we shouldn't be here. I helped to follow the sheep up hill and down dale. Unknown to him, I made the most desperate efforts—to learn the way to the shambles, and then set the butchers on.

'Now I don't say that'll haunt me for the rest of my life. In fact, I believe in rough justice—I always have. And I don't want to spill any sob-stuff—I've none to spill. But this business is so cold-blooded that it gets me under the ribs. Barabbas has gone to Biarritz, to give the women a treat: and Plato's lounging at Midian and going to have a nap after lunch. They've not the slightest idea that tonight they are going to be dead. You know it all right, of course. You've got everything cut and dried. You know when and how and where it is going to take place. But they have not been consulted upon these important points. Sheep are not consulted on matters like that.

'Well, there you are. I know I've put it badly. It looks as if I'm asking for mercy for the blackguards who did George in. But I am too tough for that. I'd be glad to know they were dead—but not that they'd died like this. And that's why I ask for their lives. No harm can come to me, for I shall be safe at Bayonne. And I don't believe for one moment that harm will come to you, because you're far too efficient to leave any hole unstopped in a case like this. But I do not want to subscribe to so cold-blooded an act. And that I shall have done, if you go to Midian tonight.'

Mansel looked very grave.

'Two months ago,' he said, 'you asked to be allowed to come in. And when I said yes you should, you threw up your hat. You knew what our object was—to put Barabbas to death. We felt that he ought to die, because he had come from France on purpose to do George in. Don't forget—there was no fair fight about that. George didn't know that he was going to die. He meant to dine with John Bagot: he never meant to die on the open road. He never knew that he'd never see Peerless again. But Barabbas did. He'd got it all arranged: but he never consulted George. Well, that was pretty cold-blooded. Sheep, shambles and butcher . . . not very far from Bedford . . . two months ago.'

'I know,' said Audrey, 'I know. The Mosaic law's behind you. I can't get away from that. But I have set eyes on Plato. More than once that day, I saw him well. And though we know he's a blackguard, he looked so pleased with life. And he saw me—he must have. And he probably thought I looked young and fresh and dashing. . . . But he never knew that all the time I was the drover, and he was the sheep . . . I was so proud of the part I'd played in this show. That night at Tours——'

'My dear,' said Mansel, 'whatever did you expect? Did you think I should call the man out?'

'I don't know what I expected. I suppose I thought that you'd lay for him—much as he lay for George, on the open road.'

'And you wouldn't have minded that?'

'No,' said Audrey, 'I wouldn't. There mayn't be very much in it, but that wouldn't be so cold-blooded as what you're proposing to do. I've only seen the place once, and I wish to God I'd never seen it at all. The moment I saw that terrace, I realized what I'd done. That is Barabbas' own bailey in which he *knows* that he is perfectly safe. And so he'll be off his guard. You know as well as I that, if you are waiting there, he won't have the ghost of a chance.'

'Do you want him to have a chance?'

'I wouldn't feel so bad if he did. I mean, even George had a chance.'

'If he had,' said Chandos, 'that wasn't Barabbas' fault.'

'That may be. But he did. Five miles from Peerless his engine might have gone wrong. And then he'd have left the car and come on by train. But here the thing has been settled. It's actually been rehearsed. And all you're worried about is my alibi.'

'Audrey,' said Mansel, 'I see your point of view. But now I'll show you another, and I want you to try and see it, because it's ours.

'Adventure has come my way—well, more than once in the past, and I've spent quite a lot of my time, to use that convenient phrase, without the law. And of Chandos, lying there, exactly the same can be said. On two or three occasions we've worked together for months on the selfsame job. And so we have learned rather more than the average man of the changes and chances of life which you must be prepared to encounter in matters like this. Our experience has made us careful, and it has taught us this—never to take a risk which you can avoid. One has to take so many which one cannot avoid, that to add only one to that number is not the way of a fool, but that of a suicide.

'Now bearing that fact in mind, consider the present case.

'We are all agreed that Barabbas is worthy of death: and every step we have taken since George's death has been taken with the object of treating him as he deserves. But please remember this. Although you've compared him to one, Barabbas is not a sheep. If he knew that we'd run him to earth, he would have but one idea—to take us to hell with him. You see he'd have nothing to lose: and a man with his back to the wall and nothing to lose is an ugly customer: and when that man is Barabbas, he's uglier still. And let me say here and now that I do not want to be killed. Neither does Chandos. And I can see no reason why Carson or Bell or Rowley should die at Barabbas' hand. And so we propose to be careful—and to take no single risk which we can avoid.

'Now supposing Midian had been impregnable. In that case we should have had to go round by some other way. We should, perhaps, have done what you wouldn't have minded our doing—that is to say, lain in wait and got him while he was abroad. I quite think we should have done that. For obvious reasons, I haven't worked it out; but all the preparation would have been easy enough. And when I say that, I mean there would have been no danger. To wait and watch is trying: but it is not dangerous. The danger would have come later on—at the actual moment of impact . . . in other words, at the moment when Barabbas was put to death.

'What is the difference between what we mean to do and what we should have done, if we could not have climbed that cliff? The answer's just twenty words long. In the first case, the approach was the danger: in the second, the danger would lie in the actual attack. That it's all plain sailing now, I frankly admit: but I cannot believe that you have any idea of the risk which Chandos ran when he went into that water two nights ago. Those rapids are deep and rough and alive with rocks. The water is cold as ice and the current as strong and as wilful as any race. And though the moon had risen, the water was dark. He had a cord about him; but that was because we wanted to save his body, if he was drowned. It wasn't the slightest use as long as he lived, for, once he had gone, we could neither see him nor hear him, and all we could do was to give him the rope he required. And for all we knew, you see, it might have been his corpse that was taking the strain. I should think that the odds against him were easily forty to one: but somebody had to take them, if we were to climb that cliff. And since, as you know, I'm very slightly lame—well, we felt that those two or three ounces might tip the scale. For all I know, they did. . . . But the point is this—that we have faced great danger to gain our ends, and the danger is now behind us instead of in front. So when you call that terrace a shambles and say that, once we are up there, Barabbas won't stand a chance, don't forget the torrent that guards it and why we fastened a cord under Chandos' arms.'

Audrey, was kneeling by Chandos, with one of his hands between hers.

'I'm sorry, Richard,' she said. 'I never meant to—to depreciate what you had done.'

Chandos looked up and smiled.

'My generous lady,' he said, 'you don't have to tell me that. But I am as anxious as Mansel that you should get things straight. You see, I know how you feel, for once—some years ago now—I was instrumental in bringing a man to death. I never meant to do that. He got in my way and I had to make him my prisoner—no matter why. Well, I brought him before my chief—the man who was running our show, the fairest, straightest man that I ever knew. He cross-examined my prisoner, who presently proved that he was not fit to live. And so he was hanged there and then, from the branch of an oak. I shall always see that tree for the rest of my life. . . .

'Well, that was cold-blooded enough. And I had brought it about. And though I never let on, I felt very badly about it, for quite a long time. And then I came to see that I had been no more than a cog in one of the wheels—the wheels of the mill called Justice, whose master we know as Fate.'

Audrey withdrew her hands and sat back on her heels.

'That's very specious,' she said. 'That doctrine, I mean. But I'll bet that if you had dared, you would have pleaded with Jonah to spare his life.'

'I couldn't do that,' said Chandos. 'The man himself had proved that he was unfit to live.'

'As has Barabbas,' said Mansel. 'We've a private grudge against him, because he caused George's death: but—well, you've seen that letter I've written to Scotland Yard. And if you saw Number Four's record, by God, it'd make you think. As you know, he is a receiver of stolen goods. But, as I have told you before, he uses his powerful position to propagate crime. He incites to robbery: and if the job entails murder, to murder, too. He says, "I want those gems: and I'll tell you how to get them—and pay you twice as much as anyone else." He doesn't care who's killed: he's safe enough, sitting at Midian: thieves can come and go, but he can't be touched. You know that three men died in the Blanche Mains show. Six weeks before that, two police were shot dead at Chester on one of his jobs. Last year eleven men died—policemen, servants or thieves, as the result of crime which Barabbas inspired . . . I'm not making this up, you know. I've seen the reports. And he really does inspire crime, for he knows that it's worth his while to pay an exceptional price. He'll pay four thousand pounds, where another fence will pay two. And so he gets exceptional service—with murder thrown in.'

There was another silence—a very much longer one. And I think we all avoided each other's eyes.

At length Audrey lifted her head.

'Give me Plato's life,' she said. 'I can't have his death on my hands.'

'No,' said Mansel. 'I'm sorry. I can't do that.'

'But he's not so bad as Barabbas. He has to do as he's told.'

'He does as he's told: but he does not have to do it. He does it, because it pays him—and pays him well.'

'Give him away to the police, but spare his life.'

'I'm sorry. That's out of the question. We—can't afford a witness of what will happen tonight.'

'Jonah, listen,' said Audrey. 'I'm not blackmailing you, because I will go to Bayonne whatever you say. And carry out every detail of what you wish me to do. But I have got some standing in this affair. In the first place, I was engaged to George. In the second place, at your request, I threw to the winds what reputation I have and pretended to be the mistress of a man that I hardly knew. In the third place, I worked very hard for more than a month, putting my heart into work which soon became very dull and which I firmly believed would prove unprofitable. Finally, I drove the Lowland from Dieppe to Tours: and though what credit there is must go to St John, if I had not played my part, the Swindon would have been lost.'

'I'll give you this,' said Mansel. 'I know no woman and only very few men who would have been so faithful and done so well.'

'Very well. That gives me some standing.'

'No doubt about that,' said Mansel. 'That's why I have taken no step without telling you first.'

'Very well. I have some standing—some right to be heard. So far I have asked you two favours: and you have refused them both. Well, now I'm going to ask you a third. I ask you to reconsider those two requests . . . to sleep on what I have said . . . and so to hold your hand for twenty-four hours. I won't come here tomorrow. And so I shan't know till later to what decision you came. But if you do decide to go through with this execution, at least I can always remember that, though I helped to kill them, I did obtain for them another twenty-four hours of the life which they may not deserve, but which they value so much.'

Two minutes must have gone by before Mansel opened his mouth.

Then he looked at Chandos.

'What do you say?' he said.

Chandos shrugged his shoulders.

'I know just how she feels,' he said, 'but the arguments against such a course are painfully clear. I can't say that they're actually fatal—I don't think they are. But they're rather compelling. . . . Apart from Audrey's feelings, there's only, to my mind, one advantage which we should gain by delay. And that is that she and John can leave Castelly tomorrow, baggage and all—give notice tonight and leave tomorrow morning, in a perfectly regular way. If they say where they're going—and go there, that is to say, to the Grand Hotel, Bayonne, and show up in Bayonne and Biarritz by day and night, they'll be off the map of suspicion for good and all. I don't think there's very much in it, to tell the truth: but, as John pointed out a while back, their failure to return to Castelly on this particular night might breed investigation. No more than that, of course, for their alibi would be sound.'

Audrey looked at Mansel.

'You hear what he says,' she said. 'Do as I ask—and make my skin safer still.'

Mansel turned to me.

'What do you think, John Bagot?'

'As an arm-chair critic,' I said, 'it's easy for me to talk.'

'Be fair to yourself,' said Mansel. 'We've all had to stand aside. But I value your opinion: and that's why I asked what you thought.'

I moistened my lips.

'I'm not going to give my opinion, because it would take too long. Arm-chair critics feel very strongly *and* fully about certain things. Instead, I will state one fact, which is perfectly true. I can't support it at all. I mean, I can't explain it. But here it is. *I shall be greatly relieved to know that Barabbas is dead.*'

Mansel regarded me keenly.

'Have you anything to go on?' he said.

'Nothing whatever,' said I. 'And so—I leave it to you to fix the date of his death. I decline to believe you'll consider sparing his life.'

'That's out of the question,' said Mansel. 'All that we have to decide is which night he shall die.'

'I've said enough,' said I. 'I leave that to you.'

'They both leave it to you,' said Audrey. 'Do as I ask. I've begged you to send that letter and let them go. But you are all three against me, and so I suppose they must die. But give them the twenty-four hours. Give me the consolation that, though they will never know it, at least I added one day to the lives which I helped to take.'

'I must think it over,' said Mansel, and, with that, he got to his feet and left us alone.

* * *

Nearly an hour went by before he came back.

He stood looking down at Audrey, while Audrey looked up.

'You shall have your wish,' he said quietly, 'if you will do exactly as William said.'

'Thank you, Jonah,' said Audrey. 'You know I'll do that.'

'Give notice tonight and leave for Bayonne tomorrow not later than ten o'clock.'

'I promise.'

'Spend the afternoon at Chiberta Club.'

'I will.'

'Dine with John at Biarritz and go on to the Casino—into the baccarat room.'

'Which means we must show our passports. I understand.'

'From there to one of the night-clubs, where you will dance till dawn.'

'Very well.'

'Then that,' said Mansel, 'is that.' He took his seat by her side. 'And now let's forget the matter.' He dabbled his powerful hand in the baby rill. 'Did William ever tell you how he and I taught Jenny to build a dam?'

* * *

The day passed quietly at Midian, so far as we saw. Plato appeared after lunch, but, after two or three minutes, withdrew to the cool of some room: and when Audrey and I left the others at half past six, the terrace was still sunlit and still unoccupied.

(Here perhaps I should say that, because of the high side walls, there must have been days when the place was unbearably hot; for unless the wind blew from the south, no breeze could ever reach it to temper the air, and the flags being so protected must have grown hotter and hotter, until they not only reflected but actually gave off heat. Still, the terrace, if sheltered, was spacious and the air, which came up from the water, must have been agreeably cool, and, had it been mine, I would not have had it altered for the sake of the few occasions on which one could not use it during the heat of the day.)

Since I was wearing no coat, Audrey took Mansel's letter and slid it into her shirt: then she put out her hands, and he took them in both of his.

'When and where?' she asked him.

'I can't say yet, my lady. I'll send you a line to Bayonne.'

'T-take care of yourself, Jonah.'

'I always do.'

He bent his handsome head and put her hands to his lips. . . .

Audrey turned to Chandos.

She did not speak to him, but she put her arms round his neck and held his face against hers. . . .

Then I shook hands with them both—and felt as though I were branded with cowardice in the field.

I could not face the servants, and that is the honest truth. And I slunk away after Audrey, and never looked back.

* * *

We never spoke a word, as we climbed to the mountain-top: but as we passed over the plateau, she put out her hand for mine.

'I've let you down,' she said. 'I should have gone back to Poitiers. Jonah asked me to: but I wouldn't . . . because of you.'

'It's quite all right,' I said somehow. 'No one can have it both ways, and—it's just the luck of the game.'

When we came to our faithful path, she let me go, for we had to tread its windings in single file: and we never spoke again, till we came to the pretty harbour in which we had left the car.

Now the end of the path was so steep that the easiest way to take it was to go down at a run, and since my lady was leading, I hung on my heel for a moment, to let her get clear. And, as she parted the bushes, I followed her down. . . .

Audrey was standing stock still on the sash of green turf. I found her attitude strange—as if, in the midst of some movement, she had been turned into stone.

For a moment I stared upon her.

Then—

'Good evening, Lady Audrey,' said Barabbas. 'And Mr John Bagot, too. Just get this once for all, will you? If either of you disobeys me, the other will immediately die.'

The man was sitting square on the stump of a tree, with an elbow cupped in a palm, and an automatic pistol covering Audrey's breast.

Behind him, 'The Kingdom of Heaven' began to shake with mirth.

CHAPTER 13

Barabbas Receives

Those frightful moments will stay with me till I die. Surprised, dismayed and confounded, I stood unable to move; while the bitter realization that, though, as I have shown, my instinct had continually warned me against such a danger as this, I had not even troubled to reconnoitre the track, lashed my understanding and cut to ribbons my heart. The sword of Damocles had fallen. I had allowed my darling to fall into the power of the dog.

Audrey was addressing Barabbas.

'We can't very well disobey you, till we know what you wish us to do.'

'I see,' said Barabbas, quietly. 'Well, let me put it like this. Don't do anything which I do not seem to desire.' Keeping his eyes upon Audrey, he spoke to me. 'Bagot, close on the lady and stop two paces away.'

Seeing nothing for it, I did as he said.

Barabbas jerked his head.

'Cuff them together, Kingdom. Go over them first.'

Plato moved towards us and out of my sight. Taking his stand behind me, he ran his hands lightly down me as far as my thighs. Audrey had to endure the same indignity. Then he stood between us, produced a pair of handcuffs and clipped one cuff on my right wrist and the other on Audrey's left.

'Sure she can't slip it?' said Barabbas.

Plato took Audrey's arm and tried to force the cuff downwards, over her slim brown hand.

As she winced, I brought over my left. . . .

At the moment at which I hit Plato, Barabbas hit me—with the butt of his pistol, full on the side of my head; so Audrey told me later, for the blow put me down and out: and when I came round, I was lying on my back on the turf, with Audrey kneeling beside me and asking me how I did.

I laughed and sat up.

'I'm all right, my beauty. How's Plato?'

Audrey looked round at that, and I followed her gaze.

Plato was lying, groaning, with a hand to the back of his head; and Barabbas was stirring the man with the toe of his boot. But while he was doing this his eyes were on us.

'Get up, you fool. You're all right.'

As he spoke, Audrey breathed in my ear.

'I need not have winced. I can slip it whenever I like.'

Her words and Plato's distress were better than any cordial for my complaint, for that might have helped my body, but she and Plato had ministered to my mind. Though my head was sore and was aching, my heart leaped up, and my brain was as clear again as it had been before I was struck.

Barabbas kicked Plato hard, and the latter yelped with pain and then got up to his knees.

Still holding the back of his head, he looked at me with a hatred which made his eyes burn in his head.

'I guess,' he said slowly, 'I guess that makes him mine.'

'Later on,' said Barabbas, roughly. 'We're getting into the car, and you're going to drive.'

'But——'

'Go and get her started,' snarled Barabbas, and lifted his foot.

Muttering, Plato rose and began to walk down the track. As I turned my head to watch him, Barabbas jammed the mouth of his pistol against my ribs.

Then he spoke between his teeth.

'Try that again,' he said, 'and Kingdom shall strip the lady before your eyes. And now follow him—and remember . . . I never speak twice.'

One thing was unpleasantly clear—that Barabbas was a passionate man and was only controlling his temper by the skin of his teeth. I had flouted his orders almost as soon as those orders had left his mouth, and Plato's contemptible conduct had fairly 'let the side down.' These things had set him on fire. His voice was shaking with wrath, and the muzzle of the pistol was trembling against my ribs. So, though I had been thinking that, with Plato ensconced in the car, I might turn to account the freedom which Audrey could give my right hand, I now dismissed this notion and determined to bide my time; for, when all is said and done, an automatic pistol can almost go off by itself, and when it is held by a man who has lost his temper, it is just about as safe as a bomb with its pin pulled out.

So we came to the mouth of the track and Barabbas' car—a handsome, 'close-coupled' Rolls, which I should have liked myself. Plato was already within, and the door on our side was open, and the bucket seat tilted forward out of the way.

'Get in,' said Barabbas, thickly. 'The girl goes first.' We both got in and sat down at the back of the car. 'I sit between you. Make room.' We made what room we could, but our arms being fastened together were still in the way. 'Lift your hands to the roof.' We did as he said, and he got into the car and took his seat. 'Now put your hands over my head and on to my knees.'

There was nothing to do but obey: so I took Audrey's fingers in mine, and we did as he said.

Barabbas slammed the door.

Then—

'Let her go,' he said to Plato. 'I'll tell you the —— way.'

The fellow made us sit back, and we could not see or be seen. Except to direct our driver, he never uttered a word: but he kept the mouth of his pistol against my groin. Since Plato was not a good driver and some of the roads we used were extremely rough, there were times when I could have spared an attention so very marked; for though I did my best to put it out of my mind, it was, after all, my flesh which was most concerned, and that refused to ignore a pressure which might any moment turn into penetration of a very unpleasant sort.

For some miles I was able to follow the way we went, but then we entered a district I did not know, and I could only be sure that we were travelling north. I had next to no doubt that we were bound for Midian, although I found it hard to believe that Barabbas would expose two captives to the eyes of his servants and guests. Still I felt we were going there and I felt it was just as well, for at least I knew something of its lay-out, and if we—or either of us—could manage to reach the terrace before it was dark, the servants would immediately see us and give the alarm.

Sure enough, after forty minutes, I saw the green meadows of Midian alight with the setting sun, and two or three moments later, Plato slowed up for an instant and then swung into the drive.

As we approached the house, I glanced to right and to left for some sign of life; but if anyone saw us coming, I never saw him, and though there may well have been someone within the stable-yard, we did not enter that, but drove straight into a garage, built into the house itself. This was little bigger than what is known as a 'lock-up' for somebody's private car, but it just accepted the Rolls, though only one door could be opened, to let any occupant out.

As Plato stopped his engine—

'Pull down the curtain,' said Barabbas.

Plato got out of the car, and a moment later I heard the steel curtain come down. Then the man must have touched some switch, for the garage was flooded with light.

It was then that I noticed a door which clearly led out of the garage and into the house itself. This was in the wall we were facing and seemed to be made of iron.

'Open the doors,' said Barabbas.

Plato did as he said, unlocking both with two keys which were fastened to that of the Rolls.

The iron door concealed another of massive oak: and when this, too, had been opened, I saw that it gave to a room which was full of light. This went to support my belief that the room in turn gave to the terrace I knew so well and I held Audrey's fingers more tightly, to try and convey to her the hopes which I had in mind. She answered this pressure at once; but whether she saw things as I did, I had, of course, no idea, and I would have given a fortune for two minutes' consultation, to settle the line we should take.

'They're getting out,' said Barabbas. 'Cover them into the room.'

Plato drew a pistol and stood to the door of the car.

Barabbas addressed us both.

'Get out of the car.'

It was Audrey's door that was open, and so I followed her out, thrusting my way past Barabbas as best I could. She led the way out of the garage and into the room, with Plato backing before her, pistol in hand.

Barabbas switched off the light and brought up the rear, locking the doors behind him by the process of pulling them to. For the locks were spring-locks.

The room was a pleasant chamber, panelled in oak: a good many books stood in cases against the walls, some nice-looking rugs were spread on the shining floor and a leather-clad sofa and chairs, with, I think, the deepest loose cushions I ever saw, were offering every comfort, not to say luxury. A second door stood in the wall through which we had passed, and between the two stood a massive writing-table, which must have been six feet square: but the sight which quickened my pulse was that of the two French windows, each of them wide open, revealing the spread of the flags and the elegant balustrade and, beyond these things, the great quilt of gay, green foliage, behind which two pairs of keen eyes were keeping their faithful watch.

'Sit down on that sofa,' said Barabbas.

The time was not yet, for Plato stood full in the way and he still had his pistol drawn. In silence we stepped to the sofa and took our seats.

The sofa was facing a fireplace, about which stood a club-kerb. Here Barabbas sat down. The man was three paces away, and his pistol was resting against the flat of his thigh.

Then he spoke to Plato again.

'Shut those shutters,' he said.

I confess those words hit me hard.

I had counted on our gaining the terrace before it was dark and so on informing Mansel of what had occurred; but, once the shutters were shut, our chances of bringing this off would be as poor as they had been excellent. But what was far worse than this set-back, his order made me wonder whether Barabbas knew that Mansel was up in those woods. . . .

I had been perfectly sure that the fellow had no idea that Mansel was anywhere near, for he kept no look-out in the glade, when we fell into his hands. But now I began to suspect that he knew far more than I thought, for, though we dashed on to the flags, cuffed as we were together, we could not have climbed a wall and so should have done no more than enter a prison-yard.

One after another, I heard the shutters clash, and the room which had been full of light became suddenly dim.

'Put up the lights,' said Barabbas.

Plato moved to the doorway and did as he said.

Barabbas surveyed us grimly.

Then he put his pistol away and fingered his chin.

'I've some questions to ask,' he said. 'If you like to lie, you can: but I don't think I should.'

'Why wouldn't you lie?' said Audrey.

'Because,' said Barabbas, slowly, 'I happen to know the answers to some of the questions which I am going to ask. And now just tell me this. Who put you on to Kingdom?'

'Look here,' said I. 'We may as well get this straight. Lady Audrey came into this show, because she's a way with a car. I had to have a good driver, if I was to do my job. But she——'

'Quite so,' said Barabbas, 'quite so. But I didn't ask that. Who put you on to Kingdom?'

I determined to do his familiar what harm I could.

'Mansel did that,' I said. 'His servant pointed him out one evening in Sermon Square. Then he got me made a member of the club to which Kingdom belongs. I used to pick him up there and watch him playing billiards, and things like that. And the club-servants knew all about him and where he lived.'

Behind me, the Kingdom of Heaven was making a choking noise.

Then he flung round the sofa and put out a shaking hand.

'It's a —— lie,' he mouthed. 'It's a pack of —— lies. He's never been into the City Conservative Club.'

'I'll describe it,' said I. 'All the ceilings are very good; but that in the smoking-room is the best of the lot. The staircase——'

'That'll do,' said Barabbas, curtly. He turned and looked at Plato, more black in the face than red. 'He used to pick you up there,' he added—between his teeth..

'And I say he's lying,' raved the other. 'He——'

'Silence,' barked Barabbas, returning to me. 'How did you know that Kingdom was going to France?'

'That was common knowledge,' said I. 'All we had to find out was when he was going to leave. So I went over to France, to be on the spot with the car, and Mansel sent me a wire as soon as he'd got the date.'

Twice Plato endeavoured to speak, but no words would come. At the third attempt—

'If you think,' he said thickly, 'that I'm going to——'

'Cut it out,' said Barabbas, sharply. 'I'm running this —— show.'

Plato sat down in a chair and wiped the sweat from his face.

Barabbas returned to me.

'When and where did the lady join you?'

It seemed best to tell him the truth.

'In Paris,' I said. 'In May. I can't remember the date.'

'Did you meet her?'

'I did. At Le Bourget.'

Barabbas turned to Plato.

'What did I tell you?' he said.

Although the other looked volumes, he made no reply.

'You say,' said Barabbas, 'that Mansel sent you a wire?'

'That's right,' I said. 'To say that Kingdom was coming and tell me when and where I could pick him up.'

'When and where did he say?'

'On Friday last, at Dieppe.'

'Did you pick him up there?'

'I did.'

'Was the lady with you?'

'She was. She was driving the car.'

'Anyone else?'

'No.'

'What car was it?'

'A Lowland. The one we were using today.'

'How did you know,' said Barabbas, 'which road he was going to take?'

'We didn't,' said I. 'We hadn't the faintest idea. We simply followed behind. Sometimes, when the road was straight, we'd pass him and lead for a bit, for we thought if we sat on his tail all the time, he might get ideas.'

'And when he stopped?' said Barabbas.

I opened my eyes.

'Well, we stopped, too,' I said. 'And waited until he went on.'

Plato was up on his feet and was sawing the air.

'He's a —— liar,' he blared. 'He wasn't working alone. And he never came in till Rouen—or later than that.'

'Don't be a fool,' said I. 'I can tell you the way you went. You turned to the right at Paletot, and then came back. A few miles further on, you turned to the left. There you stopped for a moment and sent your chauffeur back to have a look round. And then you went on to Rouen by Neufchatel.'

Plato appealed to Barabbas.

'Are you going to let him sit there and call me a fool?'

'Why not?' spat Barabbas. 'It isn't a lie, is it?' He got to his feet. 'If he called you a —— wash-out, he'd be a bit nearer the mark.' He took a step towards Plato, and Plato retired. 'Sunk by a couple of children . . . an' one of them featured that day in a paper you read.'

With that, he turned on his heel, stamped to a table by Audrey, picked up a silver cigar-box and wrenched at its lid. This gave way with a jerk, and seven or eight cigars fell on to the floor, but Barabbas let them lie and, taking one that was left, slammed the lid to and pitched the box back on the table, to ease his wrath. Then he returned to the fireplace, lit his cigar and pitched the match into the grate.

Then he spoke without looking round.

'How far did you get that day?'

I thought very fast.

'To Tours,' I said. 'But he gave us the slip that night.'

'Where did you find him again?'

'At Poitiers. I was sending a wire, and——'

'Who to?'

'To Mansel.'

'Why?'

'I'd promised to wire if I'd lost him for twenty-four hours.'

'What time was this?'

'Seven o'clock.'

Barabbas turned to Plato.

'You hear what he says.'

Plato snarled, rather than spoke.

'An' I say he wasn't there.'

'Then how,' said Barabbas, 'how did he know *you were*?'

Plato shifted his ground.

'Yes, an' what price Bogy?' he cried. 'Didn't he O.K. Bagot? Wires he's at Shepherd's Market . . . five hundred —— miles off. . . . An' all the time the ——'s standing beside me. . . . Are you going to say that's my fault?'

'Bogy be damned,' roared Barabbas. 'What's the use of a lying wire, when you've got two eyes in your head?'

With a working face, Plato sat back in his chair.

Barabbas returned to me.

'Where did you wire to Mansel?'

'I never did,' said I. 'When I saw Kingdom, I tore the telegram up.'

'Where had you addressed that wire?'

'To Cleveland Row.'

'Did you wire later on?'

'I did not.'

'Why didn't you wire later on?'

'Because I was only to wire if I'd lost him for twenty-four hours.'

'Why only then?'

I hesitated. Then—

'Because he doesn't like getting wires when he knows he's watched.'

Barabbas looked at Plato: and Plato averted his eyes.

'Have you written to Mansel?' said Barabbas.

'Yes.'

'When did you write?'

'The day before yesterday.'

'What did you say?'

'I said that Kingdom was here.'

His eyes like slits, his face like some dreadful mask, Barabbas sat still as death; and I sat still before him, watching the effect of my statement and doing my very utmost to fathom his thoughts.

I had tried to do two things. I had tried to convince him that Mansel was not at hand and to divert to Plato the beastly rage which might any moment break out. (It had gone against the grain to suppress the pungent truth that Plato himself had conveyed me for forty miles; but if I had told him that, it might have dawned upon him that some hand other than Bogy's had sent the telegram which Plato received; and that, of course, would have been fatal, for he would have known in a flash that such finesse as that had never come out of my brain.) How far my attempts had succeeded, I could not judge, for the brutal face before me gave nothing away. But I knew that he must be weighing his chances of saving the game—that is to say, his chances of dealing with Mansel, before the latter had actually opened his mouth.

Except to be seen upon the terrace, I had no plan. Indeed, I was counting upon Mansel, for I did not see how without him we could emerge from the peril in which we stood. This was extremely grave. Since Audrey was at their mercy, I dared resist no order they cared to give. Violence was out of the question: with a brace of pistols against me, all I had was a bludgeon, stuck into my sock: then again I was cuffed to Audrey, while my seat was so deep and so low that to spring to my feet was wholly beyond my power. Yet if we were to gain the terrace, we had no time to lose, for a clock behind Barabbas declared it was half past eight, and the light would begin to fail before nine o'clock.

I never looked at my lady: but I held her fingers in mine—and found them as cool and as steady as once they had been in a meadow, not very far from Dieppe. And that, to be honest, inspired me as nothing else could have done: for if she, in the face of a danger which neither Mansel nor Chandos was minded to court, could display a composure so fine, then I, 'the tougher vessel,' ought at least to be able to keep my head—and to seize and exploit, if it came, the slightest chance of bringing her out of a pass into which she should never have come.

I cannot say if Barabbas was looking at me, but that Plato was I know, for though I was watching Barabbas, I could see him with the tail of my eye. His face was as red as that of his master was gray, and was shining all over with sweat; and it seemed to be bigger than usual—perhaps, because it was charged to the full with blood; but I must confess that I did not like the look in his eyes. . . . The bright stare of Murder is not an agreeable sight.

'Where—is—Mansel—now?'

The question was bound to come, and I met it as best I could.

'I believe him to be in London. I may be wrong. He'd have got my letter this morning. I think it more than likely he'll leave tonight. But Mansel keeps his own counsel. Unless it is necessary, he never tells anyone else what he's going to do.'

Barabbas drew his pistol. Then he stepped up to the sofa and thrust the mouth of the weapon against my throat.

'Look to your right,' he ordered.

I did as he said.

I saw him place his left hand upon Audrey's curls. Then he lifted her forelock, twisted this round his finger and closed his fist. This action brought his knuckles against the top of her head. Then, without shifting his hand, he began to turn it over, towards the back of her neck . . .

I saw the lock take the strain.

The sweat was breaking on my forehead, but Audrey sat like a statue, with the faintest smile on her lips.

I saw the skin rise up—that delicate patch of skin in which were growing the roots of the lock which Barabbas held.

'Where—is—Mansel—now?'

Somehow I made answer.

'I can only tell you the truth. I think he will leave London tonight. But I do not know.'

Audrey's skin was stretched tight. In another instant, the roots of the lock would give way, and a piece of her beautiful hair would be torn from her head. And the mouth of the monster's pistol was sinking into my throat.

'Why do you do this?' I said. 'You know far better than I do where Mansel is. I don't believe he's left London; but I don't *know*. But you *do* know. If Mansel were to leave London, you know as well as I do you'd hear it within two hours.'

It was a bow at a venture. I knew—and had reason to know—that no one but Plato knew where Barabbas lived. But Barabbas did not know that I knew it. And what more natural than that I should assume that, when Plato had left for Midian, the secret had been committed to Bogy's charge?

The brutal fingers relaxed, and the tortured skin sank down. Then the pistol left my throat, and Barabbas stepped back.

Audrey was very pale. When I made to press her hand, I found that I had it fast in a grip of iron. But when I let go her fingers, they closed upon mine.

'Where is Chandos?' said Barabbas.

'I think he's at Mansel's flat.'

'Did you tell them to come to Castelly?'

'I told them that I was there.'

'Why—were—you—at—Castelly?'

'I thought it was—far enough off.'

'Why didn't you go back to England two days ago?'

'Because the arrangement was that if I ran Kingdom to earth, I was to stay somewhere near——'

'——until Mansel arrived?'

'He didn't say that. "Pending further instructions," was what he said.'

'Were you told to scout round?' said Barabbas.

I answered him bitterly.

'Mansel's not such a fool.'

'Why—did—you—scout—round?'

I put a hand to my head.

'I hoped . . . if he came . . . to be able . . . to give him some news.'

Barabbas leaned forward.

' "When"—not "if," ' he said softly. 'You hoped, *when* he came, to be able to give him some news.' He snatched his cigar from his lips, and flung it down on the floor. 'Perhaps this'll teach him not to put stage-struck Cissies into the line against me. "Mansel's not such a fool." Only a fool would have used you, you blind, —— calf. And only a —— fool would have let you tear into pieces the goods which you'd got away with by God's own accident.' He turned upon Plato, whose face was now something less red. 'Write down Bogy's number and give it to me.'

The Kingdom of Heaven stared.

'Bogy's number? You're not going to ring him up?'

Barabbas stamped upon the floor.

'Bogy's number, you ——. If Mansel's leaving London. I want to know when he goes.'

Plato got to his feet and passed to the writing-table between the doors. Then he came up to Barabbas and gave him a slip of paper, folded in two.

Barabbas glanced at this. Then he put it into his pocket and rose to his feet.

'Cover these two,' he said shortly. 'And no funny business with

Bagot. I don't want a mess on this floor.'

Plato drew his pistol and took his seat on the kerb: and Barabbas passed round the great sofa and out of my view.

I heard him stamp over the parquet and come to the door: and then he slammed it behind him, and Plato and we were alone.

* * *

Fool or no, I knew that this was our chance—our chance to gain the terrace, before the dusk had come in. And, fool or no, I knew that, if we could not escape, then I must have Plato's pistol before Barabbas came back. If not, I should surely die; for, once he had spoken with Bogy, he would have but one idea—to put an end to my life. That filthy passion which he had so long controlled would know no law but that of its own demands. And Audrey would be left to the mercy of two relentless butchers, who had their backs to the wall.

I shot a glance at the clock.

A quarter to nine.

I reckoned that I could count on a quarter of an hour: it would take at least so long for the call to be made: and whilst he was waiting, Barabbas would not come back, for he did not wish any servant to hear the number he gave.

A quarter of an hour . . . in which to knock Plato out . . . Plato, half sitting, half standing three paces away . . . whilst I was sunk in a sofa from which I could not spring up. . . . And Plato was holding a pistol: but I was cuffed to Audrey, and both my hands were bare. . . .

Audrey was scratching my palm with a fingernail—a very tiny movement, of which I was just aware.

I let my eyes travel down Plato, until they came to his feet. Then I dropped my head and stared at my own. And then, still looking down, I glanced to my right.

At first I could not think what Audrey wished to convey, for her chin was up and she was staring before her, either at Plato or at something behind his head. Then I saw a muscle move in her bare, right arm. . . .

That led me down to her hand—*which was out of sight.*

And then I perceived the truth.

Audrey was concealing some weapon which she was ready to give me and I must be ready to take.

I looked again at our warder—to meet his venomous stare and to rack my brain for some way of distracting the fellow's attention for only one moment of time.

It was the distance between us that came near to breaking my heart. From his point of view, it was perfect; he was neither too near, nor too far. He could observe the slightest movement we made. What was almost more to the point, he could have killed me twice over, before I could have left the sofa and covered the three short paces which lay between him and me.

As though he divined my thoughts, a hideous leer began to disfigure his face. Then he glanced from me to Audrey—and licked his repulsive lips.

Then he looked back at me.

'How did you know,' he said, 'that I liked them young?'

So the Kingdom of Heaven pronounced his own sentence of death. Whether I could carry it out was another matter: but the dreadful saying lent me an iron resolution, such as in all my life, I had never known. Had Audrey begged for his life, I would have laughed in her face; if she had tried to prevent me, I would have struck her aside. And it was not fear for Audrey that stopped me from standing up; but only the fear that my victim might save himself by shooting me down before I could reach his throat.

I tried to keep the blood lust out of my eyes. . . .

Plato was fingering his chin.

Then he bared his left wrist and, after a long look at me, shot a glance at his watch.

I watched him hungrily. He seemed to me to be trying to make up his mind—to decide if he could do something, before Barabbas came back.

I began to will him to do it. Whatever it was, it was better than that he should sit still, observing my every movement, three paces away.

Again he fingered his chin.

Then he glanced at the door and got to his feet.

'Put up your two hands,' he said, 'as you did in the car.'

I could hardly believe my ears.

He was going to sit down between us. . . . To spite me by fondling Audrey, *he was going to sit down between us—and hand me my heart's desire*.

I pressed Audrey's fingers twice. Then I raised my right hand up, taking her left hand with it, as I had done when Barabbas had entered the car.

Plato stepped up to the sofa and deftly passed his pistol from his right hand into his left. Then he leaned forward and down and thrust the weapon's muzzle against my ribs. Holding it there, he backed round, till he felt the edge of the sofa under his hocks.

As he turned, I put out my left hand—behind my back: and there was Audrey's right hand, with the weapon she had concealed.

As Plato took his seat, my left hand, no longer empty, sank down between my thigh and the sofa's arm.

The thing was a match-stand—a solid ball of glass, that must have weighed a pound and a half. It had been standing on the table by Audrey's side—and had been knocked off the table when Barabbas threw down the cigar-box, to ease his wrath. And Audrey's deft fingers had caught it and had whipped it on to the sofa and out of sight.

'Drop your hands to my lap,' said Plato.

We did as he said.

I looked straight ahead, as did Audrey. But Plato was looking at me. I could see him with the tail of my eye, and I dared not move.

I was armed, and he was beside me—instead of three paces away: but because of that cursed pistol, his attention must be distracted before I could strike. One instant—the fifth of a second was all I asked. But, as though he was aware of his danger, his bloodshot eyes never left me for one single moment of time.

I watched him hitch up his trousers, leg by leg. Then he put his right arm about Audrey and held her tight.

I sometimes think that he meant to force my hand—to goad me into showing him violence and so give him an excuse for taking my life. Be that as it may, I cannot believe that restraint has ever been tested as my restraint was tested that summer night.

I sat like a rock, waiting. But his eyes were fast upon me, as though he were determined to deny me the chance for which I was ready to sell my soul.

I saw his fingers appear above Audrey's breast . . . Then I saw them enter the front of her open-necked shirt. . . .

And then—*I saw his face change.*

'Hullo,' he said. 'What's this?' And, with that, he drew out

Mansel's letter . . . the letter which I had forgotten, which Audrey and I were to post.

And between his surprise and excitement, he lowered his guard. . . .

As he glanced at the superscription, the match-stand met his temple with all my might.

Although I say it, it was a sledge-hammer blow: and it cracked his skull as one cracks the shell of an egg.

He never moved and he never uttered a cry: but he just fell forward sideways, with his head against Audrey's knee.

In a flash she had slipped her cuff, and we were both up on our feet, and I had the dead man's pistol in my right hand.

'The letter,' I breathed.

'I have it.'

She touched her shirt.

'On to the terrace, then. I'll put you over the wall.'

We whipped to the nearest window.

'Watch the door,' I breathed, as I put my hand to the latch which was locking the shutters to.

Very gently I eased up the steel; and when it was free, I pushed the shutters apart.

The terrace was full of shadows: the dusk was in.

'Come,' I said. 'We'll have to chance the alarms.'

As we stepped on to the flags, I heard her catch her breath and she seized my pistol arm.

Then—

'Well done, John,' breathed Mansel. 'I knew she was safe with you.'

CHAPTER 14

Mansel Mops Up

We had to wait nearly ten minutes before Barabbas re-entered the room he had left. Though he had returned at once, the result would have been the same; but by that time all was ready for his reception.

The terrace was now in darkness, for there is next to no twilight at the foot of the Pyrénées. Audrey was standing there, with her back to one of the walls; and Bell and Rowley, both armed, were standing, one on her right and one on her left. And Carson also was there—standing with his hand on the shutters which we had put to, and watching the long façade for a sign of life.

(As though to assist our purpose, not a light went up that evening in any room facing south: but we afterwards learned that, in view, no doubt, of the capture he meant to make, Barabbas had sent the women to spend the night at Biarritz and had ordered the servants to their quarters, to stay there until he rang.)

Within the room all was in order.

Plato's body was gone; and so was the blood-stained match-stand with which I had taken his life: and so was a Persian strip which had lain in front of the sofa and so had been marked.

Mansel was standing by the doorway through which Barabbas must come—in such a way that the door, as it opened, would hide him from anyone coming in.

Wearing the dead man's jacket, Chandos had taken his seat on the tall club-kerb. He was sitting as Plato had sat—as Plato would have been sitting, but for the reckless malice which cost the blackguard his life. His right hand was holding a pistol, and the other was cupping his chin, and he would have passed for Plato—for two or three moments of time.

The sofa, of course, was empty: but that was of no account, for, because its back was as high as its seat was low, no one sitting upon it could well have been seen from the door.

And I was crouching behind a great, leather chair, on the other side of the doorway to that on which Mansel stood.

So we waited . . . in silence . . . in the shambles . . . for the sheep that we meant to kill.

It was a strange experience.

A few yards off, Barabbas was speaking to London, seeking news of the men who were now in his private room. A few yards off, the man in whose charge he had left us was lying dead. A few yards off, the lady whom he had mishandled was waiting for him to die, before leaving his grounds.

No position, I suppose, was ever so utterly reversed. Yet Barabbas had no idea that any change had been made.

I wondered what Audrey was thinking—and wished that she could have been gone: but we dared not let her go down to that angry water, until we were free to go with her and bear her up. One thing I knew very well: that was that she did not deplore the execution to come. She had had a 'close-up' of evil—had seen for herself that some men are not fit to live.

The death of Plato had not touched her, so far as I saw: she could not shrink from him living, but she had not shrunk from him dead: she had been relieved—that was all . . . immensely relieved and thankful that I had been able to put him where he belonged. But, vile as Plato was, he did not compare with Barabbas for inhumanity. The latter was monstrous. Plato was loathsome enough: but his face was not near so brutal, his form was not near so gross, and he had not that beastly presence—that savage, dominant will-power that reeked of lust and cruelty and hatred of God and man. Barabbas was the embodiment of evil—and evil paramount. Looking upon him, you knew that he was possessed.

Myself, I felt as though we were awaiting some tiger, a dangerous, man-eating brute, whose death would be hailed with relief by the district in which he moved.

With my eyes upon Mansel, I waited . . . for the beast to approach his kill. . . .

And then I saw Mansel stiffen, as though he had heard some sound.

For a moment, he listened intently.

Then he nodded his head, and stood back beside the door.

Then I heard Barabbas coming—after the way of a squall.

And, as a squall, the fellow burst into the room, spouting an oath more frightful than any I ever heard.

In fact, he threw open the door, and, as he passed in, he put out his right hand to catch it and slam it to. But before the door met its frame, Mansel had caught and was holding Barabbas' right wrist.

I heard the oath snap off short, and rose from behind my chair, to see the man standing quite still, regarding Mansel's pistol as if it were something unclean.

I had his left wrist in a flash, and Chandos rose up from the fender and came up to where we stood.

'I'll take him, John,' he said quietly. 'You take his pistol away.'

As I did this office, Barabbas spat in my face.

'You're perfectly right,' said Mansel. 'John Bagot's the rock you've split on from first to last. It was he who spotted Kingdom, and he who followed here: and, ten minutes back, he killed him—and opened the shutters for us. Oh, and by the way, my name's Mansel: and that is Richard Chandos, who now is holding your wrists.'

With that, he put up his pistol and, stepping back two paces, sat down on the arm of a chair.

Barabbas made no reply: but I think Mansel's casual demeanour had turned the iron in his soul.

His face was now contorted into the semblance of some gargoyle, designed by a mind diseased; and, as gargoyles thrust out from a gutter, so he was leaning forward and poking his dreadful head. His brutal mouth was gaping, the lips drawn clear of the teeth: his burning eyes were screwed up, as those of a baby about to burst into tears: and his skin was the colour of cigar-ash, while its many lines and creases might have been done in blue chalk.

Mansel folded his hands and crossed his legs.

'You've had quite a good run,' he said. 'You've lived damned soft and you've made a lot of money by paying less fortunate blackguards to steal and do murder for you. And you might have gone on for years . . . if you hadn't stepped out of your ground.' He unfolded a sheet of paper and held it up. 'You remember this piece of paper?' The guilty eyelids flickered. 'I see you do. That was your boast to me that Lord St Omer was dead—a man as honest and faithful as you are foul. You lay for him and you murdered him out of spite: and you may have thought that his death would frighten us off. Anyway, you made a mistake—the mistake of your life.'

Barabbas opened his mouth.

'If that dung-livered ——, Kingdom——'

'Believe me,' said Mansel, 'Kingdom took every care. But Bagot's best was rather better than his. And in any event you'll very soon see him again—and be able yourself to tell him how strongly you feel.'

Barabbas appeared to shrink. Then, without any warning, he tried to set himself free.

I know that I started forward, but Mansel caught my arm.

'Leave him to William,' he said. 'He hasn't a chance.'

So I stood and he sat, watching, while Barabbas fought for his life with a man who was stronger than he.

Barabbas was powerfully built and must have stood six feet two: then, again, he was desperate—and desperation can almost double your strength. But though he fought like a madman, he fought in vain.

Astride, like some grim Colossus, Richard Chandos might have been made of bronze. His body never moved, but only his wrists. Though these were not of steel, they did their duty as well as could have any fetters that ever were forged. Plunging, straining and writhing, Barabbas conveyed the impression that he was cuffed to some staple built into a wall; and all his frantic violence sank to the petty level of a naughty child.

Yet it was no childish violence which he displayed: before he had done, his face, which had been dry, was running with sweat and, when at last he stood still, he was breathing fast and deep, as a man who has finished some race.

As though there had been no interruption——

'One thing more,' said Mansel, 'and then I have done. I think that you ought to know that only this afternoon the lady Audrey Nuneham prayed me to spare your life. Naturally, I refused, though she did her very utmost to bring me round. Then she begged me to spare you for twenty-four hours—to kill you tomorrow evening, instead of tonight. And that request I granted, because she begged so hard. . . . Of course, that's all washed out, because when you carried her off, you forced my hand: but I think that you ought to know that the lady whom you have mishandled was your own advocate.'

Barabbas was staring at me.

Then he spoke—in a very thick voice.

'I want to be ready for Kingdom. How did you get him down?'

So far as I was concerned, that was the grimmest moment of all that terrible night, for here was a malefactor, standing upon the drop, yet so far from considering how he should meet his God, preparing to deal with his late accomplice in crime and actually seeking information to serve his filthy turn in the world to come.

His demand provoked a picture so shocking that for two or three moments I could not find my voice: then I told him the truth, because it seemed indecent to lie to a dying man.

'He sat down between us,' I said, 'and I brought over my left.'

Barabbas set his teeth.

'And Bogy?' he said. 'How did you work that wire?'

Mansel got to his feet.

'That's our secret,' he said. 'If it's any use to you, it was nobody's fault.' Then he spoke to Chandos. 'Let him go, William,' he said.

I shall never know which was the most astonished, Barabbas or I. The two of us stared upon Mansel, open-mouthed.

Then Barabbas brought round his hands, and lowered his head, as though to examine his wrists.

As he did so, Mansel hit him—on the point of the jaw.

This, with his bare fist: but Barabbas' head went back as though he had been kicked by a horse, and Chandos caught his body and held it up.

* * *

Mansel was speaking to me: but his voice seemed a great way off.

'Go out to Audrey,' he said, 'and turn her face to the wall.'

Feeling considerably shaken, I turned to do as he said. . . .

At first I could not see her. Then Rowley stepped out of the shadows.

'Her ladyship's here, sir,' he said.

Her hands came out for mine, and I carried them on to my shoulders and set my back to the wall.

We never spoke, but I held her head in my hands, while Mansel and Chandos went by—with Barabbas' body between them, to cast it over the cliff.

This done, they threw down Plato's, as well as the matchstand with which I had taken his life. But they left his coat on the terrace, as if he had flung it down before plunging into the flood.

Then Mansel came to where we were standing.

'I want you a moment, John.'

I followed him back to the room which had seen and heard so much evil and now was to know no more.

'Except for the match-stand,' said Mansel, 'did you touch anything here?'

'Only the pistols,' I said. 'And the shutter's latch.'

'Did Audrey?'

I shook my head.

Then he told me to take the two pistols and throw them over the cliff and then to ask Audrey to lend him her handkerchief.

I was as quick as I could be. When I got back, Chandos and he were going over the parquet, searching for any traces that might have been left. (It must be remembered that when they had reached the terrace, they had been dripping wet and that though they had been rubbed down and had put on trousers and socks which had been wrapped up in oiled silk, such toilet had been hastily made—and water which falls upon parquet will leave a mark unless it is wiped away.) Two or three marks there were: so I took off my shirt, which was dry, and using this as a rubber, Chandos and I between us polished them out. Whilst we were doing this, Mansel was wiping with brandy the shutter's latch I had touched: this, with the help of my lady's handkerchief, which he soaked from a massive decanter, ready to hand. And then, for good and all, we went out of that cursed room, leaving the lights full on and the shutters ajar, to find the terrace alive with little eddies of wind and see the lightning playing over the western hills.

'As I hoped and prayed,' breathed Mansel. 'A storm is just what we want. And now before we go, is there anything else?'

'The strip of carpet,' I said.

'We shall have to sink that,' said Mansel,'and hope for the best.'

Then he and Chandos and I went up to where Audrey was standing with Rowley and Bell: but Carson stood fast where he was, with his eyes on the house.

'Everyone listen,' said Mansel. 'We have but one object in view—to rush you two back to Castelly as quickly as ever we can. But you must return in the Lowland, as you set out. Chandos will see you into and out of the water and so to the Vane. Rowley will drive you to the Lowland—you'll have to show him the way. After that, you will shift for yourselves, explaining your soaked condition by saying you were caught in the storm. Tomorrow, wet or fine, you will, as usual, drive out for the whole of the day: and every day you will do that, until I send.

'One thing more. On the way to the Lowland, Rowley will stop at the barn. There he will pick up a hacksaw, to cut that cuff from John's wrist. That he will do himself, while Audrey is bringing the Lowland on to the road.

'And now, if you please, we'll be gone. You two will have to be lowered, because you've never climbed up. Chandos and Bell and Rowley will, therefore, go first.'

'And you and Carson?' said Audrey.

'We shall follow,' said Mansel. 'Those dogs have got to come out. Besides, they're just what we want to sink that strip of carpet and keep it down.'

I shall always maintain that, though she was roped, to go down that cliff in the darkness and enter that angry snow-broth was a lot to ask of a girl. But Audrey never faltered or gave any trouble at all, but did without any question exactly as she was bid.

So all went smoothly enough.

Chandos descended the cliff, with the end of the rope in his teeth. When he was ready, he signalled, by tugging it twice; and then he let his end go and I pulled it up. While Mansel made it fast about Audrey, I folded the strip of carpet and made it into a pad to lay on the balustrade: then I took hold of the rope and made ready to take the strain. Mansel tested his knots: then he picked Audrey up and swung her over the edge. . . .

Together we paid out the rope as fast as we dared: and sooner than I would have believed, we had the second signal to pull it up.

With no one to help him, Mansel lowered me down; for he dared not take Carson from his duty of watching the house.

My passage was easy enough, for Rowley was waiting to help me and a life-line had been rigged from the last of the dogs to a tree: but, as I was descending the crag, the tempest broke and the rain fell down in a fury such as I never saw—and I could not help thinking of the work which remained to be done and of Mansel and Carson, who must cling to the face of the cliff and fight to remove the handhold which kept them there.

Mansel had said that day that the danger was not in putting Barabbas to death, but in approaching the fastness in which he lay: though I needed no proof of his words, I had it that night; for, though I am a strong man, without the life-line and Rowley I should have been utterly powerless against such wrath and such cold. Between these things and the dark and the uproar the water made, I never felt so much confounded in all my life, and when Chandos put out a hand and hauled me on to the bank, I felt as though he had plucked me out of the jaws of death.

The crossing of the river was nothing after a passage so rough, and the five of us stayed together until we came up to the Vane.

There Chandos spoke in my ear.

'Come what may, Audrey must change at the barn. If not, she'll be seriously ill. Ask Rowley for a sweater and trousers, and rub her down yourself before letting her put them on: while you're doing that, Rowley must take her own things and shove them against the engine away from the fan. By the time you get to the Lowland, they ought to be fairly dry. There she must change again, so that Rowley can bring our things back.'

'I'll see that's done,' said I.

He put us into the Vane and raised his voice.

'John Bagot takes charge from now on. I trust you, Audrey, to do whatever he says.'

'I promise,' said Audrey, quietly. And then, 'You've taken such care of me: if you'd like to make me a present, take care of yourselves.'

Ten minutes later we came to the lonely barn. . . .

As if to prove Chandos right, Audrey was trembling all over when I lifted her out of the car.

Rowley moved before us lighting my steps with a torch; then he found a flask of brandy and a blanket, to serve as a towel.

Whilst he sought for a sweater and trousers, I helped my lady to strip—for she could not have stripped herself, and since the devil was driving, decency had, of course, to go by the board. Then I wrapped her up in the blanket and rubbed her down, while Rowley poured out some spirit and held the cup to her lips. Then he took her things out to the car, to do as Chandos had said, after which he came back for the hacksaw, with which to cut off my cuff.

By now she was, at least, dry: so I helped her into the clothing which Rowley had brought. Then I put on her shoes again, wrapped her once more in the blanket and carried her back to the car.

By the time we had reached the Lowland, she was as warm as toast; and since she had, as usual, a skirt in that car and since her silk shirt was now very nearly dry, the change which she had to make was of slight account. As she was now herself, I let her make this alone, because we could not go on, until Rowley had cut off my cuff.

Before this work had been done, Audrey had changed and the Lowland was out on the road, for the steel of the gyves was tough and Rowley was fearful of snapping the blade of the saw; but after a minute or two, he had his way, and I shook his hand and ran for the other car.

But Audrey would not leave until she had spoken to him; and so he came round to her door and she put out her hand for his.

I did not hear what she said, for she spoke very low: but I heard him thank her and say he was very glad.

Then she let in her clutch, and we started the last of our laps.

As before, the rain and the darkness conspired to cut down our pace, but we managed to make Castelly before eleven o'clock. And that, I think, was well done, for Barabbas' death had occurred at five minutes past nine, and, apart from anything else, we had covered thirty-five miles on the open road.

The good people who kept the inn had been very much concerned, because we had not come in on so wicked a night, and the honest burst of relief which our arrival touched off was quite embarrassing. At least, it would have been so: but there and then Audrey took charge, playing up in a way which I could never have done and telling such a tale of continuous engine-trouble and loss of way that I had nothing to do but to put the Lowland away and care for myself. (The deluge, of course, explained the state of our clothes, and my broken head, said Audrey, was due to a fall in the darkness, whilst I was trying to find out which road to take.)

Although I was now quite warm and my clothes were beginning to dry, she made me take a hot bath before she would do the same: and then we sat down to a supper which, but for her brave example, I could not have touched.

It may have been reaction: it may have been something else: but, as I sat there, glowing, and toyed with the tasty dishes which the servants were pleased to bring, I wanted to go abroad and feel the rain on my face.

I talked—for the look of the thing, as well as I could; but I felt that I could not digest the events of the last four hours, while the fortunes of Mansel and Chandos obsessed my mind.

That Audrey and I were safe, I had now no doubt. I supposed that they and the servants would disappear and successfully cover their tracks. But I wondered how they were faring and where they would go; and I wished that I could have been with them, to share the rough and tumble of speed and storm.

It was when the servants had gone that a question leaped to my lips—a question which I had smothered time and again that night.

I leaned forward and whispered to Audrey.

'How did Mansel know we were there?'

Audrey opened her eyes.

'My darling, did no one tell you?'

I shook my head.

'I never had time to ask.'

Audrey drew in her breath. Then—

'D'you remember what you said in the dell, by the side of the spur? You referred to an instinct you had, and your words were these—*I shall be greatly relieved to know that Barabbas is dead.*'

'Yes,' I said. 'I remember. But what of that?'

'This,' said Audrey. 'Jonah respects your instinct. And when you said that, you shook him—more than you thought. So much, in fact, that when we left the spur for the Lowland, he sent for Rowley and told him to follow behind us and see us into the car.'

'My God, he didn't!'

'He did—because of your words.'

'And Rowley. . . .'

'Saw everything. He had no pistol, and so he dared not be seen. But he tried to get round the glade, to take Barabbas in rear. But, before he was round, you and I had been put in the car. So he ran for the spur like a madman. . . . Bell said that when he got there, the blood was dripping out of his ears.'

So I think it may fairly be said that the stars in their courses fought against Barabbas that day. For, had Audrey and I escaped, whilst he was out of the room, he would, of course, have left Midian within the hour: and so would have saved his life, though Plato was dead.

CHAPTER 15

Aftermath

'I've had a letter,' said Audrey. 'Would you like to see what it says?'

'What d'you think?' said I, and put out my hand.

Four days had gone by, on every one of which we had driven up into the mountains or down to the sea. Neither of us was the worse for the wetting which we had received. If there was talk of what had occurred at Midian, it never came to our ears.

(The affair was not reported, except in the local press. If that may be believed, it was taken for granted that Barabbas had 'fallen' over the cliff and that Plato had dived to the rescue of his unfortunate friend.)

And now it was evening again, and the lovely world about us was black and green and gold. That is no exaggeration. The sinking sun was gilding all that it touched, and nothing could have darkened the lengthening, clean-cut shadows which all things threw: and the tilted meadows about us were all of emerald green, because they belonged to the mountains, and that is the livery mountain meadows wear.

We were sitting perhaps two thousand five hundred feet up, by the side of a leaping rill and under a chestnut tree, on a little ledge of lawn, which would have suited Horace because it was so retired. Behind us, a stout box hedge was keeping the mountain road: and there the Lowland was waiting, as she had waited so often, to carry us home.

Audrey took out the letter and put it into my hand.

Villa Carlos,
Freilles.

Dear Audrey,

We have taken this villa here for five or six weeks. William has done this for me, for the bathing is very good and I love that so. Please come to us here, and we will put you both up.

Your loving
Jenny.

Freilles is a little place, thirty miles north of Bayonne.

I put a hand to my head.

'All done in four days,' I said. 'Tracks covered: drags laid: and a perfect excuse created for being in France. You know, that pair's efficiency has me beat. Once or twice in my life I have done the "humanly possible" thing. But they seem to do nothing else. It's the way they live.'

Audrey smiled.

'It's funny your saying that. I once heard Jonah say that if rogues could only be bothered to do what was humanly possible for forty-eight hours on end, instead of for five or six and then letting up, they could get away with almost whatever they liked.'

I nodded.

'He's probably right. But you've got to know what to do.' I handed the letter back. 'She doesn't mention Mansel.'

'He'll fetch up later on. Do you want to go?'

'Orders are orders,' said I. 'What else can we do?'

'I didn't ask you that.'

'I know. I should like to go. I want us to leave Castelly. Until we leave Castelly, the curtain will not come down. And I do want the curtain down. My mind is still obsessed with what happened the other day. And until we break with Castelly, obsessed it will stay. I'll love to come back one day—when the break has been made; but I can't . . . enjoy . . . all this . . . because we have got to go back to Castelly tonight.'

Audrey raised her eyebrows.

'I find that strange,' she said. 'I knew it, of course. I knew that what happened had got you down. But I never thought that would happen—I don't know why. . . . What's so strange is that we have changed places. I was the one who begged for their lives to be spared: yet—think what you like of me, but I'm thankful they're dead. To use your own words, I am "immensely relieved." Yet you, who demanded their death——'

'Do you really think,' I said, 'that I am disturbed by the thought that I had the honour of splitting a blackguard's skull?'

Audrey looked at me sharply. Then—

'Sorry, St John. But you did say just now——'

'I know I did. I wasn't referring to that.'

'What were you referring to?'

With my eyes on the lovely landscape—

'I'll try and tell you,' I said. I took a deep breath. 'You remember that talk we had . . . the first night we spent at Castelly . . . when I said that I was uneasy when you were out of my sight?'

'Yes.'

'When I said that, I was putting it very low. Something greater than instinct—I don't know what—was insisting that you were in danger, so long as Barabbas lived. The writing was there—on the wall: but, though I could see it was there, I could not read what it said. Only, I knew its purport . . . I told myself it was nonsense, time and again. But, down in my heart, I knew that it was not nonsense, but that something which I could not define was telling the truth. I ought to have gone to Mansel and spoken out. But he had enough to think of, as both of us know. Besides, you were in my charge. It was up to me to "watch out"—and to break the back of the danger, when it appeared.

'Now, strangely enough, I felt it most at Castelly. It was always when we were there that the shadow was most pronounced. If you think things over, some creature of his must have watched us whilst we were there and must have made inquiries which we knew nothing about. It may be that I sensed his presence . . . In any event, I was glad to get you into the Lowland and out of the place. The writing receded, when we drove into the hills.

'And then—you know what happened. The hammer fell . . . And when, on that terrible evening, I ran down into the glade and saw you standing still, with a hand to your throat . . . and Barabbas covering you . . . and Plato, beside him, laughing . . . well, that is the picture I cannot hound out of my mind. I sometimes wonder if it will ever leave me . . . if in all my life I shall ever be quite the same. You see, I had been warned. But I had missed the warning, and now you were sunk. And for me, as you know, the hairs of your head are numbered. . . .

'Well, that is why I want to break with Castelly. I want to be shot of that picture and the writing upon the wall. Day and night they haunt me: every night I dream of that glade.'

Audrey sat very still. Then, looking straight before her, she spoke very low.

'I've made you tell me for nothing. I knew . . . why you wanted to go.'

Then was a little silence.

Then—

'How did you know?' I said.

'Because, the last three nights, you've talked in your sleep. . . .'

I bit my lip.

'I'm sorry for that,' I said.

Audrey was kneeling beside me, with one of my hands in hers.

'St John, my blessed, how can you?'

'Well, I am. It's stupid, my lady. And I oughtn't to be in your room. If I wasn't, I shouldn't afflict you with——'

A cool hand covered my mouth, and Audrey sat back on her heels.

'Why did I make you tell me—when I already knew?'

I shook my head.

'I don't know,' I said. 'I'm not very good at women.'

'Because I wanted to hear you say the words. Not out of vanity, dear. But because . . . I've missed your love.'

'Audrey!'

I started round, but she let fall my hand and sat sideways, just out of my reach.

'Listen, St John. I've got to go back a little—I shan't be long. We both remember Poitiers and how I told you the truth. So many men would have thrown the truth in my face . . . called me God knows what names . . . and firmly believed they were treating me as I deserved. But you—did none of those things . . . because you loved me so much.

'And then—we came to Castelly. By Jonah's orders, we had to share a room. He was right, of course: Barabbas proved him right; if I was to stay on the scene—well, we couldn't do things by halves. . . . But I'm not a fool, St John. I know how men are made. And it wasn't fair to you to ask you to carry that weight. In fact, it was outrageous. But you have never faltered. You've beaten every record that ever was made.'

'Don't say that, my beauty. After our talk at Poitiers, I *had* to let you alone.'

'I don't agree. Never mind. We came to stay at Castelly—St Antony and Delilah, the strangest bedfellows. And then—we went down, together . . . a little later than this, four evenings ago.

'For you, that moment is a nightmare. By rights, it should be for me. And yet—it isn't, St John. It's . . . anything but a nightmare. I wouldn't call it back for anything in the world. I was surprised and shaken—I'll give you that. I knew who Barabbas was, and it shook me up. And then I realized something which I had been waiting to know . . . waiting and wondering if I should ever know it . . . wanting so much to know it—so very much. I realized, my darling, that *I was mad about you*.

'Well, there you are. That discovery was so big that it made Barabbas seem small. I never had any fear. I knew it was a tight place: but you were there, and I *knew* that we should come through. The strange thing is that I wasn't afraid for you. But I never was—until he went out of the room. And then I was afraid. For I knew that his temper'd take charge, the instant he found that you'd lied about where Jonah was. . . . Then I saw that that didn't matter, because we were going to come through.

'You did it. I sat and watched you do it. Watched you side-track that monster, as if you'd rehearsed for a week. I could have sat up and shouted. You never put a foot wrong. And how did you get Plato down? By holding your fire—one of the hardest things in the world to do. . . . And then you brought me home—and cared for me by the way, as if I was a little child and you were a hospital nurse. . . . And then, the next day, when all I wanted to do was to tell you what I had found out—share with you the present *which Barabbas had given to me*, you gave me no chance. You were so quiet, my darling, so terribly quiet. . . . I put it down to reaction. After all, you'd been right through it; and you had had nothing, as I had, to lift you up. And so I thought, "Never mind: tomorrow he'll be himself." And then . . . that night . . . I heard you talk in your sleep. . . .

'It was the strangest thing. You spoke of the glade—nothing else. You dealt with those two or three moments before Barabbas spoke. And you cursed yourself, my blessed. . . . And you kept on saying over, "My darling from the power of the dog." *If you could, you would have cancelled the very event which had brought me my heart's desire*. . . .

'Why did it bring me that? Because, when I saw your danger, I knew what you meant to me. And if we had done as it had been arranged we should do—returned to Castelly and left the next day for Bayonne, you would have been in no danger, and God knows when, if *ever*, I should have found out the truth.'

For some moments I made no answer—I think, because my heart was too full. My distemper was over and gone. For the first time for ninety-six hours, the scene in the glade had receded—and the fortune I had not sought had taken its place.

It was a strange experience.

The world about me was different: yet nothing had changed. The prospect was fair as ever—meadows and hanging forests and the rock-bound peaks of mountains, standing against the blue: a neighbouring brook was still making its pretty music, and the scent of mown grass was still lading the windless air; and the sunlight was no brighter, the heaven no clearer, the kingdom of earth no richer than it had been before. But now I seemed to have been made free of these things. Five minutes before, I had been aware of them, as a man is aware of some treasure shown behind glass: but now the glass had been lowered, and colour and warmth and fragrance were all my own.

I turned and looked at Audrey.

My lady was sitting sideways, as I have said, propping herself with one arm, her pointed fingers planted upon the turf. The pose was natural, and so most elegant. Bent at the knee, her slim, bare legs remembered Arcady—nymphs and fountains and pastures and shepherds' pipes. Her slight, lithe body was neither stiff nor slack: it might have been that of some athlete, taking her ease. Her head was up, and she was looking before her, over the sweep of the valley and up at the heights beyond. Since she sat between me and the sun, her very lovely features were framed in the golden light: and this was passing through her delicate curls, turning the silk to a luminous haze of splendour, which suited her very well.

'I can stay on now,' I said. 'Castelly has lost its sting.'

The eager head came round.

'I've given notice,' said Audrey. 'I broke it to them this morning, whilst you were getting the car. I said we'd be leaving tomorrow—to stay with friends. But we will stay on . . . if you'd like to . . . my darling boy.'

I got to my feet. Then I stood over my lady and swung her up to her feet and into my arms.

'We must go, Madonna,' I said. 'If you would like to, I'd love to come back later on. You have—redeemed Castelly. But "Mr and Mrs Kingscote" can hardly be married there.'

Audrey put up her mouth.

* * *

It was half past seven o'clock, before we got back that evening—

that very beautiful evening, when earth was heaven and we were a king and a queen.

As Audrey brought the Lowland up to the door of the inn, the hostess appeared on the steps.

'Ah, *Madame* and *Monsieur* arrive. I said they would not be long.' She moistened her lips. 'Two *gendarmes* have been wishing to see them. They are now in the village, I think. They said that they would come back.'

And, with her words, 'they' entered the yard of the inn.

It seemed best to stay where we were.

'*Monsieur et Madame Kingscote?*'

'Yes,' said Audrey, 'what do you want with us?'

The sergeant glanced at the house.

'I think you have a salon,' he said.

Audrey nodded.

Then she left the car and led the way into the inn and up the stairs.

* * *

Our improvised salon was full of a sober radiance, for its windows gave to the west, but their shutters were closed.

'Monsieur does not speak French,' said Audrey. 'But I can speak for us both.'

The sergeant inclined his head.

He and his fellow had both refused to sit down. The latter was standing still with his back to the door. Audrey was sitting half on and half off the table which should have been laid for our meal, and I was standing beside her, with my eyes on the sergeant's face.

The man looked competent. His air was grave, but civil, and not officious: that he meant to do his duty was very clear.

'We have opened an inquiry,' he said, 'into a certain affair. It concerns the Château of Midian. We have some reason to think that you may be able to help us to come at the truth.'

I could understand French well enough to know what he had said. I had known he was going to say it; but that did not help me at all. I seemed to be watching the bottom fall out of my world.

I confess that I felt sick at heart.

After all the care we had taken and all that we had been through, it was very hard to founder upon some shoal we had missed.

Audrey looked from the sergeant to me and then back again.

'Do you mean that place near Orthez, where I read that two people were drowned?'

The sergeant nodded his head.

'That is the place I refer to.'

Audrey knitted her brows.

'But how on earth can we help you? We've never set eyes on the place.'

The sergeant regarded her straitly.

'Or upon its owner, *Madame*?'

Audrey stared back.

'Of course not,' she said. 'We don't even know his name.'

The sergeant raised his eyebrows.

'I need hardly counsel you, *Madame*, to tell me the truth.'

'Telling lies,' said Audrey, coldly, 'is not a habit of mine.'

'You deny that you ever saw him . . . or his—companion?'

It was that slight hesitation that made me think. 'Companion' was not the word that he had been going to use. The man knew something which did not redound to the credit of those who were dead.

'I have told you,' said Audrey, 'that, had we seen him, we should not have known who he was. We do not even know now. I did not know he had a companion, until I saw in the paper that two had been drowned.'

The sergeant fingered his chin.

'And yet,' he said, 'he was interested in you.'

Audrey opened her eyes.

'In me?'

The sergeant nodded.

'A servant of his has confessed that he was ordered to watch you and see where you went: and that he reported to his master that he had run you to earth.'

Audrey put a hand to her head.

' "Run us to earth"?' she repeated.

'That, having run you to earth, he showed his master how he could come to the place. It is an old track in the mountains. I went there yesterday . . . and found the marks of a car.'

'But what on earth,' said Audrey, 'has all this to do with us? If we were followed by someone, that is not our affair.'

The sergeant lifted a hand.

'Do you deny that four days ago you left your car on a track that runs into the woods, some seventeen miles from Castelly and four from Eauge?'

Audrey shrugged her shoulders.

'We may have done so,' she said. 'We walk for some hours every day and, if we can help it, we never leave the car on the road. But what if we did?'

'This,' said the sergeant, shortly. 'You were there, and his master knew you were there. The servant has further alleged that his master set out from Midian with the object of bringing you back. . . . That was the last time he saw him . . . . alive or dead.'

The inference was painfully obvious. But one thing was equally clear. No one could swear that we had been taken to Midian, because we had not been seen.

Audrey moistened her lips.

'But——'

'One moment, *Madame*,' said the sergeant. He raised his eyes to me. Then he touched the side of his face between his eye and his ear. 'I notice that *Monsieur* has recently hurt his head. I do not think that he did that by falling down.'

I stepped into the ring.

'Tell them the truth,' I said. 'Translate what I say.' Audrey did as I said. 'We did not report the matter, because I felt it was too unpleasant for you: but four days ago an attempt was made to abduct you, some sixteen miles from here by the track he has just described. I was just out of sight at the time, but I heard you scream: and I came up to find two fellows——'

The sergeant held up a hand.

'Describe them, plese.'

I described Barabbas and Plato, with all my might.

'Proceed.'

'I found them attempting to seize you and put you into a car.'

'Describe the car, if you please.'

I described the 'close-coupled' Rolls.

'Proceed.'

'Well, we had a dust-up. I laid one out, while the lady ran for our car: and I held the other in check, though he caught me one, as you see. Then I managed to trip him up and ran for the car myself. And then we fairly legged it—you see, they were two to one. And they had the faster car, so we drove all over the place, to cover our tracks. Result, we got properly lost. Then the storm came down and the car went wrong. We never got in that night till eleven o'clock. . . . Now if one of those swine was your man, it all fits in. He liked the look of the lady, and so he had her watched. And when he'd "run her to earth," he determined to have a stab. I need hardly say we'd no idea who he was, and it wasn't exactly convenient to ask his name. But, from what you say, I imagine it was the fellow: and all I can tell you is I'm damned glad to know he's drowned.'

The sergeant took pains to smother the ghost of a smile.

'You observe,' he said, 'the expedience of telling the truth. We were certain that you had seen him, from what the servant had said: and if you had said that you had not, we should at once have known that you had something to hide. But you should have reported the matter. If only you had done that, long before now we should have laid the two by the heels.'

'But I thought they were drowned,' said Audrey.

The sergeant shook his head.

'The birds have flown, *Madame*. Midian has not a good name, and once before there was trouble of a similar kind. But it was not so flagrant as this. Your escape, therefore, gave them the fright of their lives. They fled that night. And to cover their flight, they pretended that they had been drowned. But that is a very old trick. If you knew the place, you would know that no one could ever have fallen over that balustrade: and if you had seen the water which rages beneath, you should know that no man on earth would ever have entered that to save the life of a friend.'

With that, he signed to his fellow to open the door.

Audrey offered him some refreshment, which he declined.

'I am only sorry, *Madame*, to have interfered with your meal.'

Then he put on his hat and saluted: and the other did the same and then followed him out.

I heard them pass down the stairs.

Then I turned and looked at Audrey, to find her looking at me.

And then I saw that she was as white as a sheet.

As I picked her up, she slid an arm round my neck. . . .

I carried her into the bedroom and laid her down on a bed: and then I bathed her temples and gave her cold water to drink.

As her colour began to come back—

'High time I was married,' she said. 'And I never thought I'd say that. But I seem to need looking after. Of course, what we've just been through is bad for the heart. Oh, and thank you very much for saving your little friend.'

'The same to you,' said I. 'You made all the running. I couldn't have spoken before. My mouth wouldn't work.'

Audrey closed her eyes.

'Wasn't it awful, St John?'

'I can only say,' said I, 'that it shortened my life.'

'Shall I make a confession?' said Audrey.

'Please, Madonna,' said I.

'You know that letter of Jonah's?'

I started violently.

'My God! We meant to destroy it.'

'And never did. And it's plainly been soaked in water, and the outside envelope's gone.'

'Where is it?'

'Well, it's here now,' said Audrey, holding it up. 'By the mercy of God I saw it as we came into the room.'

Although the ink had run, the word in block letters, SECRET, was unmistakable.

I wiped the sweat from my brow.

Then—

'Where was it?' I said.

'On the table in the salon,' said Audrey. 'I was sitting on it all the time.'

* * *

Thinking things over, I cast no stone at the police. Their conclusions were hopelessly wrong: but I do not know to what others they could have come. I have said that Midian was wired: and no one would have believed that the cliff could be scaled. Though Plato had returned with the Rolls, they could not be sure that Barabbas had ever come back. That the rug and the match-stand were missing, I doubt if they ever knew. And my tale, which was founded on fact, was confirmed by the reputation which Midian bore. As time went by, I think they must sometimes have wondered that nothing was done about Midian upon Barabbas' behalf: but, so far as I know, the bodies were never recovered, and so there was nothing to prove their conclusions false. At the time, to allay suspicion that they thought otherwise, they openly subscribed to the doctrine that Barabbas and Plato were dead, and sealed all drawers and cupboards and took the keys of the cars: but what was done later on, I have no idea, though I think the ladies at Biarritz grew bolder as time went on and presently claimed the right to administer the estate. And so the matter passed into the mill of the civil law, 'and that,' said Mansel, 'is like the mills of God, for it grinds incredibly slowly and quite remarkably small.'

* * *

The next morning we left for Freilles, and were there by midday.

To say that our welcome was warm conveys nothing at all, for Jenny Chandos was dancing as we drove up to the steps, and Chandos was summoning Bell with a hunting horn.

The Villa Carlos stood five minutes' walk from the sea, yet was sunk in the pine-woods which hereabouts stretched for miles. It could not have been more private or more desirable. Freilles itself was a very modern village, very well done, while the strand which it boasted was the finest I ever saw. I have never enjoyed such bathing before or since, for the sun was immensely hot and the breeze was light, and the true, Atlantic rollers were romping, as giants at play.

Though they were in fact our hosts, Richard and Jenny Chandos ignored that rôle, and before we had been there an hour, we were just four friends together and glad to be there. No one, I think, could have helped adoring Jenny. Although she was more than twenty, she had the way of a child, and she made me think of some beautiful, forest creature, that is not wild because it has never known fear. That she thought the world of Audrey, I need not say, and Chandos later told me that Audrey and Mansel's sister were the only girls with whom she was happy to be.

Chandos led me into a salon and poured me some beer.

'I've so much to hear,' he said. 'You see, I still know nothing of the hour you spent at the château before we came. But I'd rather not hear it here. We'll talk on the sands after lunch. Walls have ears: but the sea talks too loud to itself to hear what is said. But just tell me one thing, John. That letter that Mansel wrote. What happened to that? We thought of it after you'd gone.'

'It's been destroyed,' said I. 'I burnt it myself.'

But I did not add that I had only destroyed it the evening before. And when he said 'Well done,' I felt like a thief. But I told him that afternoon, because to lie to Chandos was something I could not do.

I cannot say that we had the strand to ourselves, but, though there was room for five thousand, there were not a dozen bathers till five o'clock: and then perhaps thirty arrived. . . . And so we were able to talk to our hearts' content, while Jenny lay still and listened, with the air of a child who is hearing a fairy-tale.

The sun was low when Richard Chandos summed up.

'As I see it,' he said, 'we only made one mistake. You remember what Mansel said, when we were all in the hollow beside the spur. "Never take a risk which you can avoid." Well, that was what we did, when we let Audrey stay at Castelly, instead of at Biarritz. It wasn't much of a risk, for Castelly was twenty miles off. But it was a bit of a risk, for Audrey will not pass in a crowd. And it very nearly cost us extremely dear.

'Now if I remember aright, Mansel said that to take an avoidable risk was the way of a suicide. To that I can add a rider, and that is this. So sure as you commit that folly, you will get Fortune's goat. And that is exactly what happened. We took an avoidable risk, and Fortune resented our action and let us in.'

'How d'you make that out?' said Audrey.

'We played,' said Chandos, 'clean into Barabbas' hands. Of that there can be no doubt. It's as clear as paint. And now I'll prove what I say.' He reached for his pouch and began to fill a pipe. 'Has it ever occurred to you that, so far as you two were concerned, Barabbas was quick off the mark?'

'Yes,' said I, 'it has. Again and again. We got to Castelly on Monday. And on Wednesday he knew our movements and had us cold.'

'Exactly,' said Chandos. 'Now what is the explanation of action as swift as that? *The gendarmes gave it to you.* They said in so many words that Midian had a bad name and that *once before there was trouble of a somewhat similar kind.* Well, there you are. Barabbas had a weakness for good-looking girls and, as used to be done by so-called *grands seigneurs*, in days gone by, he had issued standing orders that he was to be informed if any attractive newcomer arrived in the neighbourhood. Well, Audrey is—very attractive: she won't mind me saying that. And . . . I don't want to shock you too much, but I think that, as likely as not, someone from your inn at Castelly sent word to some creature of Barabbas' that Audrey had come there to stay.

'Now Barabbas, as you know, was no fool. The instant he heard that a beautiful English girl had arrived at Castelly on the very same day that Plato had arrived at Midian, *he knew who she was*. Inquiry confirmed the truth—and more than the truth; for with the English girl was St Omer's "hunting crony," the "Willie they didn't know."

'And so you see, by letting you stay at Castelly, we played clean into his hands. We were taking a very slight, but *avoidable* risk: so Fortune immediately put us where we belonged.'

There was a little silence.

Then Jenny lifted her voice.

'I think the mistake,' she said, 'which you and Jonathan made was bigger than that.'

'What was it, sweetheart?' said Chandos.

'I do not think,' said Jenny, 'that Audrey should have been there. She should have stopped at Poitiers, or even at Dax.'

'You're perfectly right,' said Chandos. 'She should have stopped at Poitiers. But it wasn't our fault that she didn't, my pretty maid.'

'A-a-ah,' said Jenny. And then, 'I thought as much.'

'Tell me, Jenny,' said Audrey. 'Would you have stopped at Poitiers, while William went on?'

Jenny opened her great, blue eyes.

'Of course I shouldn't,' she said. 'But that is a different thing. I am married to William, and William is all I have.'

'I know, my darling. But I'm going to marry John—and John is all I have.'

Jenny's eyes were alight with mischievous merriment.

'I *thought* you were,' she declared, 'and I am so glad.'

'My God, so am I,' said Chandos. He sat up and put out his hands. 'And I think you deserve each other—I can't say more than that.'

* * *

And that is very nearly the end of my tale.

We stayed for three weeks at Freilles, because we could not be married until that time had elapsed. And then, one July morning, we all set out for Bordeaux.

Leaving at nine, we were there by eleven o'clock, and ten minutes later we reached the Consulate.

And there was Mansel's Rolls and Mansel himself, and Carson to open our doors, with a hand to his hat.

'Jonah, you darling,' cried Audrey. 'How sweet of you to show up.'

'My dear,' said Mansel, 'when you have hoped very hard for somebody's happiness, you simply have to be there when they haul it aboard. Add to that that I know you inside out and I'm terribly fond of you—for so many good reasons, but most of all, I think, because you've got the greatest heart of any woman I know.'

So Jenny stood beside Audrey and Chandos stood beside me, and Mansel 'gave Audrey away,' to use a term which Consulates do not know.

And then we all repaired to *Le Chapon Fin*, where Mansel had taken care to order a private room. There we were served with a 'breakfast' such as I never ate, for the wine was as good as the food, and the food was incomparable. And there we arranged our next meeting, because, of course, we could not 'talk business' there.

Mansel looked at Audrey.

'I'm told that you're going to Anise for a week or ten days.'

'That's right,' said my wife. 'Jenny and Richard, you see, have put us wise.'

'I thought they would,' said Mansel. 'I'm fond of Anise myself.'

'You found it out,' said Audrey.

'I believe I did,' said Mansel, 'a year or two back.'

'Visit us there,' said Audrey. 'And then we can talk by the stream where Richard caught Vanity Fair.'

Mansel nodded.

'I'll be there one week from today.'

'Till then,' said Jenny, 'he's going to stay with us.'

'I'd love to,' said Mansel. 'May I really go back with you?'

'What do you think?' said Jenny. 'You know that after William I love you the best in the world.'

'And after Anise?' said Chandos.

'The mountains,' said I. 'But not as seen from a certain village we know. A little further afield . . . And then—don't think us mad, but we had thought of Amiens. There's a ramshackle villa there—and we know the country about.'

Mansel laughed.

'That's just where I've come from,' he said. 'It has its faults, as a house, but it's very conveniently placed. Then, again, I like Amiens. I like the cathedral stalls. And twenty odd years ago some battles were fought near there: and Carson and I have been going over the ground. Rowley is there at the moment, keeping an eye on the cook, who thinks, of course, that she's keeping an eye on him. He tells me you're taking him on.'

'That's right,' said my wife. 'I engaged him before we were married—in case we were. That is the sort of precaution I've learned from you.'

Mansel frowned.

'Provision—not precaution,' he said.'The word "precaution" presupposes some doubt.'

Audrey appealed to me.

'Don't you believe him, St John. You're wife's a *nice* girl.'

* * *

It was while we were staying at Amiens that Audrey saw in *The Times* that Peerless was to be sold—with two hundred and fifty acres, instead of the seven thousand which George had ruled. And so, with his money, I bought it and gave it to Audrey, my wife.

It was in a way a venture, for when all was signed and sealed, I had very little left: but she had her private income, and before a year had gone by, I was at least earning my living by farming two hundred acres of those we had.

And so we both live at Peerless, as we had hoped to do, and I sometimes think that George St Omer is with us and glad that we should be there: for Audrey he loved, and I was his closest friend, and between us we brought to justice the man who had taken his life.

We seldom visit London, without dining at Cleveland Row, and sometimes we stay at Maintenance, Chandos' Wiltshire home. Then we remember together the burden of those three months and the manifold changes and chances of our excursion.

We speak of Sermon Square and the leads of the church of St Ives, and then of Dieppe at daybreak and Rouen's Cathedral *place*: we take the road to Chartres and from there to Tours, and thence to Chatellerault—in 'The Kingdom of Heaven's' car: we climb again to the telegraph-room at Poitiers, we watch the train pull out of the station at Dax, and then we go up to Midian—and matters of life and death. We see the barn and the spur, the cliff and the angry water, the glade where we hid the Lowland and the sunlit flags of the terrace we were to know: we live again those terribly crowded moments, when Audrey was actually under Barabbas' hand; and we stand again in that luxurious chamber in which, one after another, two butchers came by their own.

Of such remembrance, I think I shall never tire: and though, because of my darling, my life is as rich and as gay as that of some sparkling fountain that always plays, I must confess that there is no pursuit to compare with that which can only be followed 'without the law.' For that is the real thing, and once you have followed it, no imitation will serve.

THE END

Dornford Yates: Blind Corner

Introduced by Tom Sharpe

Three gallant Englishmen in their Rolls Royce race 'Rose' Noble and his sinister gang to an Austrian castle, where a great treasure is hidden. First published in 1927, *Blind Corner* is one of the most famous of Dornford Yates's immensely popular novels, whose stylish blend of adventure and nostalgia has kept readers enthralled for more than six decades.

Dornford Yates: Blood Royal

Introduced by A.J. Smithers

While motoring on a rainswept night in Austria, Chandos and Hanbury are ambushed by a noble Duke and become enmeshed in an intrigue of royal rivalry.

Dornford Yates: Perishable Goods

Introduced by Richard Usborne

When Adèle, beloved wife of Jonah Mansel's cousin, is kidnapped by 'Rose' Noble, Mansel, Chandos and Hanbury dash to her rescue.

Dornford Yates: She Fell Among Thieves

Introduced by Ion Trewin

One of Yates's best-loved novels, this is the story of a young girl, drugged and imprisoned in the Pyrenees, who is rescued by Richard Chandos and Jonah Mansel and is destined to marry one of them . . .

Margery Allingham: Traitor's Purse
Introduced by Jessica Mann

What should a man do when he wakes in a hospital bed to overhear that he is to be hanged for a crime that he can't remember committing? Moreover, he doesn't know what the crime is, where he is held or, more important, his own name. Witty, literate, crackling with tension, this is a magnificent thriller from the Queen of Suspense.

Eric Ambler: Epitaph for a Spy
Introduced by H.R.F. Keating

Josef Vadassy, an unassuming language teacher, is on holiday in the South of France when he is arrested on charges of espionage. The only way he can prove his innocence is by tracking down the real spy himself. First published in 1938, Ambler's spy classic brilliantly evokes the paranoia and tension of pre-War Europe.

Nicholas Blake: The Sad Variety

A brilliant professor with a secret the Russians badly want, a resourceful small girl held hostage in a snowbound cottage, and of course the supersleuth Nigel Strangeways . . . This is a cracking story from Nicholas Blake, the pen-name under which the distinguished poet Cecil Day Lewis wrote his literate and gripping crime novels.

John Buchan: Castle Gay
Introduced by David Daniell

A splendid story of intrigue and romance set in the 1920s in the heather-clad hills of Scotland, featuring some of the most engaging characters Buchan ever created. The kidnap of a newspaper magnate and the menacing machinations of rival East European factions lead to a tense climax in the library at Castle Gay.

John Buchan: The Courts of the Morning

Introduced by T.J. Binyon

Janet and Archie Roylance are on their honeymoon in South America when they get caught up in a bold revolutionary plot to overthrow a ruthless regime based on greed, corruption and drug-induced slavery.

John Buchan: The House of the Four Winds

Introduced by Simon Rees

The splendid sequel to *Huntingtower* and *Castle Gay* in which Jaikie becomes entangled in an adventure of political intrigue, kidnap and romance in Central Europe.

John Buchan: The Power-House

Introduced by Anthony Quinton

The familiar streets of London become fraught with menace for Edward Leithen when he tries to expose the fanatical ring-leader of 'the Power-House', an international conspiracy that threatens the very roots of civilisation.

Leslie Charteris: Enter the Saint

Introduced by Ion Trewin

The first famous 'Saint' novel introducing Simon Templar, a born adventurer with a lazy smile, a dubious past and impeccable taste in ties. When he tangles with the London underworld of the 1930s he may not always stay on the right side of the law, but he is clearly on the side of the angels.

Leslie Charteris: The Saint in New York
Introduced by Jack Adrian

When Simon Templar takes on an unsolved murder case he soon finds himself up against the corrupt mob who run New York City. Charteris is in peak form in this full-length novel set in 1930s American gangland.

Erskine Childers: The Riddle of the Sands
Introduced by Julian Symons

The world-weary Carruthers and his friend Davies are sailing round the Frisian Islands when they encounter some suspicious-looking Germans and decide to investigate. First published in 1903, this is probably the most famous spy story ever written as well as a classic sailing yarn.

Manning Coles: Drink to Yesterday
Introduced by T.J. Binyon

A gripping First World War thriller of exceptional literary quality and psychological subtlety, first published in 1940 and dubbed 'the book that made Manning Coles famous in a day'.

Robert Harling: The Enormous Shadow
Introduced by Matthew Coady

A spy novel of the Cold War, set in the 1950s when the Burgess/Maclean scandal was still fresh in the public mind. Well-written and pacey, with a marvellously authentic Fleet Street setting, this is a superb novel of treachery at its most chilling.

Anthony Hope: The Prisoner of Zenda

Introduced by Geoffrey Household

A masterpiece of adventure set in turn-of-the-century Europe. Rudolf Rassendyll, a well-born Englishman with a reputation for frivolity, proves his true mettle when he saves the throne of Ruritania by impersonating its King.

E.W. Hornung: The Collected Raffles

Introduced by Jeremy Lewis

At last! – The *complete* short stories which chronicle the adventures of gentleman-burglar A.J. Raffles in a single paperback, including *The Amateur Cracksman, The Black Mask* and *A Thief in the Night*. Here is the full story of how Raffles charmed, cheated and stole his way through the glittering Mayfair salons and country-house parties of late Victorian England.

Geoffrey Household: A Rough Shoot

Introduced by T.J. Binyon

Household's most famous thriller after *Rogue Male*, set deep in the Dorset countryside in the aftermath of World War II, in which a patriotic Englishman uncovers a Neo-Fascist plot.

Geoffrey Household: Watcher in the Shadows

As far as his English neighbours were concerned he was plain Charles Dennim, a mild-mannered zoologist. But when he narrowly escapes death from a parcel bomb, it is clear that someone remembers his wartime career as Von Dennim, a Gestapo officer in the concentration camp at Ravensbruck. A gripping and haunting story of pursuit and post-war retribution set in rural England.

Sax Rohmer: The Mystery of Dr Fu Manchu
Introduced by D.J. Enright

Trailing opium fumes and scents of the mysterious East, Fu Manchu has survived as one of the most sinister villains of thriller fiction. This is the first of the perennially popular Fu Manchu series, in which Nayland Smith and Dr Petrie, like an exotic Holmes and Watson, track down the oriental genius in his Limehouse lair.

'Sapper': Bulldog Drummond
Introduced by Richard Usborne

Demobbed after World War I and finding peace 'incredibly tedious', Captain Hugh Drummond places an advertisement in the newspaper soliciting adventure. A reply from the young and beautiful Phyllis launches him into a fast-paced adventure of blackmail, torture and unspeakable villainy.

Edgar Wallace: The Four Just Men
Introduced by Jack Adrian

The famous novel that launched Wallace as one of the most popular thriller writers of all time. The four just men were dedicated to preventing injustice – they judged, they sentenced, they executed. When they threatened the Foreign Secretary he was clever enough to recognise the danger, but not to escape their ingenious and fatal trap.

ORDER FORM

. . . .	**ALLINGHAM:** Traitor's Purse	£2.95
. . . .	**AMBLER:** Epitaph for a Spy	£2.50
. . . .	**BLAKE:** The Sad Variety	£3.50
. . . .	**BUCHAN:** Castle Gay	£2.95
. . . .	**BUCHAN:** The Courts of the Morning	£3.50
. . . .	**BUCHAN:** The House of the Four Winds	£2.50
. . . .	**BUCHAN:** The Power-House	£2.50
. . . .	**CHARTERIS:** Enter the Saint	£2.50
. . . .	**CHARTERIS:** The Saint in New York	£2.50
. . . .	**CHILDERS:** The Riddle of the Sands	£2.50
. . . .	**COLES:** Drink to Yesterday	£2.50
. . . .	**HARLING:** The Enormous Shadow	£2.95
. . . .	**HOPE:** The Prisoner of Zenda	£2.50
. . . .	**HORNUNG:** The Collected Raffles	£3.50
. . . .	**HOUSEHOLD:** A Rough Shoot	£2.50
. . . .	**HOUSEHOLD:** Watcher in the Shadows	£2.95
. . . .	**ROHMER:** The Mystery of Dr Fu Manchu	£2.95
. . . .	**SAPPER:** The Black Gang	£2.50
. . . .	**SAPPER:** Bulldog Drummond	£2.50
. . . .	**SAPPER:** The Final Count	£3.50
. . . .	**SAPPER:** The Third Round	£2.50
. . . .	**WALLACE:** The Four Just Men	£2.95
. . . .	**WALLACE:** The Mind of Mr J G Reeder	£2.50
. . . .	**YATES:** Blind Corner	£2.95
. . . .	**YATES:** Blood Royal	£2.50
. . . .	**YATES:** Perishable Goods	£2.50
. . . .	**YATES:** She Fell Among Thieves	£2.95
. . . .	**YATES:** Gale Warning	£3.50

All these books may be obtained through your local bookshop, or can be ordered direct from the publisher. Please indicate the number of copies required and fill in the form below.

Name .... BLOCK LETTERS PLEASE

Address ....

....

Please enclose remittance to the value of the cover price *plus* 40p per copy to a maximum of £2, for postage, and send your order to:

BP Dept, J.M. Dent & Sons Ltd, 33 Welbeck Street, London W1M 8LX

Applicable to UK only and subject to stock availability
All prices subject to alteration without notice